LIFEBOAT
NUMBER TWO

A 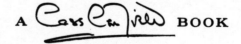 BOOK

Books by Margaret Culkin Banning

Lifeboat Number Two
Mesabi
I Took My Love to the Country
The Vine and the Olive
The Quality of Mercy
Echo Answers
The Convert
The Dowry
Fallen Away
Give Us Our Years
The Clever Sister
Conduct Yourself Accordingly
Letters from England
Salud! A South American Journal
A Week in New York
Enough to Live On
Out in Society
Too Young to Marry
You Haven't Changed
The Case for Chastity
Letters to Susan
The Iron Will
The First Woman
The Third Son
Path of True Love
Prelude to Love
Money of Her Own
Mixed Marriage
The Women of the Family
Pressure
A Handmaid of the Lord

LIFEBOAT NUMBER TWO

Margaret Culkin Banning

1817

HARPER & ROW, PUBLISHERS
New York, Evanston, San Francisco, London

FIRST U.S. EDITION

STANDARD BOOK NUMBER: 06-010204-7

LIBRARY OF CONGRESS CATALOG CARD NUMBER: 70-144188

To
Bernice Dalrymple
and
the happy memories of voyages
with both our husbands

In all my travels I have never met or known any of the characters
in this story. But I might have done so.

LIFEBOAT
NUMBER TWO

Chapter One

At three o'clock, four hours after the ship had sailed, bells clanged through the corridors and lounges and bars. They were noisy, authoritative bells meant to awake or interrupt the passengers, summoning all of them to the stations by the lifeboats to which they had been assigned by notices in each cabin. The time of the drill had also been posted on each deck of *The Seven Seas* but some had not seen it, some had forgotten it and there were always a few who would try to ignore it, as Jim Bates, the steward who stood at the end of a corridor in the bow of the boat deck, well knew. His immediate duty was to make sure that everyone in the cabins which he served would attend the drill.

Alec Goodrich, who was in cabin 4, was annoyed when he heard the bells. He was in no mood to congregate with other passengers or to have any mingling forced upon him. He had reserved a small table in a far corner of the dining room for himself alone. But he was a lawyer as well as a defeated Senator, and the habit of respecting regulations was strong in him. He threw down the magazine he had been reading—it had been infuriating him anyway with a smug postmortem on the November elections—took the life jacket down from the shelf in his wardrobe and went out to find his station.

Mr. and Mrs. Robert Cayne, who had been seen off by a very merry party of friends, appeared and they were still merry. As he had distributed telegrams and letters to the cabins and provided glasses and setups Jim Bates had sized up most of the people for whose bedroom service he would be responsible on the journey around the world. He had overheard their farewells, noted their manners and classified them roughly, although he knew from experience that a first impression could be wrong. The Caynes were on a wedding trip. He had heard the toasts of their friends. It was almost certainly not the first marriage for the robust, fiftyish Mr. Cayne but he was triumphant about this one. He grinned at the steward as he passed, out of an overflow of well-being.

At the end of the hallway Mr. Howard Demarest came out of the Mandarin suite. That was priced at twelve thousand dollars for single occupancy on the voyage and Mr. Demarest had booked it for himself. But he was not without companionship on the ship. He pressed the buzzer on the door of a cabin nearby and pushed it again impatiently before a girl opened it. Jim Bates had seen her before at the bon voyage party in the luxurious suite. Then she had been wearing white furs but now she had changed into slacks and a turtleneck sweater and become a beautiful tomboy. She was swinging her life jacket by its tapes and said helplessly, "I don't know how to get into this horrible thing!"

Demarest, a big but still shapely man, looked enormous in his orange life jacket. He took the one the girl was holding and fitted her into it, handling her as if he owned her. The two handsome women who had connecting rooms 10 and 12 noticed that as they went past. The steward had been on the lookout for them because he thought that Mrs. Barnes and Mrs. Hayward might feel that lifeboat drills were not necessary for experienced travelers like themselves. They had already impressed on him the fact that they were accustomed to travel. He had been asked to take some of their flowers to the refrigerator and to deliver a gift hamper of champagne to the wine steward. Mrs. Barnes had spoken reminiscently of other ships. Jim knew they would expect a great deal of attention and service. Both women had beauty left over from youth. It had not faded so much as been crystallized.

The passengers were assigned alphabetically to the stations on the deck and all of those for Lifeboat Number Two had to pass through the corridor where Jim Bates was standing to reach the heavy door that led to the outer deck. As they streamed through he checked off the ones who were his responsibility and there was only one who had not appeared. That was the young woman traveling alone, who was in 9. Her parents had seen her off but in the last few hours Jim had had no call from her cabin nor any glimpse of her and he wondered if she had fallen asleep. He hesitated for another two minutes, then tapped gently on her door.

"What is it?" she asked. "Come in."

She was not asleep. She was sitting on the couch-bed under her window, smoking a cigarette which had been one of many. She had not unpacked her bags or unwrapped her flowers. There were unopened letters and telegrams on the little desk. One letter had been opened and it lay on the couch beside her.

The girl had seemed very gay and happy when her parents were with her before the ship sailed and they had kept urging her to have a wonderful time. But it did not seem to have started that way. She looked at the steward as if he were a long way off, as if her mind and senses were not fitted into this compact little room even though she was in it physically.

Jim Bates said respectfully, "Pardon me, Miss, but there is a lifeboat drill. Your station is Number Two on the deck outside."

"I'll skip the drill," she said, not petulantly but without interest.

"I'm sorry, Miss, but the Commander is extremely strict about attendance of all passengers. Unless—are you feeling ill?"

"No, I'm all right—I'm fine—you mean I have to be there?"

"The officers call a roll—may I get your life jacket for you?"

He took it from the shelf of one of the wardrobes and held it open for her.

"Thank you—I can manage it—I know how it goes—"

"I'm very sorry at having had to disturb you—"

"That's all right. Are you my steward?"

"Yes, Miss."

"Please tell me your name."

"Jim Bates. Just Jim."

3

"I'm Barbara Bancroft." She spoke as if she never used the prefix Miss. She tied the strings of the jacket swiftly and correctly and moved toward the door he held open. Suddenly she smiled at him with disarming friendliness and said, "Thanks very much for keeping me in line, Jim. I'll see you later."

The lifeboats had been lowered and swung out from the railings at each of the stations which were marked at intervals around the enormous open deck. An officer stood by each one with a list in his hand and over the loudspeaker a voice explained, "Ladies and gentlemen, when your name is called please answer if you are present. It is urgently requested that all passengers attend the drills, which will not be more frequent than necessary. In case of absence a ship's officer will telephone the passenger and respectfully ask for an explanation. In the unlikely case of accident or emergency the bells will ring continuously. In that event put on your life jacket over a warm coat, wear a cap or hood, and report to the station where you are this afternoon. Use the stairs, not the elevators, except in case of disability. If you have any questions, the officer calling the roll call at your station will be glad to answer them. When the roll call is ended today the bells will ring and you will be at liberty to return to your diversions. I wish you a pleasant afternoon and thank you very much for your cooperation."

They made a grotesque group, tied into the bright orange jackets stuffed with kapok. Over the bulges they eyed each other warily. The experienced travelers knew the hazard of making acquaintances impulsively or too soon and later not finding it easy to disentangle themselves. The shy ones, like Mrs. Signe Goode, who had never been on a ship before, did not have the audacity to speak to strangers. And there were others who only wanted to be left alone, like Alec Goodrich, who lit his pipe and looked out to sea, wondering how he had been such a fool as to let himself in for this and already considering the possibility of leaving the ship at Lisbon, which would be the first stop.

4

"How many will the lifeboat hold?" someone was asking the ship's officer.

"One hundred and twenty people."

"There aren't that many at this drill."

"No sir, but the number includes the members of the ship's staff and crew who also will be assigned to this boat. They have separate drills, more frequent than the ones to which you will be subjected, for many of them have special duties in case of emergency. Now —with your permission, ladies and gentlemen—" the officer lifted his voice for attention—"I shall call the roll of those passengers listed for occupancy of Lifeboat Number Two."

It was a group introduction as well as a check on the presence of the passengers. Alida Barnes listened attentively, matching individuals to their names, sorting out expertly the ones she might want to know. Julia Hayward did not seem to listen or care. On a cruise she had rarely met anyone whose acquaintance she wanted to follow up with so much as a Christmas card.

To Alida Mr. and Mrs. Cant looked dull. She wrote them off as a typical retired couple making the most of their money. Miss Crewe was a schoolteacher type, ridiculously boaty in the plaid coat with matching cap. She reserved judgment on the Robert Caynes. Mr. and Mrs. Julian Chilton were definitely interesting. They looked aristocratic and a nurse or governess in English uniform attended their child, a little girl who might have stepped out of *Alice in Wonderland*. The Eugene Beaufort couple were charming but seemed very young for world travelers—they were probably just married and the voyage was a wedding trip. Mr. Howard Demarest —he must be very rich if he had the Mandarin suite, but he had that blonde starlet with him in the corridor and though Alida Barnes took pride in being a woman of the world and no prude she did not want to get involved with messy affairs between people out of her own social bracket.

"Mrs. Hartley Barton," called the officer. An elderly woman

supporting herself on two canes said "Present" and the way she spoke made Alida Barnes look again. She had thought at her first casual glance that an old crippled woman like that should know better than to take a long cruise. But she had answered to her name with a kind of dignity and authority that Alida Barnes associated with good background, with firm social place and servants.

A tall man with dark red hair who watched the members of the group with a glance that was more amused and cynical than friendly was identified as Mark Claypole. "Here," said Barbara Bancroft. The youth in her voice drew eyes her way but all that anyone could see of her was shoulder-long bronze-gold hair falling uncurled down the back of her dark coat. She did not turn from the railing nor look at the officer. Mrs. Signe Goode blushed when her name was called and admitted that she was there in an almost frightened way. The name of the Reverend Aloysius Duggan was called twice because the first time he actually did not hear it. He was standing off by himself, deep in the continual dialogue he was carrying on with himself, the argument as to whether he should or should not leave the priesthood of the Catholic Church. He felt lost and out of place on the ship but this journey was an obedience, perhaps his last one, to his Bishop.

The Bishop had said, "If you contemplate such a decision, Father, you must guard against impulse and haste. You must reflect, pray —try to pray," he amended gravely. "It so happens that I can arrange time for reflection for you. I have been asked to supply a chaplain for a ship which is making a long voyage, circling the globe for a period of several months. The passage is free, in consideration of the spiritual duties involved, daily Masses, confessions— and of course on such a cruise sickness or death may occur and need ministration. Usually when such an opportunity has arisen in my diocese I have sent a priest whose health would benefit from such a voyage."

"I am in good health, Bishop."

6

"You are in ill health spiritually, Father. I think this journey might be very beneficial for you. You will have considerable privacy and time to think, apart from any real or imagined pressures. You can test and measure your problems in different atmospheres, against the background of other countries. Of course you will also be of service to your fellow passengers, some of whom will be Catholics though it is probable that the majority will not be of our faith."

"Bishop, I don't deserve it. Not such a break as this trip. I have caused you great concern. I know I've been a problem to the diocese for some time and I honestly regret that more than I can say. My only excuse is that I've been tossed about in a sea of doubts—"

The Bishop smiled. "It should be good for you to toss about on the real sea for a bit, Father. I want you to do this. I do not command you. But I request it urgently. Will you go?"

Father Duggan looked at his kind superior, who was trying to hold him to a faith that he could no longer follow unquestioningly. At least he could do this, and the thought of distance and change suddenly seemed infinitely desirable.

"Yes, if you think I should, Bishop. And may I say that I am very grateful."

"There is only one condition I should like to make. Or consider it as another request. The Church has not been so scrutinized, analyzed and criticized for centuries. Among strangers you will be questioned, invited to argument. The journey will be of no benefit to you if you indulge in futile discussion. That is what I want you to get away from for a time. I send you as a priest of the Church. If, when you return, you feel that you cannot, in conscience, continue in that capacity, I shall accept your decision with sorrow but without opposition. In the meantime search your soul in solitude, let your argument be inner, with yourself and God, not with men unless indeed they be staunch priests who might help you. Do not commit scandal by exposing doubts and criticisms of the faith in

7

which you were ordained. You go as a Catholic priest. Will you respect this status?"

"Yes, Bishop," said Father Duggan, "I give you my word that I shall."

"Here," said Alec Goodrich.

His name caused no great stir of interest, though his defeat had been one of the notable upsets in the November elections. Mark Claypole half turned, quickly observant but not staring. A couple of other men seemed to be querying each other as if they were not sure if this was the same man, and then the roll call continued. Several women kept looking at Alec, for there had been no mention of any Mrs. Goodrich and he was a very handsome man. Alida Barnes wondered if by luck or good management they would include him at their table in the dining room. The girl with Howard Demarest lifted her unbelievable eyelashes and would have smiled invitingly if Alec had shown any return of interest. He did not. Alec had been getting attention of that sort from girls and women for years in every public appearance. It used to amuse him or give him a fillip of satisfaction. He had sometimes encouraged it for the votes it might be worth. But not any more. That was what had defeated him in November.

Ex-Senator Goodrich had rarely felt so out of place as he did on this January afternoon on this ship and with this company. To go on a trip around the world had been an impulsive decision and he now felt that it had been a preposterous one. His former colleague, the senior Senator from his state, Marcus O'Brien, had first put the idea into his head and it had lain fallow for some time. But Marcus O'Brien was one of the few men whom Alec still believed to have any interest in his future.

"What are your plans?" Marcus had asked when it was all over except moving Alec's personal things out of the office in the Senate Building which had been his for the last six years. "What are you going to do?"

"I have no firm plans. I'm just beginning to find out what I can't do any longer."

"It was a catastrophe. For me as well as you, in a lesser way. I figured on our going on in harness together. But you're young, Alec. You have plenty of time."

"So has Whitlock. He has six years to entrench himself in the Senate and in the party."

"I don't think he'll wear well. He's too much of an opportunist and people get on to that. And in six years you'll still be younger than he is and a whole lot younger than most of the men in the Senate. By that time all this will be forgotten."

"I doubt it. And they can always dig it up again."

"Political memories are short. Bide your time—watch for the opportunity. You are in a better position than most men when they lose an election. You don't have to worry about money—"

"They used that against me too. That was the proof that I was just a playboy in Washington."

"Rubbish," growled O'Brien. "Everybody on the Hill knows you were one of the hardest-working Senators down here. A lot of good bills had your name on them."

Alec's face tightened at the past tense and the older man said gently, "You're taking this too hard, Alec."

"It's not the defeat. I can take a licking. It's the way it was done. The way they took advantage of the situation, used the death of that poor girl to discredit me. I couldn't fight back. I was trapped. The facts were there. She was working for me in the campaign and she did kill herself in my apartment. I couldn't defend myself by attacking the character or mentality of a dead girl. So the newspapers had a field day and so did the opposition."

"You have to look beyond all that now, pick up the pieces and put them together again. I suppose you'll return to the law."

"If I could make a good connection, I probably would."

"Are you considering going back to New Alton?"

"There's nothing there to go back to. My law business in New

9

Alton was a technical partnership but Bill Warren has carried the work load for a long time. I couldn't do it because I was so busy here and my being in the Senate lent some prestige to the firm and helped Bill. But now I'd probably be a liability to him."

"I don't believe that. You must still have friends out there. And some family, haven't you?"

"Friends pretty negative after all the gossip and the way the vote piled up in my own precinct. And no close family since my aunt died last year. One good thing was that she didn't live to be humiliated by this. You know she was always deeply interested in politics and took a lot of pride in my being in the Senate. But she's gone and I'm going to put the house out there up for sale when I get around to it. I had to keep a residence in New Alton of course while I was Senator from the state and I had some feeling for the place. It's where I grew up. But it's no longer necessary."

"Then you'll be staying here?"

"I doubt it. I've seen too many has-beens around Washington, pretending they still have influence or usefulness."

Senator O'Brien did not ask the question that was in his mind but Alec answered it.

"There's nothing to keep me here," he said curtly, "my personal plans have changed."

"Too bad," muttered the Senator.

"It's not a thing I want to talk about."

"Of course not."

Alec said compulsively, "It was a mutual decision. It was a thing we had to be realistic about. The whole picture changed when I was defeated under such circumstances." He stopped abruptly and then couldn't leave it at that. He said, "I would like you to know that Cicely believed me when I told her that the girl wasn't normal and that there was nothing between us. But here in Washington we'd be haunted by the whole miserable business. It's the sort of thing that gossip columns never let go of. I've no standing in this town now."

"There are other places to live."

"Not for the Correll family. Her mother—well, you know. You've been at her parties. She lives for that sort of thing. And Cicely was brought up here. Washington's in her blood. Any other place would be exile for her. I knew that and she did too, though she wouldn't admit it. Anyway, it's all off."

"Alec," said the Senator, after the minute in which they buried the subject, "why don't you cut loose from everything for a while?"

"What do you mean? I am cut loose."

"I mean go away. Get out of Washington temporarily. Maybe travel for a while. See, as the old man said to his son, with how little wisdom the world is governed. Get a new perspective."

"Take a Grand Tour with my tail between my legs?"

"Not at all. With your head up. Go to places that are free from your habits and associations. Take a long sea voyage. I did that once. It was long before you came to Washington. I'd been overworking, had some reversals and they loomed pretty large, so large that I couldn't sleep nights. My doctor told me to take a few months off if I didn't want to crack up completely. So I did. I borrowed on my insurance and got on a ship and went out to Australia and New Zealand and put my mind on the aborigines and the sheep and the South Pacific islands, which were not so sophisticated as I guess they are now. It did me a whole lot of good, especially all the time I spent on the ship. On a ship you can separate yourself from pretty nearly everything for days. You can't do that between landing fields. I've always wanted to do something like that again. But I never could find the time. Or the money. Right now you've got plenty of both."

Alec had laughed and said it might be an idea and he'd think about it. He did not really mean to consider it. Travel might be all right for men who were sick or retired. What he wanted to do was to find a place for himself, prove himself again. But days and weeks passed with no good result. He put out feelers for offers from law firms in New York and Philadelphia but nothing materialized that would not have been demotion. He was approached by a textile combine who wanted a lobbyist in Washington, a job that seemed almost insulting, and he curtly turned it down.

In the Washington newspapers and news magazines he saw frequent pictures of the Honorable Albert Whitlock, the new Senator from his state, who had been anything but honorable in the campaign. If he happened to glance at a society page he sometimes saw that Mrs. Page Correll was still entertaining notables in that white brick mansion where he had been so welcome a couple of months ago. Where he had fallen in love. Alec had never imagined how defeating a defeat could be. He stayed in his apartment in the hours of the day when he used to be excitingly overworked. He frequented unfashionable bars and restaurants and drank more than he intended or wanted. He avoided all his former colleagues, even Marcus O'Brien, and if social invitations drifted into his mail, showing that some lists were unrevised, he threw them in the wastebasket.

The Senator's advice had been relegated to the back of Alec's mind, but not quite discarded. It lingered and every now and then pushed forward. To get away from everything was tempting. "You can separate yourself from everything on a ship," Marcus had said and God knew that was what Alec wanted to do. One day, after an encounter in the Statler barbershop with two men he had known well on the Hill and parrying their interest and suspected pity, Alec stopped at the desk of the travel agent in the lobby.

"I'm considering taking a sea voyage. Can you tell me what is available right now?"

"We've space on several Caribbean trips."

"I want to have a more extended one."

"I see." The agent thought the man's face was familiar and remembered. This was the playboy Senator. He had money. He looked over some charts and asked, "Would you be interested in a voyage around the world, sir? It just happens that this morning there was a cancellation on *The Seven Seas.* It's the flagship of the American Republic Line."

"How long is the trip?"

"Eighty-four days. Of course you touch a great many ports and can arrange shore trips to suit yourself."

And here he was. Dismayed. From the time he went up the gangplank Alec had realized that this was not what he had expected. The crowds of gay people, the bands playing on the dock and in the public rooms, the mountains of luggage, the flowers clogging the corridors—this wasn't what he had come for. But he couldn't get out of it now.

He had never even seen the departure of an ocean liner. He had never traveled for its own sake. There had never been time or opportunity. Almost since the day he had left law school he had been involved in politics and campaigns, working at first for other candidates but before too long he was one himself. He had political talent, natural charm and the gift of persuasion. He was elected to the State Senate in his late twenties, and after the sudden death of a long-time incumbent Alec had astonishingly won the subsequent race to the United States Senate though he was only one year over the minimum age requirement of thirty. Since then his life had centered in Washington, though he made periodical trips back to his home state to keep in touch with his constituents and to New Alton for short, affectionate weekends with his Aunt Lucy. He had been orphaned when he was a child and she had brought him up, instilling into him at an early age some of her own intense civic consciousness.

While he was in the Senate he had gone on several fact-finding trips abroad, one to West Germany, one to the Middle East and on the last one to Vietnam. He had been with political confrères each time and of course had traveled by air to save time. He had learned a great deal about his objectives on those journeys, usually through briefings and talks with Americans who were in the armed forces or in diplomatic service. But he had seen little of the countries and the jet plane windows showed him not much but cumulus and the monotony of airports.

So, although he was well informed about the world, he was not well acquainted with it. He had hoped that during his second term he would serve on the Foreign Relations Committee. That interest had been one of the subconscious things that had finally nudged him into the decision to take this journey. He had no errand, which made him feel strangely footloose, but the anticipation of adventure had grown during the week before he sailed. Now, standing aloof from the group at Station Two, Alec felt he had made a ridiculous blunder. This was a kind of joy ride. These people were looking for amusement, not adventure. To Alec life had never been trivial even when he enjoyed it. He was a serious man under his charm—Aunt Lucy had seen to that—and until recently he had thought he would be a useful one.

The bells rang again and with relief the passengers began to strip off their life jackets and scatter. Howard Demarest said imperiously, "Come on, Ruby. Let's dump these strait-jackets and see what's going on in the Mayfair Room."

Robert Cayne said to his wife, "Shall we take a turn around the deck? I want to show off my beautiful girl."

Mr. and Mrs. Julian Chilton told the nurse not to let Hilary out of her sight and went back to their interrupted game of bridge with friends who were not committed to Lifeboat Two. They had a few friends on board and no intention of making casual acquaintances. Alida Barnes told Julia Hayward that they had better go up to the sun deck to be sure that their chairs had been put in the right place, fairly close to the pool but where there would not be too much sun. Bettina and Gene Beaufort went to play shuffleboard. They were having a wonderful time exploring marriage and to them most of the passengers looked too old for companionship.

Signe Goode did not know where to go. She had unpacked and her cabin was in perfect order but she did not want to go back to it. It had given her a terrible feeling of isolation, almost as bad as it had been in the first weeks after Tom died. Later on she had been kept busy with the conferences with lawyers and bankers, the sale of the house where she had lived with Tom for twenty-one years and where she could not bear to be alone, and the subsequent moving to her beautiful new apartment and agreeing with the ideas of the decorator who had furnished it. The apartment had a doorman, elevators and balconies and was very expensive, but she could afford it. She could afford to have anything she wanted. It was hard to believe at first but that was what the lawyer and the banker told her.

"Your husband had become a very wealthy man," said the bank officer.

"I don't think Tom thought he was very rich," said Signe. "He never said he was. He always worried about what things cost. And taxes."

"He was accustomed to being frugal."

"We had to be," she said.

The banker smiled. "Not in the last few years. Of course the money did come rather suddenly. Tom got in on the ground floor with a remarkably enterprising and successful company, and then there was the merger and new oil discoveries, as I explained to you."

"Tom had his job. He never counted on those other things too much."

"No, I think he always felt that his fortune might disappear as quickly as it came. But I can assure you, Mrs. Goode, that it won't."

Tom Goode had been a certified public accountant and a salary of twelve thousand a year had been the top of the ladder for his position with the firm. He had made it to the top years ago, but they continued to live on a lesser amount for he had supported his mother as long as she lived and taxes were higher every year. Signe always did her own housework. She did not mind that. It would have been a nuisance to have anyone else working in her home. There were no children. That was surprising and disappointing, especially to Signe, but they grew used to it and would have been embarrassed to consult a doctor about that very private failure. So they had accumulated quite a large amount in the savings bank and, after studying the accounts that his firm handled for wealthy clients, and weighing solvency against risk very carefully, Tom Goode had finally decided to put most of his reserves into an expanding oil and gas development.

Signe knew that it had been a successful investment but she had no idea of the scope of it until her husband died. Tom had never wanted people to know he had money and possibly he did not want to have Signe tempted to extravagance or to change their way of living.

"If people get an idea that you're rich," he used to say, "if they think you've got a little extra money, they bear down on you. They're all after you, everybody with his hand out."

But the vice-president of the bank had said, "You're in a position to do almost anything you want to do, Mrs. Goode. You can live very well, spend freely, and afford to be generous to your special interests in the community. Someday I would like to go into the matter of income-tax deductions with you. It is very interesting how they work out, quite surprising sometimes."

"I don't know anything about them. Tom always did the income-tax returns."

"Well, for example, if your husband had given us the whole amount that we are trying to raise for the addition to St. Luke's Hospital, it would have diminished his estate very little, if at all. You would probably be quite as well off as you are today."

It sounded very unlikely to Signe. Anyway, Tom would certainly never have given any large amount to a hospital. He had always disliked civic money-raising campaigns. But after that conversation with her banker Signe was curious enough to buy a tax manual which she saw on a newsstand. She had always been good at doing her housekeeping accounts and enjoyed keeping a close eye on the grocery bills. When she studied the book she found that the trust official had told her the truth. If Tom had given the hospital the two million dollars the inheritance taxes would have been so much less that she would be just about as rich as they told her she was now.

Rumors of the amount that Mrs. Goode had inherited spread around and her mail soon was loaded with supplications. She discarded almost all of them, though as usual she gave ten dollars to the Red Cross solicitor, ten dollars to the Cancer Fund—her mother had died of cancer—and twenty-five dollars to the United Fund though Tom had always grumbled that she was overdoing that contribution because he had to give at the office too. But the cheery women who collected the money came after it rain or shine and she did not like to turn them down. Also she always gave a little to the Salvation Army because they worked with the down-and-outs, and in this last Christmas season she had impulsively put a twenty-dollar bill instead of a coin into one of their kettles on the street and felt a warm pleasure at the thought of the surprise it would be for the blue-uniformed girl ringing her bell.

But she made no habit of such lavishness and the Christmas season had been desolate for Signe this year. She had lived in the luxurious apartment for six months but still did not know the names of the people to whom she spoke in the elevator. This had been the first Christmas without Tom, the first Christmas in years that she did not trim a Christmas tree. She had kept the trimmings that they always used on their trees in the old house, but when she looked them over they did not fit in with the decor of the apartment. The chairs and loveseats covered with pale green velvet and gold satin made the strings of tinsel and cardboard angels and the battered star-for-the-top look tawdry. Anyway, she did not know where to buy a tree or how she could get one up in the elevator. Tom had always found a tree somewhere on the outskirts of the city and brought it home tied to the open trunk of the car. Signe put away the old decorations and bought a wreath for her outer door. She asked for one made of holly but the florist had only artificial holly and convinced Signe that a wreath with a Della Robbia design—

costing thirty dollars, which made Signe wince—would be the suitable thing in the fashionable building where she lived.

She had spent Christmas by herself. The neighbors and acquaintances that she used to have had never been intimate though they had been kind when Tom died. Some of them had tried to draw her into their groups but she had retreated from invitations, partly from shyness and partly because Tom had never wanted to belong to any clique. She had sent Christmas cards to all her former neighbors and there was a small row of greetings from them arranged on her desk. But no one had asked her to dinner.

Signe had rather wanted to go to church on Christmas Day. On Christmas and Easter she and Tom had always gone to the service at St. Mark's that had music. As a child she had been brought up as a Catholic. Her father had been Irish. He was a fireman and had been killed in a disastrous fire in Trenton and she still had some newspaper clippings which referred to him as heroic. He had been devout and parochial. But Signe's Norwegian mother had never been converted to his faith. Widowed, she went back to her job as a head waitress and was always too tired to go to any church on Sunday. Signe lost the habit of regular attendance, but there was a vestige of Catholicism in Tom's heredity and so they respected the great feast days. She had felt the lack of going to church on this last Christmas but St. Mark's was on the other side of the city from her new apartment and she dreaded the idea of making an entrance by herself. She gave up the idea and watched a Mormon service on television.

In her own house Signe had always cooked a turkey or a goose for their mid-afternoon Christmas dinner, even if it was only for the two of them after Tom's mother died. This year she had scrambled eggs and a baked potato for lunch. There was a nearby tearoom where she usually had dinner but it was not open on the holiday.

Late in the afternoon she went out for a walk to see the lighted trees on lawns and in front windows. They were very pretty but gave her no cheer. It grew dark and there had been muggings in the neighborhood so at five o'clock she went back to her apartment and mixed a Bourbon highball. Tom had always kept a bottle or two of Bourbon in the house and Signe had finally overcome her embarrassment at buying it for herself. She invariably felt guilty at drinking alone but it dulled the cutting edge of her loneliness.

She was tired of television and picked up the newspaper which she had neglected to read in the morning. She skimmed the first page, feeling remotely unhappy about all the wars and the crimes, but they seemed to be happening in a different world from her own. She turned to the women's section and found out what the President's wife had worn at a recent function, how a great house in Palm Beach was decorated and what a designer prophesied would be worn—certainly not by herself, those pants and shawls—in the spring. Idly she began to read a column that was sometimes rather interesting. It described different types of women and the way they lived and was titled "IS THIS WOMAN YOU?"

Astonishingly, on this dreary Christmas Day, it was her. Signe read about herself.

The spendthrift woman who buys what she cannot afford is to be pitied, for the day of reckoning will come. But at least she has her moments of delight. The woman who pinches every penny and must do so is also to be pitied. But she does have the satisfaction of getting her money's worth. The woman who is the most pitiable of all is the one who has plenty of money and does not know what to do with it. Her family obligations are taken care of, possibly finished, and she has an income from her father's or her husband's estate which is larger than she needs. This is the wealthy widow who could have everything and settles for little or nothing. She does not use her money for the advantage of anyone, including herself. If she ever had the spirit of adventure it has withered. Of course she might be taking a voyage to the ends of the earth—she might be watching the world go by or going along with it in Paris or Hong Kong. But inertia or fear or sometimes a guilt sense about spending her own money ties her to loneliness and monotony. There are a great many such widows. Do you know one? Is she by any chance you?

Signe read it all through again before she put down the paper. Inertia—maybe that was what was the matter with her. It was so hard to do anything that she had not done when Tom was alive. Fear, the writer said, was another reason for not doing new things. There was something in that. You were afraid of strangers, who might not like you or might make fun of you or try to take advantage of you. You were always afraid of being cheated. And she wrote that you felt guilty about spending your own money. That was so too. It was funny that even when you knew the money was there and belonged to you legally, you didn't feel right about spending too much of it.

She could go anywhere she wanted to go. The banker had said so. She remembered that she used to daydream—when she was doing the housework, especially when she was washing dishes before they had the dishwasher—that someday they might take a long trip, maybe on a ship.

There was that travel place on First Street, just the other side of the bank, with all the posters in the windows. She could go in there and ask. She wouldn't have to decide anything. She could just find out how much it would cost—to go to France maybe.

But her vague, timid query did not stop there. Almost before she realized what had happened, Signe was involved. "Would you be interested in a cruise? Let me make a little travel plan for you and if you'll come in tomorrow—it's Mrs.—? No, there's no charge, Mrs. Goode. But if you'll give me your bank as a reference—"

And here she was on a ship, sailing on the ocean, and it was worse than ever, even more alone than in the apartment. She had bought all those clothes, because one thing led to another. Signe wandered through the public rooms, trying to look as if she were used to the vast luxury. She wished she had a drink of Bourbon. That might make her feel better, give her a little Dutch courage, as Tom used to call it.

Chapter Two

The five rooms that were equipped with bars on *The Seven Seas* were differentiated from each other in size, style and usually in patronage. The Mayfair Room was the one that had the best orchestra, but a good many people, especially those who were at the first sitting for lunch and dinner, preferred to have drinks in the Sky Room with its bright blue wicker furniture and enormous windows and where there was dancing from five in the afternoon. The Embassy Café was quiet until a little before seven o'clock, when the passengers who ate at the second sitting gathered there for cocktail parties, and The Ritz drew its best crowd after the late dinner. Tonight the people who had traveled on this ship before were advising others where to go for drinks and music, and those who did not know their way around yet were experimenting.

Alec Goodrich, who was assigned to the second sitting at half past eight, asked the steward, "Jim, is there a quiet place to get a drink on board? Where there's no hullabaloo?"

"There's the Seashell, sir. That's very quiet. That's aft on the promenade deck."

"Thanks," said Alec. "I'll look in there."

Barbara Bancroft came out of her cabin a few minutes later and asked the same question.

"Where can I get a cocktail, Jim?"

"It's very pleasant in the Embassy Room, Miss Bancroft. And the orchestra in the Sky Room is very good."

"Isn't there a place where you can get a drink that isn't set to music?"

She had not changed for dinner, knowing that it was not customary on the first night out, but she had taken off her coat and brushed her hair into shining curves. She looked very attractive in her gray wool shift, and it seemed to Jim that she belonged in the Embassy Room. A girl like that would soon find friends. He said, rather reluctantly, "There's the Seashell on the promenade. But it's not so popular."

"That's fine with me," said Barbara. "How do I get there?"

"If you take the last elevator to the promenade and turn right— let me ring it up for you—"

As he pressed the button he said, "Pardon me, but I think you might enjoy the Sky Room or the Embassy more."

"Not tonight, Jim."

The Seashell bore out its name by being a small room, a curved alcove, rather dimly lit by fixtures in the shape of shells upended on the counter behind the long pink marble bar. There were a number of small tables, most of them unoccupied. A man wearing a Roman collar was sitting at the farthest one, reading or trying to read in the skimpy light from the lamp in the middle of his table, a long drink beside his book. At another table was a middle-aged woman sitting by herself. She was wearing a coral satin evening dress and looked lonely and out of place. Two men, obviously not companions, were sitting at the bar. Barbara took a bar stool at the very end of the line. She always preferred to sit at bars instead of tables. Boone used to be amused by that habit.

She asked for a martini on the rocks but delayed drinking it. There was no pressure here. There was no need to pretend, to agree without agreement. During the hours since her mother and father had gone ashore, and since she had read the letter from Boone, she had been conscious of only cessation, of an emptiness that was not even loneliness.

She had tried to carry the departure off well for their sake. There was no point in destroying their hope and delusion that this junket they had planned for her would make a difference, change her back again into that girl who didn't know anything about anything—to the child she had been before that last year in Columbia, before she met Boone, before she knew what tear gas and jail were like, before she knew what it meant to be rejected by a man. She took a sip of her drink and vaguely hoped that her mother and father would have a good time tonight, now that she was off their hands for a while. They had been so worried about her and afraid for her. They had been afraid of her too—she knew that. There was no communication whatsoever between them and herself and when they tried to be broad-minded it only made things worse and more false. Basically it was their fault that Boone did not want her. They had burdened her with possessions and what they considered privileges. They had branded her and she couldn't get rid of the brand. That was why Boone had decided that he couldn't have her in his life.

"You'd ruin me, Barb."

"How can you say that! I'd help you. I only want what you want."

"You just think so. It would be impossible to go along with me."

"Because of the color of my skin?"

"I love the color of your skin. That's what would ruin me. If we had children I probably would love the little hybrids. And I can't be on both sides of the fence. I belong with my people, the blacks."

"You didn't feel that way until lately."

"I know I didn't. I was fooling myself, cottoning up to the white liberals, going along with their pious, sentimental idea that desegregation would work. I know better now."

"It's those people you go with now. They influence you."

"That's right, they influence me. They opened my eyes. Look, Barb, I could put on quite an act about this. I could say that I'm thinking of your happiness, that I don't want to hurt you, that I'm afraid I'd make you unhappy. That's not true. I'm thinking of myself, of my own redemption as a black man with no commitments that would make me conciliate or cheat."

When Barbara had found the letter from him in the pile of bon voyage notes and telegrams every nerve had leapt and shuddered. For the ship had sailed before she saw the letter and as she tore it open she thought that he might be asking her not to leave, saying that he couldn't get along without her.

But that was not what he wrote. She knew every word of the letter, having read it many times as she sat there in her cabin for hours until the steward made her go to the boat drill. She had taken the letter with her to the deck and thrown the torn pieces of it over the rail. But she could not forget a word of it.

Boone had written,

I saw Carrie at a meeting the other night and she told me that you are going around the world on *The Seven Seas*. So I checked the day it would sail for I wanted to write you. Carrie said you asked about me and if I was all right. I am. Put me out of your mind. I shouldn't be allowed to linger in it. I have given you a bad time and the sooner you forget me the better. I won't ask you to forgive me for I don't think in those terms. It had to be that way.

I have gone through a personal evolution, changing from the person I was when we first met last year to the one I am now and must and shall continue to be. The person I now am would not attract you. The man you liked thought that to be in love with a white girl was a wonderful thing, a progress, and that if there was enough interracial love and marriage race problems would vanish. I know better now. I know that if there is any answer that is not it. And as we went along and your parents tried to face up to the possibility of marriage between us, I felt more and more of a traitor and sycophant. Traitor, I mean, to something far more important than my physical desire. I began to dislike the future I was heading into. Of course I could stand up to the snubs and the revulsions of society. That sort of defiance can be exciting but it is really a kind of adolescent delight. We would have tired of it, and soon begun to chip away at each other's personality. We would have destroyed each other even if we had some pleasure. You didn't believe that but it is true.

I am glad you are taking this journey and hope you get a lot out of it—though on a luxury cruise—I was a deckhand on one of those cruise ships one summer—most of the people who take those trips go around the world without seeing it. I hope you won't. Carrie said that you told her you did not want to go but that you felt you had to get away from New York and from your family. And from me, she implied. Personally I believe it is a good idea for you to make the break. Go away—and stay away—until you are sure of your own identity. It sounds corny but there's nothing to living except being yourself, doing your own thing.

It was a cruel letter. He had become the kind of man who could write it, without regret. Barbara had faced up to that when she threw the fragments of his farewell overboard. But that did not make it easier. He had struck her away as if she were an unwanted child clinging to him and since then she had been without any attachment that meant anything. There was no return to living at home, to being a happy daughter. She had let her parents believe what of course they wanted to believe, that she had come to her senses and broken off the relationship that had been so repulsive to them. She had not explained anything or confided in anyone. She had been civil and pliant because it didn't make any difference. But she could not go back to playing around, to the vague search for a man to marry. Graduate work at college no longer interested her. The academic world was in a mess. Taking a job would be phony. She did not need the money or want to stand behind a counter or sit at a typewriter pretending to occupation and usefulness. For a year she had been living with a cause, with a crusade, and it had been ripped out of her hands and her emotions.

She finished her drink and indicated to the barman that she would have another. He had just served the woman in the coral dress with a refill. As he put ice in another glass, the red-haired man who was sitting at the middle of the long bar spoke. He lifted his drink and let the words fall without direction. In the silent little room they came out loud and clear.

"Happy voyage to all the refugees on *The Seven Seas.*"

The others stared at him. Alec Goodrich frowned and Signe Goode looked startled and frightened. The priest looked up from his book. Barbara turned toward the stranger with curiosity. He did not seem to be drunk. His voice was amused and he smiled as he met her glance.

"Refugees? On this ship?"

"A generic term. For our fellow passengers—perhaps even for ourselves?"

"That's a rather obnoxious statement," said Alec Goodrich.

"But it's interesting," Barbara said. "Are you a refugee, Mr.—?"

"Mark Claypole. Oh yes. I suppose most of the people on the ship are escaping from something. Not the young and old honeymooners, not Pat here behind the bar and the rest of the ones who keep the ship afloat and serviced. But, in the main, passengers on a journey like this are bound to be on the run from trouble or grief or disappointment. Don't you think so?"

"I wouldn't know."

"I know what you mean," the woman in satin said in a sudden explosion of words. Three drinks had made it possible for Signe Goode to speak to strangers. She had found this room before dinner and come back after she had dressed, to get more courage.

Mark Claypole glanced at her. "Won't you join us at the bar, Madam?" he asked and without waiting for an answer he went to her table and escorted Signe and her drink and fur stole to the bar. She hoisted herself to a bar stool for the first time in her life, the folds of her fine dress spilling brilliantly down its length.

"I'm very grateful to have you say that you understand me," said Claypole.

"Well—sometimes you want to get away from everything, that's what I mean—my husband—Mr. Goode, I'm Mrs. Signe Goode—died a year ago and when you live alone—well, after a while it gets on your nerves—"

"And you become a fugitive from loneliness," he prompted.

"I guess that's it. I read a piece that said travel was one thing that women like me should do—I don't know how true it is—it does seem very queer to be on the ocean on a ship and not know a soul."

"Something must be done about that. May I introduce myself—I'm Mark Claypole—and this young lady is—"

"I'm Barbara Bancroft."

"Senator Goodrich at the other end of the bar." And as Alec stiffened at being identified with his former title Mark Claypole went on smoothly, "Father Duggan is also with us. Could you be persuaded to join our little group, Father? We are discussing refugeeism."

"I'm afraid I have nothing to contribute to the conversation."

Father Duggan spoke quietly and lowered his glance again to his book. He had been listening and watching the incident. The man called Claypole was making a fool of the woman with that exaggerated, mocking courtesy. But his words had struck home to the priest. It was true. He was on the run. Fleeing from decision.

Signe was very glad that the priest stayed at his table. When she was a little girl she had gone to parochial school and respect and awe of nuns and priests had been instilled in her. Something of that feeling lingered. Priests were different from other men. She could remember how all-powerful they had seemed in the confessional. She had not practiced her religion in years. But she had been surprised and slightly shocked when the priest came into this cocktail room and ordered a drink. Of course he was reading his prayerbook. Priests had to do that every day. Signe remembered that.

Barbara said to Mark Claypole, "No, I think what you say is terribly exaggerated. Most of the people on this cruise must want to see the world. That's what it's for, why they're taking it."

"I'm sure that they'd tell you that. Maybe even believe it."

"Are you a psychiatrist?" inquired Alec.

"No. Only a writer. My job involves exploring motives."

"Or imagining them," muttered Alec.

He disliked journalists and people who wrote about others for a living. Most of them were unscrupulous. At the height of his career he had got along well with the press but after the tragedy it was different. The publicity had been merciless and slanted, exaggerat-

27

ing his wealth and ambition, playing up his engagement to a girl with social position. They added these things up so there was more to pull down with a crash after a girl who had worked in his campaign was found dead in his apartment. It was an obvious suicide but the journalists and reporters had draped it in innuendo. They would not spoil such a human-interest story with the true facts that the girl had been a nuisance in the organization, that the Senator had been embarrassed by her devotion but could not possibly have guessed that the public announcement of his engagement to Cicely Correll would send her over the edge.

Reporters had turned Alec's brief statements upside down, interpreted his silences to suit themselves. And here was another of the ghouls, at it again, singling him out by name insolently in a public place. Alec wanted to let his anger loose and leave the room but he knew that Claypole would make something of that. Stubbornly he stayed where he was.

"Are you going to write a story about this cruise?" Signe Goode was asking.

"That is the question to which there never is an answer," said Mark Claypole.

If he did write one he probably could not sell it. The picture had changed. A few years ago they were clamoring for anything he wrote. His prices were steadily going up. But now the editors were difficult to please and even his agent was more evasive than hopeful.

Milton Knott, his literary agent, who had made a nice piece of money on the ten percent commissions he received for selling Claypole's work in the beginning, said that he didn't know why it was or what it was. The market had changed. He dwelt on that. Many of the periodicals that had published fiction had folded in the last ten years and the ones that were left were buying controversy or scandal, not much good prose.

"They want revelations about people in the news, they want super true confessions. The magazines don't give a damn whether a person can write well or not, Mark. The bright boys on their staffs rewrite the stuff anyway."

"They never had to rewrite my stuff."

"No," said Milton gloomily, as if that might be the trouble.

"Have you had any word yet from Hollywood about *Summer of Fancy*?"

"The trouble is that out there they aren't buying anything except the top best sellers. If they are sexy enough or far offbeat."

Claypole's first book had sold a hundred thousand copies. His last one had sold less than six thousand.

He asked, "Where are you going to send *Bird of Passage* now that Boardwalk has turned it down?"

"It's pretty well made the rounds," said Milton uncomfortably. "Phil Prentiss liked it but was not quite convinced enough to buy. He almost took it."

"That's rubbing it in."

"He did say one thing that might interest you. He said that he could use a story on travel, if he could get one with a new angle."

"What kind of angle?"

"He didn't specify. What he feels is that hundreds of thousands of people travel these days and they would identify with the right story."

"Would that be a firm offer?"

"I asked him that—talked about your Palm Beach story and the profile you did of Chicago—and Phil said that he thinks you can make places come alive through people better than almost anyone. But he wouldn't make a commitment. He said that the thing was so vague in his own mind that he'd have to see the story first."

"So he could turn it down."

"I don't think he would. I believe it might be worth a try. I have faith in your work. You know that."

"I wish I had," said Claypole.

So here he was, taking on a crazy, expensive gamble, looking for a story without a contract for it. With only a little more than ten thousand dollars left, now that he had sold his car and his equity in the apartment and paid for his passage in one of the cheapest inside cabins on the ship. And the alimony was continually bleeding him.

At the time of the divorce he hadn't objected too strenuously to the amount of money that Suzanne's lawyer demanded. It was worth paying the money to be rid of her and their marriage. For if he was free he was sure that he could get back to work, to the kind of work that had brought him notice and praise at twenty-five. There would be no more of the incessant arguments or the quarrels or the senseless parties where people talked about writing when they should have been doing it. The seven years with Suzanne had been one long drift in the wrong direction. Suzanne had fooled him at first. He had thought she was interested in his work. But what she wanted was the periphery of the profession, the glamour and publicity that went along with a writer's success. When those things had begun to diminish for Mark she had been unhappy and then resentful because he did not force his way back into the limelight. She believed that was a matter of making and keeping up contacts with influential people in the literary world, but Mark knew better. While they were breaking up he had a vision of recreating his former industry, of spending long days and nights at the typewriter, of feeling the old verve and enjoyment with exhaustion in his work. After the financial and legal details were settled, when the divorce was at last final, next month—

Now it was nearly twenty months and he had not restored either his diligence or his success. He wasn't fluent any more. If he had an idea it often withered before he got it down on paper. He wrote without zest or faith. He wasn't confident and he had become cynical, almost meeting defeat on the way. He knew that today he should have taken his typewriter out of its case and pounded out his first impressions of the voyage. Of that little tugboat pushing the great liner away from the dock and out of the harbor, and the sharp contrast between the men in oily working clothes on the tug and the people watching from the decks of *The Seven Seas*. His imagination was pricked as he saw the old woman propelling herself laboriously on two canes to the lifeboat drill with a look that was curiously enraptured—as if she had managed to make the start of the journey against all odds. There was the lifeboat drill, assembling the group of strangers who conceivably might have to die together—the exit of Howard Demarest with the woman called Mrs. Signe Goode would be an unlikely combination.

He had meant to work today but his typewriter was still covered. Since the sailing he had been as idle as a boy on a street corner watching the girls go by. Then he had finally come into this bar after sizing up the other ones, which reminded him too much of all the futile cocktail parties he had gone through in the last few years. He drank slowly and was able to carry his liquor well so he had been there for a long time, making an occasional wisecrack to the bartender. The thing about refugees had come into his mind and he had spoken it aloud because the mocking toast seemed amusing at the moment. Mark Claypole had begun to do perverse things before the divorce, unexpected and out-of-line things, sometimes to annoy Suzanne and plague her snobbery, sometimes to display his indifference to opinion, to show that he didn't care whom he annoyed or pleased. Like needling this Senator who had taken such a beating. And playing up the middle-aged widow instead of the pretty girl.

He wasn't sorry that he had decided to come, useless junket though it might be as far as writing went. The faint throb of the ship meant that he was putting distance between himself and the scene of his frustration. He didn't have to write a story. He didn't have to go back. He could get lost somewhere in Africa or Asia. Men often disappeared, completely changed their way of life, shucked off previous associations. Some of them became beachcombers. Anything was possible.

Signe Goode took a cigarette from her bag and fumbled in it for a match. Claypole quickly bent closer to her, snapping open his lighter. He noticed that her skin was quite beautiful, without a blemish though she was probably close to forty if not already there. As she held the cigarette to the flame he saw the rings on her hand. There was a gold wedding band and another set with a very small solitaire diamond. They told Mark Claypole that she had always worn those rings since her husband gave them to her and that he couldn't afford more than a very little diamond at first. But he must have left her well fixed. She had no jewelry but her beaded evening bag must have cost more than her engagement ring, and the fur stole that he had carried from her table to the bar was certainly Russian sable. Suzanne had begged for a piece of sable and he had given her one when he made his first sale to a book club. He knew what that furry lightness cost.

A page went down the corridor outside the room, playing a light tune on a bugle.

"That must be the call for the second sitting," Mark Claypole explained to Signe Goode. "They're ready for us in the dining room. Tonight I suppose we have to find our regular seats."

"I'm at table 24," said Signe.

"I forgot my card. I'll have to ask the steward where they have planted me," he said.

Barbara had already gone, leaving a half-filled glass behind. The priest closed his book and signed the chit for his single drink. Alec Goodrich was the last to leave, waiting until he was sure the others must have reached the elevators, thinking with satisfaction that he would have a table by himself. He wanted no more of Claypole's talk.

The young men who arranged the shore trips offered during the cruise at ports of call had been placed, by their own request, at a table by themselves at the second sitting. This would protect them, while they were eating, from criticism, questions and even praise for the excursions ashore. They had been very busy this afternoon, getting their office in order, and cables had been constantly coming in which would make changes in their arrangements necessary.

This was annoying to both the travel agents and the passengers but was bound to happen. The long safaris in Africa took complicated planning and there were often disappointments. A guide who was relied upon would die or disappear. Guides were a continual problem. Some were stupid, some arrogant. But the rule was that in almost every port native guides must be employed in addition to the young men from the travel bureau who acted as escorts on important tours.

Cars and buses that had been promised at the docks sometimes did not show up. Hotels and planes oversold their space. This afternoon they had heard that the ship's arrival would clash with an International Rotary Convention in Lisbon which had unexpectedly altered its schedule, and some of the reservations for dinner at good hotels for passengers on *The Seven Seas* would have to be canceled. That had meant ship-to-shore telephoning to other hotels and night clubs in Lisbon and had been expensive.

There were four travel agents listed as part of the ship's staff and they had several assistants who filled in when necessary, as well as a bookkeeper and two typists. These ate at the first sitting. The four head men had a general attitude of slight superciliousness, but this was to some extent a protective covering from the constant demands and whims of passengers. They were on the whole competent young men who enjoyed travel and had picked up a considerable amount of knowledge about the countries and the ports which they touched.

Percy Blake was the oldest and had saved nearly enough money to open his own travel bureau in a year or two. Jim Hicks was the youngest and had joined the agency after he got out of the Navy because he wanted to see more of the world. Cecil Brettingham was British and his BBC accent had somehow affected the others, so that they all spoke in clipped sentences. Harold Monk cultivated a manner of indifference to the whole job but his associates knew that he always did his share of the work and on the trips which he personally chaperoned no one ever lost a suitcase.

They had their own status on the ship. They did not command the same respect as the German professor who gave the lectures did. Nor did they have the authority of the purser and the chief steward. But they had good cabins on the upper deck and a well-placed table in the dining room from which they were tonight observing the passengers. They were welcome and useful at all the public parties on board and invited to many of the private ones. They danced well. They were extremely well dressed for they knew the places in Singapore and Hong Kong where well-tailored clothes could be bought for very little money. None of them was married at present. Percy Blake never wanted to try it again and though Brettingham fully intended to marry a wealthy and beautiful woman he had not found the right one yet. Some woman on every voyage would always try to break down Harold Monk's indifference and up to a point he would let her try.

Already they had identified some of the people on board. Demarest had introduced himself and stated various requirements for his shore trips. They did not like him but it was necessary to walk softly where a director of the Line was concerned. The Chiltons would have special attention. The ex-Senator had not come into the travel office. He might not know the ropes about shore trips. The pretty girl in gray had not been in the Mayfair Room where the travel agents had cocktails tonight before dinner. The old lady with the canes was out of the past but it wasn't her first time on a ship. Like Jim Bates, the agents made their quiet ratings.

In the Captain's sitting room, forward on the navigating bridge deck, Commodore Rudolph James was talking to the cruise director and the social director, Mrs. Joan Scofield.

"When you have your first daily program printed, Harold, be sure to put in the usual item about the fact that during the cruise I shall invite all the passengers to have dinner with me at one time or another and that there is absolutely no order of preference."

"I'll make it the first announcement, Captain."

"How many are we finally?"

"Five hundred and seventy-six passengers."

Joan Scofield, who was as beautiful and brisk and charming as her job demanded, said, "It will mean about sixty at each dinner if you have one every week."

"I'm sure you'll arrange the lists so that everyone is taken care of in groups that are as congenial as possible. Mr. Howard Demarest is on board and he's a director of the Line so he probably should be at the first party."

"There is a young lady on board who seems to be a close friend of Mr. Demarest," Joan Scofield said with so little emphasis that it was meaningful.

"Pretty?"

"Very."

"Then we surely can take care of her," said the Commodore, smiling. "Is there anyone else who should have special attention? I know there's no preference but some things have to be considered."

"Mr. Alexander Goodrich was a United States Senator."

"I've heard of him. I'll remember and look out for him."

"And when I went over the list I saw the name of Mr. Mark Claypole. If he's the writer—if it's the same one—he was very good. I'll find out," said Joan. "It looks like a very nice crowd for this voyage."

"Good," said the Commodore. "About the dinners—I was thinking that another year we might do the job a bit more informally—"

He stopped, feeling as queer as the others were embarrassed. It was a slip of the mind as well as the tongue because this was the last world cruise that Commodore James would command on *The Seven Seas.* He was being retired and though he constantly reminded himself and everyone else that this was his final voyage, the fact hadn't quite come true to himself.

He laughed and said, "Well, another year that won't be my

worry. There's the bugle for the second sitting. Better get down while things are hot. Goodnight."

He was having dinner by himself tonight instead of with the ship's officers. There were some details he wanted to think out, for at the last moment he might have to make a change in the route around Africa and omit a couple of ports. The passengers always complained when that happened but Commodore James did not want to run into any disturbances and he had been told that trouble might be brewing in Durban, which could mean strikes on the docks, delay or tie-ups and possible shore dangers for the passengers. The itinerary had been planned to the hour for eighty days and any change would be disrupting.

He did not ring for dinner immediately but went to the windows at the front of the sitting room and looked out, savoring the sight, reminding himself that he would not see it from this viewpoint again, nor while he had this authority. The ship was alone on the ocean, casting beams of light on waves that were curled with white foam. The voyage was under way and after sixteen years of world cruises Commodore James knew all that it meant. Five hundred and seventy-six passengers—*The Seven Seas* could carry twice that number on a transatlantic trip with first- and second-class passengers, but on her cruises around the world all the passengers were first class and the number was limited. The crew and staff numbered slightly more than six hundred, including the paid entertainers. Twenty-four ports would be entered if the schedule was kept. It was difficult to maneuver in and out of some of them and a few might be slightly hostile, with world conditions what they were.

He had these things and also his staff in mind. Karl Van Sant, his Chief Officer, was certainly aware that he would move up to Commander, but he wasn't putting on any airs about that. The cruise director, Harold Fuller, was a man who knew his business and would keep things moving. Commodore James was not so satisfied with the shore excursion staff, who were under the direction of their travel agency, though of course he himself had ultimate authority if anything serious came up. The young men seemed to regard themselves as members of the Department of State. So the purser had acidly remarked, but the purser had ulcers and his point of view had to be somewhat discounted. The young men would probably do their jobs well enough, and the women passengers would like their fancy manners.

His responsibility did not prey on Commodore James. He enjoyed its weight and intricacy. But he knew that only a man in his position could fully realize what was necessary to keep all these people safe and fed and, in so far as possible, happy and comfortable for eighty days. Some were bound to get sick. There was usually a death during a voyage as long as this one. The eighteen elevators had to be constantly checked, the plants that distilled sea water into the enormous fresh water supply had to be carefully tended, the decks closed off when they became slippery, lifeboat drills regularly carried out. Thousands of details were delegated to the hierarchies of ship's officers and stewards and sailors and cooks and entertainers but the ultimate power rested with the Captain, as did the mood of the voyage. He had to be friendly enough and sufficiently aloof. He had to give the passengers an event to remember when they dined with him by the written invitation that Joan would send around. She was a great hostess—Joan was a whirlwind, the Commodore often said. It would have been very easy to make his feeling for her more than admiration and enjoyment in having her around, but that sort of thing was very bad for morale on a ship and the Commodore did not permit himself or his officers such indulgence.

He rang for a menu and when it came he ordered oysters—they would be unavailable after a few days at sea—and the filet mignon, which would not yet be frozen. No dessert. He was careful to keep his weight down and his tall figure trim. Commodore James certainly did not look sixty-six. Nor feel it.

Chapter Three

Since he had come this far and would probably have trouble getting his fare refunded, Alec Goodrich reasoned, he might as well have a look at Casablanca and Las Palmas, which was a matter of only three more days after leaving Lisbon. By that time he would have made up his mind whether he wanted to continue with the eight days of cruising during which the ship would cross the equator and arrive in South Africa. He could fly back from Capetown if he felt like it.

The week he had already spent at sea had gone very fast once he had established his own routine. He liked all the stewards who served him—Jim Bates in his cabin, Dennis in the dining room, and Anatole, the wine steward with the golden chain around his neck, who gave him special attention and at dinner would suggest a choice of wine in a conspiratorial way. It was not hard to keep himself to himself as Alec had feared it would be. He looked at the printed program for the day which was shoved under his cabin door each morning and could tell at a glance what he wanted to avoid, such as the "boost your own state" night—Alec did not want to call any attention to his present relations with his state—and the special cocktail party for those who were traveling alone, "so that they could meet each other," and the midnight buffets with the hard-drinking group who never wanted to go to bed and called themselves the Night Owls.

But the motion pictures were excellent and the young history professor who gave travel talks about the ports where the ship would pause was thoroughly educated and interesting. Several times Alec had played shuffleboard with a few men who didn't try to develop the game into later social occasions. He usually drank at the Seashell bar but did not see there again any of the ones who had been his companions on the first night. Sometimes he passed the priest on deck and exchanged a few comments on the weather. The priest did not seem to be seeking company or converts. Alec saw Claypole daily in the dining room but the writer was at a satisfactory distance, flanked at a large table with other men and women, including Mrs. Goode. The Bancroft girl was at a table in the middle of the dining room, obviously the star table, for Howard Demarest and his girl were also seated there. Barbara was very beautiful in evening clothes and when she wore them would pile her hair high.

Mrs. Barnes had managed an introduction to Alec and asked him one night if he would fill in at a bridge table. It would have been openly rude to refuse and she and her friends played a superb game so the competition was stimulating. But when she said he must call her Alida and that they must play again, he managed to be inaccessible in the theater the next night. What Alec had enjoyed most so far was to pull on a sweater, walk on the high boat deck where there were no steamer chairs and let the wind whip around him. Then he would think it all over, and each time it was a little less painful to do it, as if the wind and the solitude took the sting out of the wound.

In Lisbon he had left the ship and walked from the dock to the city and at a large hotel found a taxi whose driver could talk fairly good English. He remembered what the young professor had said in his lecture about the city and asked to be driven through the old city where the streets were hardly more than ancient paved paths and wound and wound up the hills. He sat with the driver, who became friendly and translated the names of the streets—the Street of the Little Angels, the Street of the Sad Virgin, the Street of the Man Who Talks to Himself. I should get out here, thought Alec with amused irony as the driver named that street.

It was surprising to feel, when he finally went back to the ship, a sense of being in place. He had been dislocated for months and to have Jim say that he hoped Mr. Goodrich had enjoyed himself and Anatole remark, "Ah, tonight you must have a wine of Portugal, yes?" was oddly agreeable.

There was the same feeling when he returned from a long day in Casablanca. He had known many historical and political facts about the city but he had not anticipated its astonishing whiteness and wealth. He avoided the bazaars—there was nothing he wanted to possess and no one for whom he wanted to buy anything—but he found his way to the Anfa Hotel and went inside to look around, because he remembered that this was where Churchill and Roosevelt had met for their famous Casablanca conference. Sitting on a divan in the lounge and ordering the mint tea, which the professor had said was the drink of Morocco, his mind dwelt on the two statesmen. When they had met here they had been at the height of their political power. They would have been wary of each other with great cordiality. It was an unsafe game even at their level. Churchill found that out when the war was over. He must have been bitter to his bones.

Someone said, "Hello, Senator," and he looked up to see Mark Claypole's slightly satirical grin. Signe Goode was with him, carrying some sort of embroidered garment or scarf over her arm.

"This girl is a great shopper," said Claypole.

"I'm really not. I never have been. But the things are so beautiful and so different," Signe said. "It's all so wonderful!"

"And this is where the great rascals plotted," said Claypole.

Signe did not know what he was talking about, and Alec did not want to talk history with a journalist.

"I don't think they look like rascals," said Signe, "and I haven't seen a single beggar."

Alec beckoned the waiter. He said it was a very interesting city, more modern than he had expected, and escaped after a few more flavorless remarks. To get back to the ship and unlock his cabin door gave him again that pleasant feeling of having a place of his own.

"Wonderful city, Jim," he said in quite a different tone from the one that he had used with Mark Claypole, "and now I'd like a double Scotch right here in the room. I'm not much for peppermint tea. My aunt used to give it to me when I had a stomach ache."

"I'll bring it right away, sir."

Father Duggan had gone ashore soon after the ship docked. He was restless. At times this journey to which he was committed seemed unbearably long and he could not bring himself to any close companionship with his fellow passengers. He had expected that there would be other chaplains aboard to take care of the passengers who were Jews and Protestants. But when he inquired about this the head steward had told him apologetically that the rabbi who had been booked for the voyage had been taken ill and forced to cancel and for the Protestant services they usually relied on a passenger who was familiar with them and willing to conduct them on Sunday. So the priest had done the obligatory things, said Mass daily in the theater where the stewards would place a temporary altar. A few people attended every day and a larger number had come to the Sunday service, when he had tried to give a sermon that would mean something, especially to the young members of the crew who sat in one row. But it had seemed to him as artificial as the pictures that had flickered on the screen last night. And he had wondered whether, if the trappings and beauty of churches were taken away, religion would stand by itself.

He had no plans for the day but obviously most of the passengers were bristling with them. There were private cars, taxis and buses lined up, some already assigned, some idle and waiting, with their drivers shrewdly measuring the tourists and accosting the ones who seemed affable and might be generous. Howard Demarest was immediately paged over the loudspeaker and the priest watched him go to a limousine, his girl with her usual manner of going along as she was told. She wore the shortest possible dress of peacock blue and was already tanned to a flawless brown.

Mr. and Mrs. Chilton had brought their little girl and her nurse, and a private car was waiting for them. The child was the only one on the ship. Father Duggan pitied her, surrounded by too much wealth and too much protection. She had probably never been let loose on a playground.

Mr. and Mrs. Robert Cayne paused to say good morning to him. Mr. Cayne knew everyone and didn't leave out the priest. He had told Father Duggan that his first wife had been a Catholic. "She was very devout," he said. "I never objected. I know a good many Catholics—we have some in Rotary who are very fine citizens. But as far as I'm concerned, if you don't mind my saying so, there are some things I couldn't go along with personally in the Catholic religion. I guess I just think my sins are my own business."

Cayne was wearing a very gay floral sport shirt this morning and was harnessed with camera equipment. "Stand still, darling," he said suddenly, "right where you are. I want a picture of you with the natives in the background and we'll tell the folks you met up with some of your cousins in Morocco." He swung the lens. "Father, I'd like a shot of you."

Father Duggan held up a protesting hand and quickly moved out of range. He saw the writer who had been so talkative on that first night aboard and he was with the woman he had picked up there. The acquaintance had progressed, apparently. They were hailing a taxi. The beautiful Bancroft girl was getting on a bus, mingling with the others but not blending with them as usual. She managed that very well. The priest had often observed her in the dining room. She was gay but he believed she was not happy. Certainly she was not a party girl, as they were called, like the one with Demarest.

The priest was still a young man, who would become forty in the course of this voyage, but he had been ordained at twenty-six and in fourteen years of work in both wealthy and poor parishes, hearing confessions, celebrating marriages, listening to human problems and visiting in houses of illness and death, he had developed a sympathy so deep that it gave him extraordinary insight into conditions of grief and confusion. People did not have to tell him when they were carrying burdens. He usually knew by looking at them.

After a few years he had begun to share many of the burdens even while he prescribed doctrine for them. The sullen or bitter pregnant women whose tenement homes were already crowded with underfed children, black boys growing up in hate and violence beyond the persuasion of religion or the discipline of law, mismated husbands and wives who could never live together in peace or usefulness but were denied divorce, corruption that was sometimes tolerated or forgiven because of affluence or political power—all these things preyed upon him. The advice he was obliged to offer as a priest often seemed hypocritical to him for he knew that it did not meet the problems or resolve the tensions and would probably be rejected.

He had tried to close his mind to his own criticisms. He tried to find satisfaction in the relaxation of some dogmas and precepts. Fasts were being abolished, services simplified, laymen now read prayers from the altars and there were folk masses where long-haired boys strummed guitars and chorused ancient responses to the beat of pop music. But to him the changes were palliatives. Sometimes they seemed to Father Duggan to be almost bribes. In the parishes where he had served for the past few years the innovations had not increased faith or devotion. They resulted in more-unkempt congregations who spent less time in their churches. More Catholics received the Blessed Sacrament on Sundays than ever before, but what disturbed him was that they did it as a matter of course, without sufficient preparation or contrition, probably often without being in a state of grace. He had no desire to see the old stringencies and bigotries revived. But he thought the Church was making small concessions to comfort and convenience and not attacking the major problems of modern living and deteriorating morality.

He knew that he was only one of many troubled priests. There was a generation gap in the Catholic clergy and many of the younger men were half in and half out of the institution. They ignored the admonitions of their Bishops, gave unauthorized interviews and opinions to the press, argued against celibacy and yet did not completely sever their ties with the hierarchy. They joined and led street marches to demonstrate for peace or integration or better housing or more welfare. Father Duggan had done his share of marching but for him that had been an outlet to nothing.

The pronouncement of Pope Paul against birth control had shocked him to bitterness. It seemed a blind decision to cling to outworn patterns for sex relations and family life.

"Catholics won't go along with it," he said to the Bishop.

"I suppose some may not. We must do all we can to make them feel that the Holy Father knows what is right and can be permitted."

"But how can this be right when it will make more women stay away from the confessionals or tell lies in them and more men shrug their shoulders and say that they'll decide for themselves? If there is a general breakdown in obedience on one point, there will soon be a breakdown on another. If the Pope loses authority, the Church will dissolve."

"Your duty is clear then. To help maintain his authority."

"But the Pope doesn't seem to realize what the world is like today."

"I am quite sure that he does," said the Bishop dryly.

"What I hear in the confessional—what people tell me—"

"Yes, you are on the firing line, I know. But you love the Church, don't you, Father Aloysius?"

"I have loved it all my life."

That was what made it so fearful a struggle. Sometimes the thought that he might never again say a Mass would almost overcome him with pain. Yet to continue to make use of the great privilege while disbelieving in the judgment of the head of the Church would make him both traitor and sinner.

One of the travel agents spoke to him. "There is a seat left in the last bus, Father. You're going with us to Marrakesh, I hope?"

The crowd of tourists had thinned. Father Duggan said absently, "Thank you—yes, I think I shall—I was given a ticket," and mounted the steps of the bus. He went down the aisle and saw that there was only one vacant place, beside the Bancroft girl, who sat next to the window, watching the natives on the dock.

"May I sit here?" he asked. The bus was moving and it was too late for retreat.

"Of course," said Barbara, and moved a little to give him more room. She glanced up and he saw her face closely for the first time. The smile was pleasant enough, but his gift of intuition told him that this was not a happy young woman.

As Alec Goodrich went through the hotel door Mark Claypole said, "You can't really blame him. He was a pretty good Senator, as they go, and he must have actually liked the racket."

"He doesn't seem very friendly," Signe said, "he has a table all by himself in the dining room."

"Taking no risks."

"What do you mean?"

"He was caught up in a scandal—you must have heard about it. It killed him off politically. One of the girls who worked in his campaign committed suicide and there was a lot of talk. My guess is that it probably wasn't his fault. Those girls who go political are very uptight. But they didn't like it in the Middle West."

"Oh," said Signe, "I think I did read something about it. But he wasn't the Senator from our state. I don't know much about politics. Of course I always voted—I did when Tom was alive. He was a Republican."

"I'm sure he would have been."

"Yes, he always voted the straight ticket. He'd bring home a sample ballot and go over it with me. I haven't voted since. I suppose I should. But unless you know the people who are running for office it's so confusing."

"To all of us," said Mark.

After ten days he knew a great deal about Signe Goode. Possibly more than she herself knew. As she had told him about her life and her environment he expertly related the facts to their causes. His imagination could see the little house, looking much like the other ones in the block to everyone but the Goodes, with the leather armchair "that Tom never would give up" before the television set, "we never had one in color but I have one of those now in the apartment."

He also understood Tom Goode better than his wife ever had. There must have been some quality of the miser in him and probably a basic distrust of society. He would provide adequately for his wife as well as for his mother, who must have been an old harridan. But in so far as possible he had kept his home as a small comfortable fortress against social and financial demands, and voted Republican as the lesser evil. He had been shown the picture of Tom Goode that Signe carried in her handbag. No one would have looked at him twice on the street but he had made a fortune.

Signe had not talked freely to anyone in a long while but perhaps because he was so carelessly friendly, or possibly because he had broken through her misery on that first night aboard, she had talked to Mark almost without being questioned. Sometimes during the days he would stop by her steamer chair and if the one next to it was empty he would stretch himself out there and listen as the pattern of her life evolved from its details. As he had been listening idly one morning a week ago.

"They are so good-looking." That was when Mrs. Hayward and Mrs. Barnes went by, wearing beautifully matched sweaters and pants. "I never wear slacks. Tom didn't like them. But now everyone seems to, in the very best society. You know I was really sort of scared when I found I was at the table with those two." She paused to give a still timid smile at them as they passed, polite in greeting but not stopping.

"Scared? Why on earth?"

"Well, I've never known society women. And you can see that they are."

Mark said lazily, "They are women who are spending a lengthening age over a small card table and going round and round a diminishing world to avoid the exigencies of their middle-aged sons and daughters."

"Do they have families?" she asked, picking up the last bit.

"I have no idea. That was just a quotation. From a book called *Tales of Manhattan*. Alida and Julia are very Manhattan."

"I don't call them by their first names." Signe laughed. "I just say 'you.'"

"You say Mark."

"That's different. I feel as if I know you."

His denial was a silent one, and Signe went on: "We never went out much. Of course for a long time we couldn't. Tom's mother lived with us for years. His stepbrother had a big family and lived out West and when his father died Tom said, 'It's up to us, Signe.' And it was—we had the extra room in our house. But it was rather hard on Tom, for she failed and you know how old people get confused and difficult and think they're being neglected. We never left her alone the last year—one or the other of us was always in the house in case anything should happen. I sometimes think of how different it would have been if we'd had more money when she was living with us."

"Nice to have money any time."

"Sometimes more than others. I wish Tom had taken a trip like this just once. He could have, after he made those investments. But we didn't know what was going to happen. He should have had a checkup. But I never could get Tom to a doctor."

He didn't want to spend the money. And he distrusted doctors.

It fitted into Mark's picture of Tom Goode.

"He was only forty-six. We'd just had our anniversary, our twentieth, and he always gave me as many roses as the years we'd been married. American Beauties. Tom used to say that I was his child bride and that he'd robbed the cradle because I was only eighteen when we were married. But I never felt any difference in our ages, except that he knew so much more about everything."

There was no difference between her age and that of Mark Claypole. He noted that, wondering vaguely why he had assumed she was older. Some of Tom Goode's age must have rubbed off on her.

"Anyway, I wish that he had taken some of that money and spent it on himself. I certainly don't need so much."

"Is there ever too much money for a woman?" he asked.

He hadn't been probing but that was when she told him about her interview with the trust officer and mentioned figures.

"I was just astonished," she finished.

With no change of expression Mark too was astonished.

"I had no idea," she said, "but I guess it just happens that way with oil and gas."

"They seem to gush when people least expect it and not when they do. Anyway you have learned from sad experience to spend your money while you can."

"I just don't know how, Mark. If you don't need things it seems sort of foolish to buy them. Almost wrong. Sometimes I do worry about where the money would go if I should die. If we'd had children it would be different."

"Haven't you made a will?" he asked with curiosity now.

"Not yet. Tom never did and that was why I got everything. The vice-president of the bank, Mr. Magee, said that I should make a will. He wanted to help me do it. But he is very interested in hospitals and charities and I rather thought—"

"That he hoped to feather the nests of his projects?"

"Well, he's a very nice man but so many people want money for things. I get ever so many letters. From people I don't know. But

48

Tom never liked what he called the do-gooders. And it's his money. I wanted to wait and think it over. If anything should happen to me as things are now it would all go to his stepbrother. I suppose that would be right in a way. But—"

"Why don't you like his stepbrother?" asked Mark, skipping one question.

She hesitated and he did not press for an answer. But after a moment she explained, "Tom and George were never really close. Tom always took the responsibility and George did pretty much what he pleased. He's been married twice—that's why he has all those children. And then—I've never told this to anyone else—"

"People are always telling things to writers. No one seems to know why. But don't tell me if you're going to be unhappy that you did."

"It's kind of a relief. To tell someone and get it out of my system. Tom was very good to George. He was very generous. He lent him money."

To Mark that figured. Tom Goode would take care of his own —his petulant, senile mother, his irresponsible stepbrother, and his wife to whom he brought those carefully counted roses. But he did not want any of them to know how he was fixed because they might demand more than he could give. Probably he always made a poorer mouth than necessary, even to his wife. And when suddenly he had a great deal of money—that could have been unexpected to him also—the habit of financial reticence was formed. It grew stronger because there was more to be grabbed for. So he had told Signe very little about the burgeoning investments. Perhaps he was afraid she would get extravagant ideas and he would have to give up the old leather chair.

"He gave George a great deal of money over the years," said Signe. "I knew he helped him out but I didn't know how often and how much it came to. But after Tom died I was going through his desk and there was a sealed envelope in one drawer that he always kept locked. It was business stuff, he told me, that he wanted to keep separate. I had the key to it after he died, of course—it was on the same ring with his safety-deposit key—and I opened the envelope so I know how much he did give George. He had sent him a check for three hundred dollars just a few days before he died. George had never paid anything back."

"That happens."

"It wasn't the money I cared about. I tore up all those pieces of paper that George had signed. The last one too. But George didn't even come to the funeral. When I finally got him on the phone he said he was sorry but he couldn't make it. But he could have. He had that last check from Tom."

Mark heard the resentment and the pain and the shame. She had been the only member of Tom Goode's family to follow in the undertaker's limousine to his grave. That had been the final hurt, the plunge into loneliness, and Mark Claypole felt a flame of sympathy lick across his mind. For just a second he identified with her desolation. That used to happen to him, as it had when he was writing his first book about a misunderstood boy in a small town and he had been emotionally torn to pieces as he wrote. It hadn't happened in a long time.

The second passed. This was a very commonplace woman though an amazingly rich one.

"George didn't know about your husband's money?"

"He found out about that later somehow. Then he wanted to come and see me. He wanted to make a fuss. The lawyer and the bank wouldn't let him."

Mark lounged to his feet. "Better not think of it, dear," he said. He was not going to take on Signe Goode or let her begin to cling.

At Casablanca he intended to spend the day ashore on a beach. He had been there once before, on an assignment for *Journey,* and he remembered a long, shining beach. He would find it, have a long swim and then lie on the sand and not think. He had roamed the ship looking for the story that eluded him. He had filled his wastebasket with false starts and unsatisfactory pages.

When the ship docked he put his bathing trunks in the pocket of his raincoat and joined the crowd that was flocking to the gangplank. People were gathering in twos and threes and larger clots of companions for the day, and he looked forward to being rid of the lot of them. Then he saw Signe Goode standing alone. She wasn't dressed right. She wore a checked suit that would be too hot for the day. It should have been a cool plain sleeveless linen dress of the sort that made Julia Hayward so more than usually handsome. She and Alida Barnes were as usual ignoring Signe, who looked alone and unplanned. Mark wondered caustically if it would make a difference in their attitude if they knew how really rich Signe was.

She smiled at seeing him and said, "I hope you have a good day."

"You too," he said. "Are you off to Marrakesh or Rabat?"

"There weren't any tickets left. I'm just going to look around."

"You aren't tied up?" he asked against his will and good sense.

"No," said Signe and he could hear the hope.

"Why not join up with me?"

"I don't want to be a nuisance. Where are you going?"

"To a beach," he said. "Do you swim?"

"I just love to!"

"Then get your suit and come along. We'll have a swim and then lunch at a beautiful hotel."

Signe said diffidently, "If you'll let me pay for the lunch."

"I'd be delighted."

He had been surprised at the litheness of her figure without the elaborate and too bulky suit. Also at her swimming.

"You're pretty expert in the water, Signe."

"I used to teach swimming when I was a counselor one summer at a Girl Scout camp. Before I was married. And sometimes, when we could get away, Tom and I—"

"No, don't tell me where you went on Sunday afternoons. Don't make me jealous."

He was making fun of her and he knew that she must realize it.

She did, but she didn't mind. She wasn't going to be alone all day. He could tease her as much as he liked. They swam for an hour and afterward Mark fell asleep on the sand. Signe, drying out under an umbrella supplied by the Ain Diab Beach Club, soaked in the bright beauty of the shore, and watched the tiredness and defeat in Mark's face destroy his mask of cynicism. She noted how much gray there was in his thatch of red hair. And she saw that the raincoat tossed over his body to shield it from the sun was very shabby.

Later they wandered through the open stalls of the bazaars. Suddenly Signe caught the fever of buying. Everything glittered and the merchants were very determined to sell.

"Wait until you get home," advised Mark. "You can get the same things at Macy's more cheaply."

But she bought the gold caftan. The persistent little native said it was very beautiful on the lady and with his greedy eyes as a mirror the lady felt beautiful. It was expensive and she cashed a large traveler's check, and asked for the change in American currency.

In the taxi on the way to the Hotel Anfa she took a bill out of her purse, put it shyly in his nearby pocket and said, "It's my lunch, remember. But will you take care of it for me?"

He hoped it was fifty dollars, not ten. At the hotel he took a look and found it was a hundred. Why not, he thought—all those millions going to waste—and ordered an unforgettable lunch, beginning with melon dipped in candied ginger.

Chapter Four

Julia Hayward looked through the stone arches of the hotel terrace at the sumptuous gardens which she had seen five years ago when last she had been in Marrakesh. They were as beautiful as before but she felt no revival of delight or wonder at the exotic colors and luxuriant blossoms. Seen from the back by passing hotel guests she looked like a girl with a slim, beautiful figure and a crest of dark hair that was styled in an individual way. There was no one in front of her to see the carefully tended face which was not young and held no expectations, and the somber eyes which did not really see the gardens for she was contemplating things within her mind.

Five years ago she had been here on the trip with the Byrds and the Haltons. It hadn't worked out too well. She was an extra woman and that was always basically humiliating. It was better like this, even if Alida did keep rambling on about who was connected with who, and magnified her petty discontents with the service and food.

Julia did not care about the cross-social-puzzle game, as she had once described it, and she ate so little that she was not an epicure. Also she was given good service without demanding it because of something in her natural manner. She did not travel for the same reason Alida did, which was that everyone in her income bracket and on her social level went away from New York during the cold months. For ten years, since her divorce, Julia had traveled to elude memories and in the recurrent hope—always disappointed—that unknown and strange places would give her life a new impetus. She never considered leaving New York permanently. She was locked into it by her associations. But its air would become stale with repetitions of people and places and a journey was the often-tried remedy.

Alida had bought some postcards and was at a desk in the lounge writing messages. They would read as they always did—"Lunching here at the Mamounia, divine hotel"—"Perfect weather so far" —"Only wish you were with us"—"Love always." She would send them to her son in Washington, to her daughter who was wintering in Arizona, to a bachelor in New York who had sheered away from marrying her but was still available as an escort to the opera or as an extra man at dinner parties, to various friends in Palm Beach or California or the Virgin Islands at the moment, and to her cook and caretaker. She would leave out the "Love" on the card to the bachelor and the servants. Alida carried a small address book with a jeweled cover in her handbag, so that she could always keep up with people and remind them of herself.

Julia never sent postcards to anyone. She had mailed her itinerary to Peter before she sailed, on the off chance that a letter from him might reach her at one of the ship's ports of call. There had been none at Casablanca and Julia had disciplined herself into never being hurt by anything her son might or might not do. But the lack of a letter had forced her to think of Peter now as she gazed at the gardens. Peter and Christine went their own way. Julia did not know whether it was the same way any longer. She did not think they were happy. But what young married people were happy today? The question was a kind of tranquilizer. She asked herself that as she thought of her son's married life. The younger crowd didn't think in terms of happiness or unhappiness. They talked of communication and wanted sexual novelty and variety in relationships and there seemed to be no rules but only experiments. Julia accepted that because there was nothing to do except take the fact of the strange new freedoms without a blush. But ten years ago when she had divorced her husband there had been a few rules left. He had broken all of them and thrown the pieces in her face. She couldn't live with him.

54

So she had decided at the time. But sometimes, as now, with Peter and Christine and their child hovering in her mind, she wondered about that decision. If she couldn't put up with him, she should have married again. Before she was forty there had been opportunities she had thrown away or not wanted to develop. She wished she could tell Christine that a husband was the best answer even if he was difficult or she did not like him very well. Of course Peter must be hard to live with. On the edge of being a manic-depressive, the psychoanalyst had said and added that his trouble obviously began when Julia got her divorce though it was not evident at that time.

She turned from the window and her thoughts. Alida was still writing. With the beautiful handwriting they had both been taught at Miss Blake's School for Girls. Julia had known Alida since they were young, before they were debutantes. Now she was divorced, Alida had been twice widowed, and a great deal of gay and expensive life had flowed under the bridge since they were beautiful girls. Alida had two children and two stepchildren and a scattering of grandchildren but she did not want to be put in a corner like an old woman yet, she often said laughingly. Actually as far as Julia knew there was no family corner to which she could be relegated. The younger members were all too busy with their personal lives to take her on. Alida kept in touch with them by letters and postcards and brief visits and her children kept in touch with Alida's generous checkbook. They always sent her extravagant flowers when she took a cruise.

Alida loved to travel. To her each journey was like picking up a new hand of cards at bridge, like playing duplicate, talking post-mortems and figuring how it could be played better. She had traveled with both husbands and since the last one had died four years ago in an airplane crash it was wonderful to have Julia. They had met after his death at a dinner party and Alida had suggested that they take a cruise together.

Julia was at loose ends that season. She had tried so many things.

She had gone with the Applebys on their yacht to the Mediterranean, to Australia and the South Pacific, loosely joined to the Frinton Smiths who were on the same ship, and in an effort at independence she had gone alone to Guadeloupe, which had left a horrid memory of doing little except walking miles on the beach by herself and reading herself to sleep with mystery stories. The next year she was persuaded by her travel agent to join a group of women who went to Moscow and Leningrad and Bucharest and she was glad she had done that, though she would never want to do it twice or to see any of those companions again. Alida's suggestion had come at the right time and they had traveled together for the last three years. Julia was fond of Alida and more than a little grateful. For Alida paid her full share of the expenses and often insisted on doing more, for she knew that Julia never had quite enough money to live as she did. Her personal income had seemed enough at the time of the divorce and she had refused alimony, insisting instead that her husband set up an irrevocable trust for Peter.

She crossed the room to where Alida wrote.

"Are you writing a book?" she asked.

"I've just a few more cards. I want to send a couple to Jim's boys at school—it's educational for them to see pictures of a place like this—and then I must write a note to Alma to remind her about having the floors waxed. Servants need to be jacked up when you aren't there. You know how it is."

"Not any more. I think I'll go over to the square and look at the snake charmers that somebody talked about yesterday."

Alida shuddered.

"I won't be long," said Julia.

She took a taxi because she was not sure of the way and the doorman who called it for her said to watch her purse carefully. When she reached the square she told the driver to wait on the street, and he told her to watch her purse, there were many people who thieved.

"Yes, I will," said Julia.

She saw the extraordinary snake charmers, gave them a few coins and then wandered to the end of the square, where an old gray-bearded Moroccan sat on a rag of carpet, surrounded by a circle of natives. Some of them were old and some were young and they all bore the stamp of deep poverty. They stood or squatted, listening to the old man who was telling them a story. Julia had heard about this performance, but when she was here before her friends had been more interested in shopping than in sightseeing and she had not come into this part of the city.

She went as close to the group of natives as she dared, and stood there, listening with them. She could not understand the language but the concentration of the people and the voice of the storyteller fascinated her. It was the voice of a great actor who needed neither scenery nor costume to hold the attention of his audience. The faces around him grew serious and despairing as he told the tale. Some writhed their bodies in grief. Suddenly Julia felt tears behind her own eyes. He seemed to be telling of her own lonely unhappiness, of her failure to give Peter the strength and courage he needed, of her futile life.

The voice was sad. Then it condoned, forgave, ceased. As the story ended Julia felt a tug at her wrist and her purse was gone. She turned and saw a small brown figure running across the square. No one moved in pursuit.

"Did that boy grab your purse?" She saw the priest who was on the ship coming quickly toward her. The Bancroft girl was with him.

"I saw him behind you," said Barbara, "but I thought he was just listening to the story."

"I'll see if I can find a policeman," said Father Duggan.

"No," said Julia, "it doesn't matter that much. It was an old bag and there wasn't much in it. The courier on the train has my passport, luckily, and I've a friend at the hotel who will pay for my taxi when I get back. Let the little vandal have the purse. It's a small

57

price of admission to that wonderful storytelling."

The priest gave her a smile of admiration.

"Wasn't it wonderful!" said Barbara. "Do you understand Arabic?"

"Not a word. But I felt as if I knew the story he was telling."

"Sorrow is the same in all languages," said the priest.

Joan Scofield had not left the ship during its day at Casablanca. That gave her a chance to catch up with things, work on the social schedule, make up a list of guests for the Captain's next dinner and have her hair done.

She had been a social hostess on passenger ships for five years. This job on *The Seven Seas* was the biggest one she had ever had, and she was now making the world cruise on it for the second time. She was thirty-five years old and could look twenty-five unless the day had been too harassing. She had two assistants, one who taught French and one who was in charge of gymnastics. But most of the planning of activities for the women passengers was done by Joan herself.

She had been the wife of an army officer who was killed in Vietnam. The shock of his cruel death resulted in a miscarriage, and some months later an aunt had taken her on a cruise in the Caribbean to help her forget her double tragedy. On the ship Joan did not take part in the games and amusements but sometimes, watching the efforts of the hostess, she thought she could do a better job of organizing and entertaining travelers. She knew that she must find a job to supplement her small widow's pension and she did not want to go back to the exhausting sympathy of her friends and relatives. One day she asked the hostess how one could get such a job and found out where to apply. Within six months she was on another liner sailing to South America, planning social events and bringing strangers together.

It was a variegated job and Joan loved its lack of monotony. Some of the women travelers had charm and wit, even talent. Some were pitiful and others taught her only to control contempt. She had established a "Questions and Answers Hour" which had been a success on various ships. It was a great joke with the ship's officers, who continually kidded her about it, asking her ridiculous or bawdy questions, but Joan said that it cleared the air and saved the rest of the staff from a lot of complaints. At eleven o'clock in the morning, when the ship was at sea, she would take a chair in the front of the lounge on the lower promenade and brace herself for questions that were answerable or unanswerable, and also for criticisms.

"This is the first cruise I've ever been on when people dressed for dinner on Sunday night. Isn't that very bad form?"

"Miss Scofield, the schedule of the ship doesn't give us nearly enough time to shop in Singapore. Couldn't you ask the Commodore to change it?"

"I hate to bring this up, Miss Scofield, but something should be done about the hairdressing parlor. I had an appointment and was kept waiting for forty-five minutes."

And always the question, "How much should I tip?"

Joan placated and explained. She advised them what to shop for and what not to eat in various ports and what was best to wear. She was aware of course that the more intelligent women aboard never came near her question hour. But they were not her charges as these others were.

She also had to decide what prizes should be given in the dance contests, to choose a pretty girl who would call the numbers for Harold Fuller on Bingo nights, to organize the French class for Mademoiselle Michel, and to encourage the women who were "reducing to rhythm" with Miss Tobin. She was expected to know everyone and remember names when she received with the Commodore before his dinners. Her evening clothes had to be dramatic enough to give style to the innumerable shipboard parties. She had to be admired, gay and amusing but keep the men from making passes at her.

After the first week of a cruise Joan would have the passengers sorted out in her mind, by their social usefulness on the ship as well as by name. When she had first seen the list she had been pleased to see that several men were traveling alone, for there was always an imbalance of available men for unattached women. But Howard Demarest had Ruby Canaday, technically not traveling with him but never far away. Joan had begun to think that was a situation which might become troublesome, for she had seen flashes of quarrels between them already.

Alec Goodrich was not responsive to invitations or to games. Joan had seated him next to Barbara Bancroft at the first dinner given by the Commodore. They made a very handsome picture, which the ship's photographer snapped at once, and the next day it was pinned with forty or fifty others on the bulletin board. But it was not a picture of having fun, like the one of Mrs. Robert Caynes. Alec was usually as alone on deck as he was at his table in the dining room, and Barbara took little part in the organized programs. Joan guessed at a mutilated love affair in Barbara's background.

Searching her memory after she was sure he was an author, Joan remembered the name of a book that Mark Claypole had written. She had read it some years before and the story came back with the title. When she met him one day in the first week she said with a smile that usually created a responding warmth, "You really are the writer, aren't you?"

"Which writer?"

"The one who wrote *Father to the Man*?"

The look of resentment on his face surprised her.

"And if I did?"

She went on as best she could. "Nothing, except that I wanted to tell you that I loved the book. It was so beautifully written. I shall never forget that boy."

"Thank you. That is very interesting coming from the hostess of the ship."

He managed to put contempt for her position into his words and it angered Joan.

"Why should it be interesting?" she asked. "Didn't you think that people in my profession could read and write?"

"Sorry," he said, "I certainly did not mean to intimate anything of the sort. But you seem so extremely busy with all the games and edifying classes and general togetherness that I wondered how you could spare the time to read."

"I wasn't on a ship when I read your book. It was quite a long time ago."

"Yes, quite a long time ago when anyone read it." He switched the subject. "Is it amusing, your job of hostessing?"

"I don't laugh at it," said Joan.

"I'm sure you don't. But do you really enjoy presiding over those antics? I glanced through the window of the lounge when I was prowling the deck the other morning and there were dozens of adult women lying on the floor and kicking their legs up and down. I found it hard to credit my eyes."

"It's very good exercise. And they love it. Why shouldn't they kick their legs if they want to?"

"You have me there," he said, and as someone stopped to speak to Joan the conversation ended.

It was not renewed. Joan did not like Mark Claypole. He did not seem the kind of person who could have written such a tender, pitiful story. She decided that he was probably spoiled by success and sophistication.

Sitting under the hair dryer at the end of her supposedly free day in Casablanca, Joan looked over the advance copy of the program for the next day. There was something planned for everybody— televised news, trap shooting, the flower-arrangement class, the first lecture on Africa, rhythmic reducing, horse racing—plenty for Mark Claypole to satirize. Let him, thought Joan. Hundreds of thousands of people look forward and backward at cruises like this as the best times of their lives.

She considered the present one. Each journey was different from every other one. The weather was always a gamble and invariably there were special excitements—love affairs, thefts, an occasional attempt at suicide. And certain passengers left the mark of their temperaments on each cruise. It bothered Joan that there seemed to be too many loners on this ship and she wondered if she could do something about that, somehow assimilate them. For she hoped this cruise would be the best *The Seven Seas* had ever undertaken. It was the Commodore's last voyage and she wanted it to be happy and brilliant. He hated to give up his command of the ship, no matter what he said. Joan was sure, though he had never told her so outright, that he was going back to nothing he wanted.

She noted something else on the program and pushed back the hood of the dryer.

"Lifeboat drill for the crew tomorrow, Mignon," she said to the operator, "at two o'clock."

"But we have had that," protested Mignon.

"I know. But we have to keep in practice."

"I lose a customer. I lose six dollars each time these drills. This ship—she never sink."

"I don't expect so. But it's Captain's orders. Aren't you in Lifeboat Two with me, Mignon?"

"I forget."

"You'd better not," said Joan. "I think I'm dry."

The ship was due to sail from Casablanca at seven in the evening and before six-thirty the Commander was on the bridge checking final details with his officers. The train from Marrakesh and the motorcoach from Rabat had returned, and in the twilight the Commander could recognize some of the passengers who were going up the gangplank. He saw the writer who had asked him so many questions one day, not only about the engineering of the ship but about his experiences. Rather smart questions. Commander James had given him a few facts—the fellow had to earn his living by picking other people's brains, he supposed—but he had cut him off abruptly when the writer had asked a question about his retirement.

There was a woman with the writer this evening, carrying what looked like a native dress over one arm and holding a clump of mimosa and bird of paradise flowers with the other. The priest came along with a pretty girl whom the Commander had noticed and he thought with amusement that in spite of his collar the priest knew how to pick them. He also saw the two handsome women, Mrs. Hayward and Mrs. Barnes, whose names he remembered because he had gone to a cocktail party they had given the other night.

"Fifteen minutes," he said to his chief officer. "The gangplank goes up on the dot. The stewards have checked of course to make sure that everyone is on board."

"Calling Mr. Howard Demarest," came over the loudspeaker at almost the next moment. "Calling Miss Ruby Canaday. Calling Mr. Howard Demarest. Calling Miss Ruby Canaday."

"They can't be on board yet," said the chief officer. "I think they went off with some big shot in Morocco. I suppose he has connections in every port and introductions to the top people."

"We sail at seven," said the Commander. "If they aren't on board when the gangplank goes up they will have to fly to Capetown and rejoin the ship there."

"He'd make a hell of a row."

"We sail on schedule."

"Yes, sir."

There was no one on the gangplank now except a ship's officer. On the dock lingered a mixed crowd of people who had been visiting the ship while it was in port, idling natives and street peddlers gathering up their wares. Twelve minutes after the Commander's ultimatum a limousine glided up the dock and stopped at the side of the ship. Before the chauffeur could leave his seat Demarest flung open the rear door and got out. He moved heavily. Ruby Canaday tumbled out after him and without his help. She ran toward the ship and almost fell on the rough platform of the dock, and everyone who stood at the railings above saw Demarest grab her arm and then slap her violently as she tried to release herself from his rough grip. She slumped against him and they made their way to the gangplank, followed by the black chauffeur of the car until the officer in white took over.

Mrs. Hartley Barton, leaning on her two canes, gave a shocked sigh. She always watched when the ship on which she was a passenger left a port though now it was very hard to stand very long. She was thinking of how many happy sailings she and her husband had known when she saw the blow. It ruined her recollection, reminded her that she was an old woman and that the world of manners and decency had changed. She sighed. Others laughed. A man made a joke meant to be heard at large.

Joan Scofield, at the side of the boat deck, frowned with worry at the ugly little scene. She glanced up to the bridge where the Commander was standing. From his position he must have seen what had happened, but he had not moved. His ship was sailing on schedule.

Chapter Five

The travel lecturer told his audience in the theater—every seat was taken for he had become popular and also it was a misty morning —that Africa was four times as large as the United States and the second-largest land mass in the world. Great civilizations had waxed and waned there while Europe was still barbaric, dwelling in caves and wearing animal skins. He explained that Gao on the Niger had once been a center of the arts, and that the inhabitants of that city were reading and writing in Arabic for centuries before the era of exploration to the West.

A number of his hearers knew these things and would nod their heads wisely in agreement to show that they did. Alec Goodrich did not nod. He had known most of the facts but they had become alive now that he himself was cruising near the coast of Africa, past Cap Blanc, past Cap Vert. He was beginning to sense the continent as if he were feeling it on a relief map. Behind the few ports on this tremendously long coastline rose the high plateaus and then the great mountains.

"Africa contains more than fifty countries, many of which are larger in area than the few colonial powers that still occupy them and the ex-colonial ones that conquered them in the past."

Alec had listened to many speeches in the Senate about American relations with underdeveloped countries but he had never realized the scope of the problems as he did now. Or of the possibilities. He had a feeling of being cut down to size and expanding at the same time. When the brief travel talks were finished he often supplemented them, pursuing the facts by reading books he found in the ship's library or by walking the decks and making his own analysis and projection.

A restless woman climbed over his knees to get out of the theater. Two people behind him were whispering, not too softly, about something irrelevant. But Alec was not so annoyed by interruptions and trivialities as he had been when his mind had seemed empty of everything except injustice and defeat.

"Mali," said Dr. Hermann, with the careful articulation that did not destroy a faint German accent, "had been great for four centuries. It had iron, gold and salt and had become tremendously wealthy. It had a very effective political system. Then Songhai became great in the fifteenth and sixteenth centuries as Mali was fading."

The lecture came to an end. As Alec left the theater he carried with him the question of why Mali had faded out. Why had its political system become ineffective if it had worked well for a time? Was it the same story as long ago as that? The wrong men were elected? Factions fought to a stalemate? Political loyalty didn't last? Or maybe a younger generation wanted a new leader and a different kind of civilization.

Father Aloysius Duggan was going out on deck through the same door that Alec had headed for. Holding it open for the priest Alec asked, "Did you hear the lecture?"

"Yes. It was very interesting."

"He knows his stuff certainly."

"I understand he is German born and is a professor of history in some Western college. Making good use of his sabbatical year."

"I wondered how they got hold of a man like that. Good deal for him, a holiday with pay. I thought I recognized the academic manner. I listened to him as if I wanted credit for the course."

The priest laughed. He and Alec fell into step and Alec said, "What I was wondering, when he called it a day, was why the political system of Mali lost out, if it had been very effective. I suppose nobody knows when there's such a time gap."

Father Duggan asked, "Don't political organizations—perhaps all organizations—wear out?"

"If you don't mind my saying so, Father, your organization, the Roman Catholic Church, seems to have done very well. For nineteen centuries and still going strong."

Father Duggan did not think it was going strong. The Church was in great trouble, in confusion. He had an impulse that was almost a desire to discuss that with this man who was obviously thoughtful. He knew that Alec Goodrich had been in the United States Senate and his point of view would be interesting. But he had promised the Bishop not to talk about the problems of the Church, not to give scandal by telling of his own doubts.

He said, "The Church has found it wise to make many innovations in its organization as times have changed."

"But it has always maintained the same hierarchy, with the Pope of Rome as its head."

"That is true."

"I've been told and I've read," said Alec, "that it has made recent changes in its ritual and is dropping the use of Latin. But it has not altered its stand on birth control or divorce at all, has it?"

"No," said Father Duggan.

"I should think, with conditions as they are today, that must make it difficult for many of your people. I mean that the rising cost of living and the crowding into the cities doesn't make it easy or even feasible to feed and house big families."

"It presents a serious problem."

He doesn't want to open up, thought Alec. I suppose he can't, under the rules. But Alec himself had become hungry for conversation. There used to be so much good talk around him. He felt on the verge of it now and went on, "And another problem is that there are all these marriages of students and even high-school kids that are part of the pattern now—from statistics I saw when I was looking into that"—he paused for a second or two, too clearly remembering those meetings of the Committee on Education and Labor, stinging again at being able to have no further part in them just as he had been getting some things under way. He finished rather abruptly, "The divorce rate is very high in that group. It seems to indicate that many of those kids didn't really know what they were getting into."

"I am sure that they often don't know," said Father Duggan.

"But your Church won't let them have another chance, will it? I mean that if a boy or a girl or the two of them find there's been a mistake, there's no out, is there, if they want to remain Catholics?"

"The Church allows legal separation for sufficient cause. It does not permit remarriage."

"Isn't that pretty hard on human nature?"

No one knew better than the priest how hard it was on human nature. All those troubled confessions. All the appeals for dispensations. All the explanations that seemed reasonable. And all the rebellions because human nature couldn't stand it, and the Church lost boys and girls who needed it as much as it needed them.

"I'm speaking out of turn, I'm afraid," said Alec into the lack of answer. "I apologize."

"There's no reason to. Personal problems—even individual tragedies—do exist. But sometimes we cannot see the wood for the trees, not the entire justice for the small injustices."

Alec gave a quick side glance at the priest. What did he mean by that?

Father Duggan did not notice the glance. He thought he had made a weak, evasive answer and was ashamed of doing no better. But he must not speak out. He had promised the Bishop.

Alec Goodrich said, "That's quite a thought."

Neither of them went on talking. They both had become afraid of saying too much. At the next entrance Alec said, "Well, I think I'll see what the stock-market report looks like today."

The priest continued around the deck, feeling more of a hypocrite than ever.

It was a long journey between Casablanca and Capetown, and in the eight days between the two ports routines became more deeply

68

established. People had found their own level at the bridge tables. On the Lido deck, where buffet lunch was served on sunny days and by the open swimming pool groups of almost naked passengers browned and ate. In the evenings when the dance music began the dancers could be easily classified. There were those who were almost professionals, those who were being taught by professionals and working excitedly at new and intricate steps, and those who, after a few drinks, would try a fox trot or a waltz and feel graceful and light-footed.

Cocktail parties multiplied. Jim Bates delivered invitations to the passengers on his end of the boat deck and he knew that Mrs. Barnes and Mrs. Hayward were invited to many of them. The Honorable Alexander Goodrich seemed to be asked to all of them. But he usually drank by himself. Mrs. Goode received comparatively few of the square white cards supplied by the head steward's office on request and needing to have only the names of guest and host written in.

Jim liked Mrs. Goode. He had recognized her inexperience even before she told him she had never taken a sea voyage before. He was rather protective toward her, suggesting that when the sun was high it was well to keep out of it even if she liked to swim. He saw that she sunburned instead of browning. Jim admired Mrs. Hayward's smooth tan but he always kept at a respectful distance from her and she never talked to him as Mrs. Goode did. Mrs. Barnes made him a good deal of trouble—the toast would be cold on her breakfast tray or she would want a dress pressed within the hour and that meant difficulty with the valet service for Jim—but she was, as he had hoped, generous at the end of the first week when tipping was in order.

Barbara Bancroft was his favorite passenger on this trip, but Jim did not think she was enjoying the cruise as much as she should. Invitations that he slipped under her door were sometimes lying there unopened when he made up her room hours later. On the night when Howard Demarest was giving a very lavish party in his suite before the second sitting, she asked Jim to bring a lamb-chop supper with a double martini to her own cabin. She always looked right for any time of day or occasion, whether in shorts or bikini or dinner dress, but she did not seem to seek or even enjoy attention or admiration. At the end of the week her tip was just the amount that in Jim's category it should be, and she offered it to him as one person to another who deserved the money, with a few extra words of thanks.

Howard Demarest was not methodical in his tipping but it averaged out all right. He would give Jim five or ten dollars when it was not necessary or expected and forget to tip when normally it should have been forthcoming. Jim had no illusions about the relationship between Demarest and Miss Canaday. All the stewards took that for what it certainly must be. Jim was often summoned to bring splits of champagne to the big suite before Demarest and the girl would go down to the bar or to some party, and sometimes Demarest would act like the minister coming to call, as Jim would describe it, and sometimes recently requited passion would be in the air, or he would feel the rough edges of a quickly silenced quarrel. There had been a noisy row on the night they sailed from Casablanca. The girl was crying and a bit hysterical when they got off the elevator and Demarest finally left her in the corridor and slammed his door. She rang for ice later and Jim saw the mark on her cheek that was becoming black and blue. She did not get up until the middle of the afternoon the next day and all that time her telephone was off the hook. But a few days after that Demarest gave the big party and she was there, looking very beautiful and acting as if nothing had happened.

Jim did what Ruby Canaday told him to do but he didn't hurry to do it. When she gave him orders he knew well enough that she wasn't used to giving orders. There was something stagy about her manners as if she had learned them from movies or television. But when Demarest gave an order Jim wasted no time in carrying it out. Not that he liked Demarest but he was a director of the Line and it was obvious that he was accustomed to having people jump when he spoke. The Canaday, as Jim thought of her, was in his opinion letting herself in for something.

Sometimes, as he shaved or knotted his tie, Howard Demarest would stare at his face in the mirror as if he were looking for something. Sometimes he would have a feeling of revulsion as he saw what thirty years had done to a young man of twenty. Then again it wasn't so bad. The bold courage was still there in the eyes that had become heavy-lidded, the features were thickened with flesh but still in good proportion. The high forehead was unwrinkled, for he was a man of action, not of thought. The lines that dragged his face down were dug in from his nose to the corners of his mouth. He would search for himself in the mirror and as a rule, unless he had a bad hangover, be reassured by the reflection.

He had begun his career with a number of natural assets. His ego never had been burdened with humility. Even as a young man he woke in the morning not with a feeling of meeting the day but rather that the day would meet him and be the better for it. He had an unusual aptitude for mathematics, and figures excited as well as interested him, so he rated high in the business school of the university. Also—and this he never underestimated—he had the body of an athlete, graceful and vigorous, and a very handsome face. The scouts from the banks and industries and law firms who came to recruit college students before their graduation noticed him immediately in any group.

He chose industry, but not with any idea of making his way step by step within the structure of the one in which he began. He intended to move about, watch for opportunity, and he hoped with confidence that before too long he would be a man to be bargained for and bid for by competitive organizations. In the next twenty years he learned almost all there was to know about industrial chemicals and coatings, electronic devices and computers. Naturally he became familiar with methods of financing and advertising as he went along. His picture was in *Fortune* twice before he was forty, as a featured young executive in two different organizations. He was a pioneer in building up conglomerates and that was one of the reasons why he was a passenger on *The Seven Seas.*

The American Republic Line, which had owned the big ship and a number of smaller ones, had a long history of profit and self-sufficiency. But competition with air travel and the doubling and trebling of the costs of services and supplies had finally made refinancing necessary. The Line had been acquired by a corporation which also owned a railroad which handled only freight, a productive chemical division, and an insurance company, and was making a very good thing out of nationally distributed cheese products. It was at a meeting of the Thermal Company, the parent through adoption of these diverse interests, that some doubt about the value of the shipping Line had been discussed last November. Mr. Curtis and Mr. Welch were not sure it would have any value in a few years and said so.

"Passenger ships are going to be obsolete," said Welch. "Years ago they were the big thing. But they aren't any more. With the superairliners that are being constructed they haven't a chance."

"I'm not convinced of that," said Mr. Davis. "There are still many people who prefer to travel by sea."

"Look at the ships that have been laid up already."

"The transatlantic and transpacific runs are losing out. But we're promoting cruise travel, Caribbean jaunts and South American trips. And *The Seven Seas* has had a world cruise for the last nine years. Always practically sold out."

"Does it make money with present costs?"

"It's more than broken even to date."

"Who takes these world cruises?" asked Curtis.

"I don't really know. I've never taken one," admitted Mr. Davis. "People take them for a rest, I suppose. Or to see the world. If they can afford it. I guess they go to whoop it up too. There is a lot of entertainment provided on cruises, even if you only go as far as

Bermuda. And a lot of liquor, which of course is always profitable. As I say, they seem to be very popular but I don't know too much about them at first hand."

"We should have more information."

"There is a brochure," said the secretary.

"That's not information," said Curtis, "that's advertising. I mean that we should have a breakdown of the whole thing. Look into not only the obvious costs but dig into wastage and advisable cuts. We need a survey of the labor situation too, as regards the flagship and the little ones that go to the islands, to find out whether the service on them is blown up."

"We cut out stewardesses on *The Seven Seas* last year, you know."

"And had to employ more stewards and nurses."

"We talked about abolishing tips and raising the fare but nothing was done about it."

"It's a tricky business to do away with tips. We weren't sure it was even feasible."

Curtis said, "I still think we ought to explore the cruise business thoroughly. Our profit on the Line isn't large enough to absorb any big drain, like a strike for example. Personally I'd like to know more about the clientele on our world cruises and how long we can count on it, if we can. There aren't going to be so many rich, retired people in the near future as I see it and that's the group we draw from, I suppose."

"The rich widows."

"Widows in the future aren't going to be so rich if they have to pay capital gains on their husbands' estates. Mine isn't."

They laughed and then a director asked, "How would we go about getting someone competent to appraise the whole situation? Even if we could find the right person these experts have their own staffs and their charges are terrific."

"Perhaps I could do it," said Howard Demarest. "Maybe I could be trouble-shooter for this particular job."

"How do you mean, Howard?"

"Well, my doctor has been breathing down my neck about my getting away for a change," said Demarest. "As a matter of fact he suggested an ocean trip. I haven't decided on anything, but I know that *The Seven Seas* takes off on that world job sometime in late January. I might sign on and kill two birds with one stone, satisfy my doctor—of course he's a bit of an alarmist—and bring back a report on the makeup and so forth of one of these cruises. I don't think it would be wise to be tagged as an observer for the company or an analyst. I wouldn't want the ship's officers to have an idea that I was anything of that sort or they'd clam up or show off. Of course they'd know that I am a director of the Line but I'd go as an ordinary passenger and see what the deal is. I've looked over a good many enterprises to see what they're worth."

"You certainly have. It would be very useful," said Curtis, "but can you spare the time?"

"I've damned well got my orders to spare it."

The discussion drifted into hearsay about cruises until Mr. Welch brought it to conclusion.

"I suggest we postpone further consideration of our policy toward our passenger ships until we see what Howard comes up with, if he decides to make the trip."

"I can tell you right now that you can count on it if you believe it would be useful."

"Then I say that we lay this matter on the table and proceed with the agenda."

The doctor had surprised Howard Demarest more than he had frightened him.

"I don't like the sound of your heart too much, Howard. Or your description of that pain you had. You have to let up."

"What do you mean, let up?"

"Give your heart a chance to rest. Get away from pressure for a while. I don't think this is anything serious. Not yet. But it could become that unless you change your pace."

"There must be medicines. There are drugs for everything to-day."

"Yes. I'm going to give you some pills and a prescription for them that you can fill anywhere at any time."

"What are they?"

"Nitroglycerin."

"I know about those. I know men who take them all the time."

"They're frequently used. And very effective. If you get a pain or feel on the edge of one put one under your tongue. If you don't have pain keep them handy just as a safeguard."

"And that will fix me up?"

"No. You should stop smoking."

"You're not going to make me give up liquor too? Or try to make a eunuch out of me?"

"Not at this time. Take one instead of two drinks in an hour and limit your drinking hours. Don't spend every night with a lady. Limit that too. But the main thing is to relax your tensions. It would be a good thing for you to go off somewhere and fish for a month."

"I'd go nuts. Fishing has never been up my alley."

"Then take an ocean voyage. A long one. Go round the world."

It had seemed made to order. The day after the directors' meeting Howard Demarest had called the passenger agent of the Line, and the agent, who knew on which side his bread was buttered, set things in motion. He changed a couple of reservations with falsified excuses, so that the Mandarin suite was available for Mr. Demarest, informed the head steward and the purser that the director would be taking the cruise and that a complimentary cocktail party should be set up in his rooms on the day of embarkation. He did not get in touch with the Commodore, knowing that he would not welcome suggestions from the booking office, but he was sure that the identity of this special passenger would soon get around to the ship's officers.

Demarest told one of his secretaries to get him information about the ship's schedule and its ports of call. When he looked them over he dictated some letters to persons of importance in New York and Washington who in turn would undoubtedly dictate others so that good introductions would be forthcoming. In Lisbon he had lunched with a leading banker and sent Ruby off to see the castles in Sintra. In Casablanca Henri Latour had offered to be his host, cabling Demarest before the ship's arrival there that it would be a pleasure to show him the city and to have him visit his country house. The cable had added that if he was traveling with family or companions they would also be most welcome. So he had taken Ruby along. She was looking beautiful that morning and Demarest had started out by being pleased with her and anticipating showing her off. But the day had been a catastrophe.

The Latours lived in the country but with elegance. They had chosen to stay in Morocco after the French formal control had terminated. Henri Latour was too well bred to boast but it became evident to Howard Demarest as they drove through the city and places were pointed out that his host had been a member of one of the great colonizing families and undoubtedly still owned a fraction of the metropolis with its handsome buildings and magnificent boulevards. He was a little out of his depth socially and even financially and he realized that before they reached the Latour estate. There he heard the wife of Henri Latour addressed by servants as Comtesse. There were other guests for the late luncheon, most of them bilingual but politely careful to speak excellent English to him. He sensed that life in the white mansion by the sea might be informal but nothing was casual. And he soon wished that he hadn't brought Ruby. He could have carried the occasion off by himself, but under the worldly, courteous eyes of these people she was embarrassing.

Ruby was completely out of place, but instead of admitting it and being wide-eyed and simple she assumed an air of sophistication, as if she had been everywhere and seen everything already. It was a transparent pose and Demarest knew that it fooled no one.

An apéritif was served before lunch and Ruby, who had never

tried French vermouth without gin or vodka dominating, made a slightly wry face. One of the guests said quickly that mademoiselle would like a cocktail perhaps—it would be a privilege to make her a cocktail and he had learned the art in the States. She said she would love it, that she liked six to one. The man made cocktails for both Ruby and himself, and she had several, which destroyed her attitude of hauteur but made her flirtatious. It amused the men but Demarest could feel the appraisals of his hostess and the other very chic women who were there.

At lunch two wines were served and he saw with controlled anger that Ruby was getting drunk. There seemed nothing he could do about that or about her maneuvers with the men. The afternoon was a long one. The Latours did not hurry anything. He was shown the grounds and the private beach and the stables. There was conversation, questions about the foreign policy of the United States, and Ruby said, "They seem to expect us to take care of the whole world!" Faces went rather blank at that remark but nobody argued the point. When it was past five o'clock Demarest said that they would have to leave because it was a long drive and the ship sailed at seven. Ruby said, "Don't worry, they wouldn't dare go without you!" She was then drinking a highball, supplied by the man who knew American habits and had made the cocktails.

Henri Latour said that he would have the car brought around at once and apologized for not being able to leave his guests and drive back with them. Demarest knew that there would be lifted eyebrows and probably some laughter after he and Ruby had gone. He had made a very poor impression, been personally diminished by the girl, and it galled him. He sat in the car without speaking until she said, "They must be awfully rich."

"They are better than rich," said Demarest, "they are distinguished."

"Well, I don't like French people very much."

"And what in God's name do you think they thought of you?"

"What do you mean? What did I do?"

77

"Shut up," he muttered because though there was a glass pane between them and the chauffeur the man might be able to hear.

"Don't speak to me like that."

"I said be quiet."

She turned her head away and Demarest stared out at the strange dark trees and then the first lights of the long white city. He thought of Katherine. She was a lady. If she'd stayed with him, if she'd been with him today—

Ruby had fallen asleep and breathed heavily, for she was still a little drunk. When they reached the pier he shook her to wake her and she straightened up and got out of the car after him. But the boards of the pier were rough and she was unsteady. As she stumbled he dragged her to her feet, and when she tried to pull away anger at her and at himself went out of control and he struck her.

He had struck Katherine once and that had been the end of his marriage. It had lasted for nearly nine years, and though it had not been as happy a marriage as it looked to other people it had steadied his success and given him a better place in the social world than he had ever had before. He had been with an electronics company in Cincinnati when he met her and he was definitely looking for a wife.

She belonged to a wealthy and devout Roman Catholic family which had bred a bishop and a monsignor. She measured up to everything young Demarest wanted. Her religion was rather boring but he was sure he could calm her down about that when they were married. Katherine was romantically in love and intended to convert him to her faith after they were married. It was some time before she realized that neither her prayers nor her example would accomplish that. She told no one but her confessor of her hope and failure. He said that she should not reject her husband, and she tried to obey but she did not welcome Demarest nor want him, and of course he knew it. One night his humiliation had risen to anger and he had struck her.

She had left him. They were separated legally but not divorced and Katherine had been given custody of the children. She had gone to Ireland with their children and was bringing them up there. She had bought a small castle and he had been told that it was beautiful, but there had been no direct communication between them for nearly ten years.

Demarest had not suffered greatly because of the break, even at first. When Katherine left him he had been considering moving on to New York anyway, where a new business connection had been offered him. He accepted it and his headquarters had been in New York ever since, combining companies, building them up, selling when the profit was ripe. He had an apartment with a good address and belonged to several clubs. Katherine would not divorce him because of her religion, and although his lawyer told Demarest that he could divorce her on grounds of desertion, or after two years of separation, he had let the matter stand as it was. He did not want to marry again. And in some ways having an undivorced wife was a protection from other women. He was occasionally curious about the children, especially the boy, but as he saw the adolescents in New York and heard about their habits, he thought shrewdly that they were better off in their castle in Ireland than in America. Someday he would look up the boy, arrange it through his lawyer.

He had very little social life except at his clubs, but there were always available women and when he had time or desire for it he established a temporary relationship. Ruby had been the last one. She was a model and he had come upon her at a night club. She was beautiful and the type of city girl who is both wise and ignorant. She had not been in his plan for this journey but one night when he was in her apartment—he always came to her, not she to him—he thought that he would miss her and also that it would be fun to have her on the ship and he asked her if she would like to go along.

"A cruise!" she exclaimed with delight. "I've never been on one. It would be wonderful. But you have to have all sorts of clothes. I've seen them in the shops. I've modeled some of them!"

"We'll fix you up," he said.

But he was cautious. She was to buy her own ticket and have her own cabin. He called the booking agent and said that a niece of his was also taking the trip and he would appreciate it if she could have a cabin on the boat deck. He was lavish with money but he gave it to Ruby in cash. Technically she was on her own and he knew that an affair on shipboard was no novelty.

It was, as he had figured, fun to have her along at first, but she was beginning to be too demanding and he had to slap her down occasionally. The contrast between Ruby and Barbara Bancroft at the same table could be irritating. But things had been all right until the day at Casablanca. To set them straight again he had given a cocktail party and nearly everyone came. Mrs. Barnes and Mrs. Hayward were there, and the writer and Mrs. Goode, and the Commodore and Joan Scofield looked in for a few minutes. The Robert Caynes were there, of course, but not Alec Goodrich. Nor Barbara Bancroft.

Demarest had not been neglecting the job he was doing on the side, inspecting the ship and analyzing costs and wastes as well as figuring out whether this type of travel had a future and was worth an investment. He had made many mental notes but come to no decision. The huge smorgasbord midnight feasts that were set up every night could be cut down. There were more paid entertainers on board than were necessary. Such things were easy to put a finger on. But travel by sea and expeditions in foreign ports might be on the increase or on the way out. At this point he wasn't sure. He found that he himself liked being on the sea, and in spite of the rather continuous drinking he felt better than he had for some time. He could sleep until noon. There was no mail pouring in. And in spite of the incident at Casablanca it was worth it just to have seen that city, how those French people held on, and the style they lived in.

Chapter Six

Before the ship reached Capetown Alec Goodrich had received a cable. It came from Senator Marcus O'Brien in Washington and was brief and cryptic: LETTER MAILED TO REACH YOU CAPETOWN IF NOT RECEIVED TRY TELEPHONE ME.

The letter was there. Jim Bates brought it before eight o'clock and Alec was surprised to see that it was written by hand, very unusual for a man with a staff of secretaries. Alec realized that it must contain some top-secret information. Sitting on the edge of his bed he read it, then read it again and then sat there, filling in the story between the lines. He was deeply touched.

I am writing this by hand because very few people know that this project is in formation and I would not write at all unless I were sure that you can be involved in it, if you think well of it. It is soon to be announced that a commission will be set up to reexamine in depth the relations between the federal government and state universities. Privately supported educational institutions not to be included. Problems of better financing, collaboration and discipline to be studied. Two-year grant for expenses assured. Your name has been suggested as chairman because of your experience on Committee on Education and Labor. No Senate confirmation necessary as this will be done under Presidential authority. Personally consider this a very rewarding job—no fanfare, hard work, plenty of prestige and national notice. Would have to return at once so cable me soonest. Hope your trip has been enjoyable to date. Have missed you. Your shoes are badly filled.

It was completely obvious that when this commission had been planned on the highest level, Senator O'Brien had seen its possibilities as a comeback for his former junior colleague and had wangled it so that Alec could have the chairmanship. He might have asked that as a personal favor for himself. Perhaps he had made a promise of support for some legislation that the President wanted, or made a trade. But it would have been an honorable trade. Alec knew Senator O'Brien well enough to be sure of that.

There were innumerable commissions set up and of course their reports usually gathered dust. But now and then one caught the public imagination or was a test flight for an administration project. This one involved money, which made it important, and Marcus would not have recommended it if he had not thought there was a bite in the proposition. It could be a very useful commission. Alec knew it was needed. Better and less volatile relations should exist between the government at all levels and the universities which lived on state funds and federal grants. It was all tax money and Alec liked the exclusion of private colleges, whose trustees often had a sense of personal ownership. The relations between the federal government and the state universities could set the pace, set an example. There was too much favoritism now, too often political pressure. It would be a tough job but it should be done.

Reading the letter again the words "prestige and national notice" stood out. The grand old man did not overlook that chance for a comeback. Nor did Alec. He must cable at once and the message must show that he realized what was being done for him.

The cable office was on the top deck, near the officers' quarters. But the window was closed. Alec rapped on the glass. A young man slid the pane back and Alec said that he wanted to send a cable.

"We can't accept cables when the ship is in port, sir. It's a regulation."

"But this is important."

"I'm sorry, sir, but you will have to send it on shore."

"Where do I go to do that?"

"From a hotel or the post office. The post office is best. It's not at a great distance. Any policeman on the dock can direct you."

Alec went back to his cabin. Jim Bates had already finished

82

making up the bed. He said, "Have a good day, sir. Have you been to Capetown before?"

"No, I never have, Jim."

"You'll enjoy it. It's different in a way, with all those mountains just about on top of it. Some people like it better than Durban. But when you get out of Durban just a little way into the Bantu country you see more of the old South Africa."

Alec was realizing that he was not going to see any more of South Africa at all. A feeling of disappointment and regret came over him from nowhere. Tonight, or at the latest tomorrow, before the ship sailed, he would be on a plane.

"Have a good day, sir," repeated Jim and went out with the sheets for the laundry.

Alec followed after a few minutes. The ship was in the usual medley after arrival in a port and before the passengers were given clearance to go ashore, but the crowds were on the lower decks and Alec stayed on the upper one, looking at the peak that he knew must be Table Mountain, with its white cloud tablecloth, and at the surrounding summits which he could not identify.

"The tablecloth looks a bit dirty this morning," said Mark Claypole, joining him at the rail. "Going on to Johannesburg for a few days, Senator?"

"No, I can't make it," said Alec. He had made a reservation for that trip but when the cable came he had decided he had better wait and see what was on Senator O'Brien's mind. He looked down at his fellow travelers with curious envy. They were not friends but he knew many of them by sight or through slight contacts and he felt, now that he was about to leave them, that they were a pretty good bunch of people.

"Do you still think they're all refugees?" he suddenly asked Mark Claypole.

Claypole smiled in his crooked way. "What do you think by this time?"

"I think they're all right," said Alec. "At least they aren't sitting on their hands. Most of them seem to want to see things, find out what goes on outside their own bailiwick, for one reason or another."

"You're generous. I suppose a public figure has to be."

"I am not a public figure, Claypole," said Alec shortly.

"Sorry."

"Quite all right but I make the point."

"I'll keep it in mind. I'm going down to have some breakfast. Had yours yet?"

That was an invitation, for in port the tables in the dining room were not reserved. But Alec said, "I'll wait a bit," and Claypole left him.

Alec was astonished at how churned up he was. He thought of Washington as he viewed the strange mountains, seeing it not only with clarity as a city but with the habits and confrontations his return and acceptance of a new job would mean. He would have the news hounds asking questions, trying to put words and prophecies in his mouth. There would be jealousy, competition, the inevitable political struggle, no matter what his backing was. If he put the proposed job over in a big way, the people who had veered away would come back again. And if Cicely had not yet found another man—how would she feel and what would she do? He had not allowed himself to think of Cicely since he had refused to hold her to their engagement, but now he remembered her beauty, her gaiety, her flashes of insight and intelligence and her ambition for him. When he went back—he found himself resenting return. His thought was like a spoken word, an admission. This is the first time that I've had the freedom to be my own man since I went into politics.

Even before that. His early life had been shaped by Aunt Lucy's interest in politics, her insular patriotism—she had been so proud of his part in those first small political battles and the victories he had won. Of course by that time he had already discounted and been amused by her Daughter of the American Revolution attitude, which regarded the world outside the United States with pity or dislike or condescension. He had become interested in the foreign relations of his own country, based campaign speeches upon them. But his rhetoric had not made the world as real as the two weeks of this journey had made it. He was moving about in it, not as a politician but as a traveler with no strings attached. He had not known how much he had enjoyed the brief freedom until he faced the loss of it. Get some coffee and a couple of eggs, he directed himself, and then, as soon as you can get off the ship, find out where that post office is and cable Marcus that you appreciate what he's done and will try to do him credit in the job. You must phrase it pretty carefully so that if the message got into the wrong hands it couldn't be interpreted as any kind of conspiracy.

The post office was big and bare except in the center, where a large writing table was surrounded by red chairs upholstered in leather. A sign on the wall back of the table read FOR EUROPEANS ONLY. Alec did not sit down in one of the chairs. He contemplated them, a dozen questions in his mind. He had read about apartheid but to see it was something else. Could it possibly last? He saw a black man slowly and apparently serenely sweeping the floor beside the writing table. There was so much he did not know and should know.

"Can I help you?" asked a guard in English.

"Where do I send a cable?" asked Alec.

"The last window on the left, sir."

Standing at a shelf beside the window Alec wrote the Senator's name and address on a blank cablegram. He did not hesitate after that. The message read: RECEIVED LETTER DEEPLY APPRECIATE SUGGESTION AND POSSIBILITIES BUT FEEL SHOULD TAKE YOUR PREVIOUS ADVICE AND PROCEED ON JOURNEY. YOU WERE RIGHT. IT WAS THE THING TO DO. EVER IN YOUR DEBT. ALEC GOODRICH.

The schedule of the cruise allowed two days in Capetown and from there many of the passengers would be scattering on trips by train or plane that would take them to Johannesburg or Kruger National Park and let them rejoin the ship at its next stop at Durban. Those tours were expensive but even if he could have afforded it Father Duggan had no desire to visit the financial capital of the Republic of South Africa, to see lions and giraffes in their national preserves or to visit scenic waterfalls. His plan for the two days was simple. Tomorrow he would take the twelve-dollar bus ride that circled the mountains and the shores of both the Atlantic and Indian oceans. But on this first day that he would set foot in Africa he wanted to be alone and form his own impressions without the clacking of a guide. He had read about a church that he very much wanted to see.

During the last few years he had organized desegregated Catholic groups in his own parish and done what he could to destroy distrust and resentment. He had not always been successful but his sympathies with the blacks ran deep. His fears ran deeper and today he hoped that he might learn a little that might be useful when he went back to America, whether or not as a priest. So he walked through the city for hours, less interested in its surprisingly modern aspects than in the variety of color in the skins of the people on the streets, the obviously disciplined segregation and the signs of Dutch and English colonization that showed in the names of shops and banks. He stopped in a tearoom and described the church that he wanted to visit, and the proprietor, who had a Cockney accent, knew where it was and gave him directions.

The day had become very hot and he was one of the few white persons exposing themselves to the sun. He rested for a few moments in a small park, studied his map again, and found with satisfaction that he was close to the church he was seeking. He went on and saw it was simply built, approached by high, wide wooden steps. From the outside, an ordinary house of worship. But when he went inside it was different from any Catholic church that the priest had ever seen.

The stripped body of Christ on the crucifix above the high altar was black, the statues of the Virgin and the saints in painted red or blue robes and with golden halos had black faces. The figures on the Stations of the Cross that surrounded the walls were black.

He knelt for a few moments at the altar rail, deeply affected emotionally, and prayed for the people who had wanted to claim Christ for their race. He prayed for complete understanding and compassion and for an end to his own confusions. As he rose he remembered that when he was a child he had been told that three prayers said in a church which had never before been visited by the one who prayed would always be granted. He wished that he could still believe it.

The church had been empty when he entered but as he studied the figures he heard the door open and close. He turned and saw Barbara Bancroft coming slowly down the center aisle. Her eyes were on the crucifix but as he moved she recognized him.

She said aloud in a still, hard voice, without smile or greeting, "They don't want even Jesus Christ unless he is black, do they!"

She stared around, then turned and almost fled toward the door. Father Duggan followed. She must not feel like that about this church. On the high steps of the church she stood with her hands before her eyes. She was shivering in the heat.

He said quietly, "It seems strange, of course, but you must not be shocked."

"Oh, I'm not shocked," she said, "it isn't that it shocks me. I know how they feel. I know all about it."

"What is it that disturbs you then?"

"It surprised me, that's all. I was tired of walking and I came inside to rest. Rest! There it was waiting for me, saying it again."

"Come out of the sun," said the priest. "There's a park down the street. You should sit down. Please come with me."

She came without resistance and he guided her to a bench shadowed by the huge leaves of an exotic tree. He sat at the other end of it and waited for her to recover herself. This was not the girl with whom he had spent a pleasant tourist's afternoon in Marrakesh. She had been interested in what they saw there but impersonal. It was quite different now. He knew that he was close to the source of her trouble and unhappiness. But he asked no questions. She had pressed her hands against her eyes again and he was sure that she was silently weeping. Then she lifted her shoulders in a gesture of control and looked straight ahead, facing something that he was sure she had faced before.

She said finally, "It is wrong, isn't it?"

"What is wrong?"

"The blacks cutting us off. Cutting themselves off from all whites."

"They are seeking to establish their racial dignity. They feel that they can only do it by themselves."

"I know," she answered bitterly. "I know—would you like to hear why I know?"

"I would like to know why you are unhappy, Barbara, but only if it would help you to tell me.

She said, after a moment's pause, "I had a black friend. He was more than a friend. I loved him. And he loved me. For a while. We were going to be married. Then he changed. He told me that he didn't want to marry me, that I would ruin his life. Because I was white! That was the reason, the only reason. He said that to marry me would make him a traitor to his race. It wasn't that he didn't want me—as a woman. But he would not let that matter."

"It must have been very hard. For both of you."

Barbara said, "We were in college together. That was where I met him. He was older—a leader. He had terrific potential. Everyone thought so, even the people who objected to things we did. We were—you know—protesters. We struck and made trouble because there was so much discrimination and injustice. The police were very rough—they used a lot of tear gas and once I was in jail for a couple of nights. But I was never so happy in my life. I was working for something and trying to break down a lot of barriers and stupid rules—he and I were working together for the same thing. That was at first. Then he changed, suddenly. He was doing graduate work in law and he was going to be a civil-rights lawyer. But he left the university. He started to go around with people who didn't believe that integration would work, who despised the very idea of it—well, like in that church. Everything and everyone had to be black. When I saw that figure on the cross, rejecting me just as—"

"Christ was not rejecting you."

"It felt that way."

"Have you been alone in all this trouble and confusion? Without any help?"

"How could anyone help? Oh, some people tried, who used to be friends of both Boone and me. But it was no use."

"Your family?"

"There's just my mother and father and we don't talk the same language. Of course they were horrified when I said I was going to marry Boone. Then they tried to be broad-minded and civil to Boone and that was almost worse because he knew how they felt about him. When we broke it off they were so happy. And painfully kind and forgiving. I didn't tell them that he was the one who had done it. They never would have been able to understand that. They had no idea of how I felt. I didn't want them to know. Not because of my pride but because I couldn't talk about it. It was a thing I had to bear myself. But today in that church—have I shocked you, Father?"

"Of course not. I am only sorry for the anguish that this man caused you."

"Thank you."

A blossom fell from the tree to the bench. She picked it up. It was a curious color, blending scarlet and pink, and the huge petals caressed her fingers. "What a strange flower," said Barbara, "and how strange to be here, telling you all this. I feel better than I have in a long time. Does confession always do that to people?"

"It should," said Aloysius.

He did not feel like a confessor at the moment. He was very conscious of her beauty, heightened now for him because he knew what had erased gaiety and happiness from her face. He felt a personal desire to restore it, to relieve her from shocks and suffering.

"Barbara," he said, "will you do something for me?"

"I'd certainly like to."

"Let's go back to the church. For just a few minutes. I don't want you to remember it as you saw it before."

She hesitated, said, "I'd rather not. But if you want me to, all right."

"I'll be with you," he told her, "you won't feel rejected."

Mark Claypole could not afford the excursion to Nairobi. It would ravage the small bundle of traveler's checks that he had left, and he knew that his balance in the bank in New York would be low after the alimony for the next two months was paid. He had told his banker to take care of that at the usual time and asked Milton Knott to deposit to his account any money that might come in for him through the agent. There were still small drifts of that now and then—sometimes from a secondary sale to a magazine in Australia or Denmark—and there was an occasional windfall in royalties from the condensed book version of his first novel. And Mark had not quite let go of the hope that Hollywood might come across, that a producer might see that the last novel had film possibilities.

Anyway he wanted to take this shore trip. For Nairobi was the approach to Hemingway country and Mark had never seen Mount Kilimanjaro. He did not expect to find a story in the place—the best story had already been written—but he wanted to get the feel as well as the sight of the region that Hemingway had made so real through the eyes and emotions of characters who were strangers there. That was Mark's own line. He often thought of Hemingway with caustic understanding, of that long slide from brilliant work to frustration and despair. He would not have to slide so far in his own case but he knew the sensation.

As he considered the journey he vaguely wondered whether, if he took up the matter with Signe Goode and asked her to come along, she would pay for both of them. He could be casually frank about not being able to afford it. But he rejected the idea. He did not want her ingenuousness interfering with his attempt to reincarnate the inspiration of a great writer, whose work she most certainly would not have read.

When he counted his checks again after he had booked and paid for the shore journey he thought that if it did become necessary he could get a loan from her. That idle fortune of hers should have a workout now and then. He could give her the worth of the money in one way or another, spend some of it on her. Tom Goode hadn't done much of that when he had it.

He had told Signe, when she asked what he was going to do in Capetown, that he was taking off early the next morning for Nairobi. He left it at that and Signe said, rather quickly, that she wanted to stay in Capetown for the two days that the ship would be docked there and go on with it to Durban. She was going to shop for some thin dresses and Joan Scofield had told her that there were some wonderful department stores in Capetown.

"Blue dresses," said Mark, "white. Don't buy those LSD-trip prints. Solid colors for you."

She looked surprised and pleased. "That's what I like. But when I was getting ready for this trip the saleswoman said prints were the things I'd need."

"Don't let anyone sell you things, dear. Buy from instinct."

Signe knew now that the dear meant nothing. It was his way of talking to women.

"And don't spend all your time in Capetown in department stores," he added.

"I'm not going to. Joan says I should take a bus trip that's scheduled for the second day. You see two oceans," said Signe. "First you drive along the Atlantic coast and through the mountains and then cross over and come back on the other side along the—I looked it up on the map but I forget—"

"The Indian Ocean," said Mark.

"That's it. I talked it over with one of the men in the travel office and he said that if I went on one of the long trips like the one you're taking I'd miss the one from Durban to a place called the Valley of the Thousand Hills—isn't that a lovely name?"

"It is indeed. I hope it's as lovely as it sounds."

"It's where you see the Zulu dances. And honestly I'd rather see the Africans than a lot of those wild beasts that they say you see on these other tours ashore."

"You've got brains."

"No—but you can always go to the zoo at home. When will you be back from your trip?"

"I'm not sure," said Mark. "I'll fly back, probably, just before the ship sails from Durban."

He hoped that he could arrange to spend an extra day in the Tanganyika territory near the great mountain, bypass the visits to the game reserves and the stop in Johannesburg, shaking off the companionship of other people who might be on the tour and doing his own thing. When he saw Demarest and his girl at the airport he was glad he had planned it that way. The young Beauforts were there also but they were never a nuisance. They were locked in their own company, a living example of the generation gap. They gazed across it, talked politely across it and stayed on their own side. Eugene Beaufort had finished his time in the Army and this trip with his new wife was a wedding present from her family. He was a lean young man with immensely becoming long sideburns which made Mark remember the pictures of the good young men in early editions of Dickens. He sat on one of the benches and Bettina rested her head on his shoulder and slept. It was early morning and the Beauforts always danced every night as long as the

92

musicians would play. She was wearing a pants suit and looked tired and tousled, and pretty.

Howard Demarest was in very good spirits this morning. He greeted Mark cordially and Mark responded with protective indifference. He was very glad to hear that they were not staying in Nairobi but flying back from there almost immediately to Johannesburg, by private plane. Demarest explained to Mark, who did not listen with interest, that he had business connections with some Johannesburg people.

"They're taking good care of us, showing us every courtesy," said Demarest. "I'm looking forward to seeing Johannesburg. Of course it's full of millionaires. Johannesburg was built on solid gold. But they tell me that though it's a big city it's still got the frontier spirit. I understand that it can be a very rough city, more dangerous than New York or Chicago in some sections. But the Europeans—that's what they call all the white people over here, you know—"

"I know," said Mark.

"It's a mixed batch in Johannesburg. Dutch, British, Afrikaners and there are quite a lot of Jews. South Africans don't have any prejudice against them. They're cosmopolitan minded. Though of course they draw the line at color."

"What color?" asked Mark. "There's a broad spectrum in these African cities."

Demarest laughed. "Well, I suppose there's plenty of tarbrush. There always is, in any place where there is a big proportion of Negroes. But the thing is that in South Africa when they say segregation they mean it and they seem to be able to handle it. A nonwhite has his own place and he has to keep it. There's none of this deliberate-speed hokum about integration out here."

"No," said Mark, "if you sleep with a gun beside you and have a pack of fierce dogs I suppose you can enforce segregation."

"It's their way," said Demarest. He grinned at Ruby and said to her, "If you get any more of that tan on you, they'll try to segregate you."

She stroked one of her bare arms with a slim hand on which the long oval nails were so polished that they seemed almost to reflect the light. She was breathing in the admiration of the men in the waiting room, the bold looks and the sly looks. Her dress was the color of ripe watermelon, ending high above her smooth, bare knees. A leopard-skin coat lay on the bench beside her but she was standing for better display, constantly moving her body a little, rhythmically, as she had been taught to do when she modeled.

Mark Claypole glanced at her as if she were the cover girl on a magazine that he would not buy. The story that went with that picture would be the same old one, with new names and incidents brought up to the mores of the minute, but there would be nothing original about it. He had no desire to write that story, though there was always a reading public for a tale about the aging lover and the sex-career girl and the brutalities of their relationship. Mark did not like Demarest or Ruby Canaday but they stirred a faint curiosity. The desire for personal recognition was unusually magnified in Demarest, who must have all the money and power he needed in his own world. But he was almost defensive. It seemed to Mark that he was continually selling himself to himself as well as to other people. He was giving the girl her keep in luxury but obviously that wasn't enough for her. She wanted men, an audience of men, not one of them. And Demarest wasn't getting all he expected or wanted. There had been that blow at Casablanca.

Mark looked at his watch and saw that it was past time for the plane's departure to be announced. Crossing the room he asked the travel agent in charge when they would take off.

"We're waiting for another member of the tour, Mr. Claypole. Mrs. Hartley Barton. She's on her way. It won't be long now."

As he spoke the waiting-room door opened and Mark saw the elderly woman he had noticed on the day of sailing—he put her age as past seventy—come in, pulling herself along on her two canes.

There was the same look of delight and anticipation on her face as he had seen on that first day. She smiled—the smile of a lady who was gracious from long habit—and said in a voice that was surprisingly young, "I do hope I haven't kept everyone waiting. Just as I was leaving the ship there was a long-distance call from Nairobi that I couldn't ignore."

"She must be crazy," said Howard Demarest to Ruby, "a crippled old woman taking a shore trip like this. They shouldn't let her."

But the travel agent was paying Mrs. Barton special attention, personally taking her out to the plane before he called the other passengers. She had a front seat for herself and her canes and sat on the aisle, saying cheerfully that it would be less trouble to get out from that place. The young Beauforts helped her take off her coat when they got on and wanted to know if she was comfortable, as if they were used to elderly ladies. They sat behind Mrs. Barton and Demarest was across the narrow aisle.

He said toward her, as they leveled off in the air, "This may be a hard trip."

Mrs. Barton had immediately recognized him. She had often seen him on deck but she remembered him as the man who had hit the girl at Casablanca. She answered pleasantly but not as if she intended to continue conversation, "I've always enjoyed it. And it is not so difficult as it used to be."

The reply astonished him. He couldn't let it alone. He had decided she was an old schoolteacher who'd saved up for this cruise and wouldn't miss anything.

He asked, "You've been here before?"

"Oh yes. I always enjoy Africa."

"You travel a lot?"

Her eyebrows lifted. "We've always traveled—at our pleasure. I would not know if it would be considered a lot."

Young Beaufort heard the interchange and grinned. He murmured to Bettina, "Just like Grandma. She put him in his place."

95

Demarest persisted. "I suppose it gets in some people's blood. But I don't know how long these cruises will last. They're taking off a good many passenger ships. Planes get there quicker. And it costs less."

Mrs. Barton looked at him, examined him. She said, "My dear sir, people will always want to travel by sea. Just as they will always want to ride horses."

She turned her head just enough to exclude him, dismiss him. Demarest grinned and pinched Ruby. "Wonder if she tries to ride a horse too," he muttered under his breath.

He did not attempt to draw Mrs. Barton into conversation again. But he was irritated. The familiar annoyance of not having someone realize his importance itched. It was an old itch. For some reason the old woman reminded him of his wife's mother, who always thought she was better than anyone else. The plane flew on jerkily. Beaufort brought his wife and Mrs. Barton paper cups of mineral water. He squatted down beside her seat and talked to her. Easily. They must know each other. He heard mention of names. Demarest thought of being met at Nairobi. Probably in style. He'd be taken care of—he did not quite admit to himself that he would like to have that old woman see how he himself traveled.

It was a long, tiresome flight punctuated by a box lunch that few people ate. The descent was fairly abrupt and Demarest felt that it was careless and considered making a complaint about it. The relief could be felt as a general mood when the plane finally touched down. Bettina Beaufort looked more untidy, not quite so pretty. Mrs. Barton straightened her hat, which was the only one on the plane of course. She had not taken it off and under its brim her face was gray with fatigue. She reached for her canes and the guard and Gene Beaufort carefully helped her to her feet. The other passengers waited and Demarest said to Ruby that it was a damned nuisance having a person in that condition on a plane.

Someone was being paged. He heard the loudspeaker before he deplaned. The name was not clear. It was probably for him.

"Mrs. Hartley Barton," came over the microphone.

She stood waiting, dark dress crumpled, face serene and unsurprised.

A chauffeur hurried forward. The guard indicated Mrs. Barton. And Demarest heard, "The car is waiting, Madam. Sir Maurice and Lady Mary send warmest greetings."

Chapter Seven

The motorcoach in Durban which had been reserved for the ride to the Valley of the Thousand Hills was fresh with bright blue paint outside and very clean inside. It was filled. Father Duggan had seen Barbara Bancroft mount the steps of the bus and was careful not to follow closely. He found a seat well back of hers. He did not want or intend to intrude upon her. She might very possibly regret that outburst of confidence in the park the other day. Also she had been very much—overmuch, he was afraid—in his thoughts since then. It was involuntary and rather frightened him. He had not had such a personal feeling about a woman in years, not since he had been ordained. He had been friendly with many girls and women, fond of some of them, but it was the fondness of a father and a priest.

The Robert Caynes were on the bus. They had stayed with the ship instead of taking one of the longer trips to the game reserves or to other African cities. They had considered one of them but the cost was eight hundred and ninety dollars, which, as Robert Cayne said, meant a thousand before they were through. They had already become aware that this cruise was going to cost far more than they had originally figured, with tips and wines and films and shopping and entertaining. Robert Cayne blustered generously that it was once in a lifetime and was their wedding trip and he did not care what it cost. But he did care, for he knew from the daily bulletins that were posted that the market had been going steadily down since they had left New York, and when they returned income taxes had to be faced. He was well satisfied this morning to know that he would spend less than twenty dollars today and was not going to be out a thousand for a five-and-a-half-day junket.

"We'll see just as much from the bus probably," he said to his wife, "and be more comfortable sleeping on the ship instead of in some lodge in one of those parks, probably being bitten to death by bugs."

Kitty Cayne, who had been a secretary in the investment-banking firm of which Cayne was one of the many vice-presidents, said she thought so too. She was being very feminine since her marriage but she knew the money score.

Signe Goode had reverted today to her original shipboard shyness. The bus trip from ocean to ocean which she had taken in Capetown had been very scenic but she had felt lonely and unplaced. She did not want to sit by Julia Hayward this morning, but Signe had been one of the last to board the bus and by the time she did there was only the choice of taking the aisle seat beside Julia or the other unoccupied one by the priest. That she could not face. She wouldn't know what to say to him or not to say. She asked Julia if the seat next to her was being held for anyone. Julia said no.

"Then may I sit here?"

"Of course, Mrs. Goode. Would you like to sit by the window?"

"Oh no, thank you." They agreed that it would be a hot day and then conversation lapsed. Julia turned again to the window. This was bad luck for her. She had hoped that the aisle seat would stay vacant or be taken by someone who was a complete stranger.

She was by herself for Alida had gone to Kruger Park for several days. She had urged Julia to come with her but without success.

"It's a small, very nice group," Alida had said. "That young Britisher with the travel bureau is conducting it. Did you know he went to Oxford? That interesting couple from Canada are going and the Julian Chiltons. Marcia Chilton didn't know what to do. Her husband is terribly keen on seeing the park but they didn't want to take Hilary along for it would be a hard trip for a child and she might catch some infection. So they finally decided to leave her on board with the nurse as far as Durban, where we'll all rejoin the ship. The nurse is utterly reliable—she's been with them for years but Marcia worries. Of course they had that horrible experience."

Julia didn't inquire into the experience. Alida had established a connection between the Chiltons and herself for they knew some of the same people in California.

"It will be fun," Alida had said, "and we must sign up at once for the membership is limited on that tour."

"I'm not signing up," Julia answered. "I can't afford it."

"But you don't want to miss it! Look, Julia, it will be my treat."

"No, there have been too many of your treats, though I thank you very much. Just forget about me and go along with the Chiltons and have a grand time."

"What would you do?"

"I'll wander around Capetown. And on the day that the ship will be docked in Durban there's a bus trip that might be interesting. To native territory. It's before you'll get back to the ship."

She was firm and Alida had to yield after more offers and protestations. Julia was not only willing but glad to have a few days by herself. In Capetown she found a bookstore and went to a theater. She also did some figuring about the erosion of her income by the increased cost of everything, especially rent and clothes. She thought of moving to a smaller apartment in New York when she went back. If she could earn something—but what could she do at her age and with no training? Occasionally she looked at Joan Scofield with envy. If, right after the divorce, she had gone into something like Joan's kind of work—but it was too late now and anyway she knew she would not be good at it. She couldn't tolerate all those women.

When the ship sailed for Durban, it seemed to her to be pleasantly empty and relaxed. The run took only a night and a day and Julia had her meals brought to her cabin. There was no one left at her usual table in the dining room except Signe Goode—the others had all gone off on tours—and Julia found it difficult to talk to Mrs. Goode about anything except scenery and weather.

At Durban there had been a letter for her. Not from Peter but from Christine. It had been delivered to her this morning, a short letter in Christine's sprawling handwriting, which could use up a page of onionskin paper with twenty words.

Dearest Julia—

Pete says that we ought to let you know what's with us. Of course he should write you himself but he asked if I would so I'm elected harbinger of news. We're divorcing. Nothing is working right for us—it hasn't for ages. He is terribly edgy and nervous, either indifferent or jealous, and frankly I've had it. I still love the lad but living with him is something else. He feels the same way—I haven't been much to come home to. So he doesn't. He's moved to the Field Club here and I'm going to Mexico, which is handy and quick. It should be all over by the time you are back in New York. We won't divide Tony. Pete agrees that I should have him, if he can see Tony now and then. Tony won't know about this until he comes—probably here for I expect to stay on with the shop—for his summer vacation, but Pete didn't want you to pick up the news from somebody you might meet in some port or get it in a letter from one of your friends. This sort of thing gets around. I have some dazzling decorating jobs in prospect so don't give me a thought. I'll keep in touch and Tony and I will always welcome his grandmother and have a bed and a bite for her any time you come our way.

All love,
Christine

There was nothing Julia could do about it. Flying back from Africa to try to hold them together would be preposterous and they certainly would resent it if she did. Christine would be as casual and determined as her letter. Pete would be civil and unreachable. Julia wondered if he was still in analysis, if he was drinking more heavily. Would Tony be scarred by this divorce as his father had been subconsciously at twelve years old? There was nothing she could do about it. The thought swung back and forth in her mind like the pendulum of a metronome.

The motorcoach lumbered through the city. It was air-conditioned but the heat outside was obvious. The windows were wide and from where she sat Signe Goode could see the fantasy of the streets, the rickshaw boys with their headdresses of feathers, horns and beads, the people dressed as race and religion required—women in silk saris, bearded Mohammedans wearing red fezzes, half-naked boys holding monkeys. Everywhere flowers blazed on the shrubs and trees—at hotel entrances, in public parks, in niches between buildings, in bouquets at flower stalls and in the miles of sunken gardens along a waterfront which the guide announced was very famous Durban Bay.

He was a native guide and used a small microphone. His English was sketchy and so accented that Signe could not understand much of what he said. She yearned for company, for someone to whom she could exclaim and pass on her wonder at the brilliance and the strangeness. But it was obvious that Mrs. Hayward did not want to share enthusiasm. She did not seem impressed. Probably she had been here before, Signe decided. She must have been everywhere.

The coach began to climb to higher altitudes and behind gates and walls and more massed flowers Signe glimpsed big houses.

"Here is very, very rich people living," said the guide.

"I'll bet," agreed Robert Cayne aloud and roused a general laugh, but Julia Hayward did not smile.

"Now we go to Valley of Thousand Hills," the guide informed them.

"How long will it take to get there, Joe?" asked Cayne.

"One hour and few minutes. We stop take pictures when we see Zulus on road. Children dance. You get good pictures Zulu children."

Barbara Bancroft was sitting beside a man she did not know by name though she had seen him on deck. She had been briefly civil and then fallen into silence, absorbed by the sight of this mosaic of color and race. It was unsettling. It proved something possible—something that she had made herself stop trying to prove.

Then she saw the first group of Zulus by the side of the road. It was made up of women and children, and as the bus came closer to them the children went into a frenzy of dance, each by himself. They were nearly all naked, and as they danced they held out their hands and shouted, "Money, please, nickel, dime, money."

"You want stop take pictures?" the guide asked.

Cayne said, "You bet," and readied his motion-picture camera. When the bus stopped he was the first to get off, feeling in his pocket for small change.

They leaped as he tossed it to them. They jumped like animals, did special antics for the camera. A child who could not be more than two years old lay on the edge of the dusty grass and slowly revolved himself.

Barbara felt sick.

"Just like monkeys," giggled a woman.

A girl with a child on her back came under Barbara's window and stretched out her hand. She had one eye and broken teeth but her body was young, her breasts high and firm.

"And they call themselves 'people of heaven'! Isn't that something?"

Father Duggan cut the laugh short.

"Who knows? It could be true," he said with quiet authority.

Barbara turned to give him a look of gratitude. Signe Goode did not turn but she heard what he said and the priest did not seem so formidable to her. Signe did not like to see those children exposing themselves like that. Some of them were pretty or would be if they were clean. She wondered what their homes were like. She remembered, not too distinctly, the pictures of foreign black children on brochures which had been sent to her with requests for money.

She stirred and Julia Hayward was conscious of it and glanced at her seat mate. She saw that Mrs. Goode was not bad looking. She had a good skin but she made herself up badly. Vaguely Julia was curious about where the woman came from, why she was going around the world. But the curiosity did not rise to question.

The group stopped for lunch at a roadside inn, which had a shop plastered with racks of postcards and counters displaying souvenirs that had been made in Germany, Japan and America. There were also plastic bags of hard candy for sale. Barbara bought several of them and put them in the big purse she was carrying. If she saw more children she would have something to give them. Candy, not money, and she wouldn't throw it at them.

Like monkeys, those people said. Boone had said bitterly once— she let herself remember how he looked, how handsome he was, how pride and anger would flash in his mobile face: "A lot of people think of us as monkeys, a cut above apes. There used to be slave owners in the South who would dress up the little black boys in red coats like the monkeys with organ grinders and teach them tricks. That was a hundred years ago but plenty of people still feel like that about Negroes. And the blacks are the only ones who can change it, not by kowtowing and trying to mix but by building up the black race. All over the world."

If he had seen that man throwing money to those children—

"Aren't you having lunch, Miss Bancroft?"

"I'm settling for a Coca-Cola."

On the way to the Zulu enclosure of the Valley of the Thousand Hills, where the tourists were to see native dancing, the guide talked incessantly. The Zulus bought their wives with cattle. For a good cow a man could buy a woman to work for him for life. If he wanted to return her, he would want his cow back. Laughter. The unmarried girls wore beads as love letters and the colors of the beads showed if they were ready. Laughter. The guide was condescending. The Zulus were a national problem. But he too had a black skin.

Boone had said, "They must be taught not to despise their own people, not to feel inferior."

The dances were not beautiful. Unshapely men and women with large, bare, pendulous breasts capered around in a circle of sand to the sound of a beaten drum. They had been rehearsed as to when to stop for money or grin for a photograph. Barbara wandered away from the circle of watching tourists and found the place which served as a tiny hamlet for nearby natives. It was a collection of round huts, a few roughly thatched, the others made of mud and clay and manure, without windows and with a low aperture for going in and out. A small thin child crawled out of one of the outlets as Barbara watched. There was no one else around. Bedded-down fires smoldered beside most of the huts.

The child struggled to its feet, teaching itself to walk. Barbara bent down to give it a piece of candy and as she looked through the entrance she saw that there was no furniture at all. It was merely shelter. The child sucked at the candy and a look of pleasure, almost a smile, came over his face. Barbara touched his head with her hand and the child tumbled back to get inside his home again. She knelt down and tried to coax him out but without any result. She got up and went back along the rude path that she had come, and suddenly there were small boys and girls following her craftily in a growing pack. They had seen the candy and she portioned it out into their little greedy claws—hands hard as implements and used for all purposes. When she took out the third bag a boy snatched it from her and ran and the rest went in pursuit, streaking back to cry, "dime—nickel."

She shook her head, closed her purse firmly and said, "No more." She was not frightened and she would not treat them as animals. She smiled at them and they stared and repeated their chant for money. Father Duggan, on the top of a hillock—for he had left the dances and was unadmittedly looking for Barbara—saw the smile and to him it was sad. He knew what and of whom she was thinking and went down to be with her.

Commodore James had taken Joan Scofield to dinner in Durban. He had a favorite restaurant in the city which he usually visited when his ship was long enough in port. It was quite unlike the beachfront castle hotels, only a couple of darkish rooms with walls decorated with gold and silver filigree and there were rare birds in cages hanging from the rafters. It was cool with darkness and age.

Almost all the patrons were men, though the high, precise voice of an Englishwoman could be heard now and then above the low male conversations. The setting gave Joan and the Commodore a sense of remoteness and intimacy.

"This is the kind of place tourists never see," Joan said.

"That's why I brought you here. You see enough of our passengers."

"How did you find it?"

"A Greek merchant on the ship one year told me about it. I have a favorite haunt in almost every port. I won't be seeing this one again. Do you like the wine?"

"It's perfect," said Joan but wouldn't be diverted. "You'll miss your haunts, won't you?"

"Oh, Lord, yes."

"But you'll be free to travel where you please."

"Travel costs too much unless it's part of your job. No, I'll be stuck. I'll sit on a bench in a park and whittle."

"It's all wrong. It makes no sense. You're a wonderful commander. I know because I've seen others on ships where I've been hostess. Don't they know how stupid they are to lose you?"

"It's automatic. Not personal. If the Line were independent, as it used to be, things might be different. If seamen were at the top. But now the Line is amalgamated with big business and men like Demarest make the rules, run the show."

"I don't like him."

"He's sharp," said the Commodore. "Between ourselves I don't think he's on the ship just to give his girl a boat ride. There's more to it than that."

"What do you mean?"

"He's a kind of scout, I think. For the holding company."

"If he's that, I like him even less. He does ask a lot of questions."

"Let him ask. Give him the answers. We've nothing to hide. It's a good ship. The passengers get their money's worth. Maybe there's a bit too much plush but that's not up to me. Not unless there's something dishonest about it, and there isn't on *The Seven Seas.* "

Joan said, "I love the ship. But I don't know whether I want to stay with it without you."

"It's a good berth, Joan. And nobody does a better job than you. It's been a pleasure to have you around."

"Don't," she said, "you make me feel miserable. I've been so happy being your hostess."

"I wish you were more than that," he said. "I shouldn't say that. I'm an old man being turned out to pasture. But I'm not sorry I did say it."

"I'm glad you did." It was almost a whisper and he reached to touch her hand.

"We have a few more weeks," she said after a minute. "Can I have some more wine?"

He poured it and they talked of wines and Africa and the next run of the ship, which was across the Indian Ocean. It was late when they went back to the ship, which was to sail at seven o'clock the next morning.

The Commodore paid off the taxi and they walked toward *The Seven Seas,* which lay enormous beside the dock, gleaming white and with lights at almost every porthole and window.

"Isn't she beautiful?" said Joan.

"Hard to beat."

"It's a funny thing," Joan said, "on board there's that mixture of strangers—most of them never saw each other until two weeks ago—and yet when they come back to the ship tonight there'll be a sort of family feeling. It's like that after shore trips. They come home."

"A happy family?" asked the Commodore with a skeptical grin.

"I wouldn't say that. Most families aren't happy. But they thrive on their irritations."

Chapter Eight

Mark Claypole came back to the ship earlier than he had expected or intended. The journey to Nairobi had turned out to be a fool's expedition as far as he was concerned. To be sure, he had seen Kilimanjaro, wearing its insolent snowcap in the midst of a steamingly hot country, and he had understood why Africans had always prayed to it and identified it with divinity. But he could not project himself into their reverent worship. He could not even manage to be alone with the mountain, for small herds of tourists were not only interruptions with their incessant cameras, but the results of conforming the jungle to their comforts were obvious everywhere.

Mark did not go on safari. He had not signed up for one of the trips to the game reserves and after a few hours in Nairobi he was sick of the very word *safari*, advertised on all sides in connection with boots, tents and shaving lotions. There was no bite left in it and the pretense of hardship had become commercial. He looked at some posters which pictured the well-known "Treetops" lodgings, from which it was promised that elephants, rhinos and buffalo could be seen by hundreds every night, and figured that the sight of animals which had been observed so often was not worth the money. They too were up for sale.

None the less he watched Kilimanjaro from several vantage points for a long time, fully realized its beauty and mightiness with no emotional reaction, and then had dinner at a lodge at the entrance to the jungle, recommended by the driver of the car he had hired for himself in the city. It was a disconcertingly good dinner, with almost French cuisine, and coffee was served in the lounge. He spent the night within hearing of occasional strange roarings and trumpetings, feeling stupidly safe and almost undisturbed. The disappointment of his unadmitted hopes oppressed him. He could only get away from it by leaving in the morning, writing the place off and writing off a little more of himself into the bargain.

His driver, whom Mark kept in a state of astonishment, took him out to the airfield again and he was lucky enough to hop a little six-seater plane that was headed for Durban. After a few hours of bumping and sweating he was back on the ship with a mixed feeling of relief and lethargy, followed by annoyance when he found that the bars would not be open for some time. Nearly everyone, including the bartenders, was still on shore.

With the two-week-old copy of *Time* which he had bought in the city, he wandered into the empty smoking room and settled into one of the huge upholstered chairs in front of the windows that faced the harbor. It was a moment before he saw that he was not alone. The ship's only child passenger was almost lost to sight in an adjoining chair.

Mark had noticed her many times, always with her parents or nurse. She pleased him. Like all people of intelligence he treasured *Alice in Wonderland,* the fantasy that time and cynicism could not erode. This child had not only the smooth, almost lank hair always credited to Alice but the expectant, meditative expression of the Tenniel illustrations. Her skirt was full, the small sleeves were puffed. No doubt it was a modern child's fashion, but the effect was right. She wore no apron but a pocket on each side of her skirt served as well.

He said, "Well, hello. How are you today?"

She made no answer, looking steadfastly ahead and not at him.

"That's not very polite," he said gently and teasingly. "Won't you speak to me?"

She said, "I am not allowed to speak to strangers. Or to take candy."

"Oh," said Mark, "I see. No candy. I haven't any to offer you, anyway. And that's very sensible, not talking to strangers. But people who are traveling on the same ship aren't strangers. How could they be?"

She thought and asked, "Why aren't they?"

"Because it's like living in the same house. You can't be strangers when you live for weeks on the same boat."

Hilary said, "I don't know. Nobody told me that."

"There's an element of truth in it. But we needn't go into that. Where is your family today? And that omnipresent nurse of yours?"

"My father and my mother have gone on a trip to see the beasts. And Cora is sick. She was not supposed to let me out of her sight. So my mother will not worry and have a nervous breakdown."

She even talks like Alice, with the same straightforwardness and logic, thought Mark.

"That's a bad thing to have certainly," he said.

"Yes. She had one when they stole my brother."

Mark was putting the facts together. Careful not to press her lest she run or possibly vanish. He said quietly, "I hope you got him back."

"Well," said Hilary, "after a long while they did. But he was dead then. He was mutilated."

The fact, stated so calmly, and the incongruous word on the child's lips, gave Mark a twinge of horror. He asked no further question but Hilary was talking now.

"Cora is sick to her stomach," she explained. "She was sick all night while I was asleep. She has to go to the bathroom all the time."

Mark said reassuringly, "That happens to a lot of people when they go traveling. They get over it but it isn't much fun while it lasts. Is she in bed?"

"No, she was better so we came out of the cabin and down here. But she was sick again and had to run to the ladies' room. She left me in there—" Hilary pointed to the adjoining library—"but the men came with vacuum cleaners so I came in here."

"It's comfortable here," said Mark, "isn't it?"

"I like it. I like being by myself."

"I often feel that way. Don't you go to school?"

"In New York I do. But Cora takes me and comes for me. Or my mother does sometimes. I would like to go by myself but I am not allowed."

"Oh, well," said Mark, "when you get older they'll let you."

"Yes," agreed Hilary, "and when I get older I can run away."

"That shouldn't be necessary."

"Lots of girls do. Don't you know that?"

"I've heard rumors. It seems rather a stupid thing to do."

"They like to. They hide," said Hilary. "I've read all about it in the magazines. And the newspapers."

"How old are you?" asked Mark.

"I'm ten. I think I would have to be about thirteen to run away."

"Did you get that interesting advice from the newspapers too?"

She nodded gravely. "There are lots of girls under sixteen who run away. They take drugs. We don't have any drugs in my school. It's not allowed."

"Look," Mark began and was interrupted by hearing a frightened woman's voice almost screaming in the lounge and a steward's protesting answer.

"But I left her in this room! In this chair! Hilary!"

Mark stood up. "The little girl is in here," he called.

The nurse rushed in. Her face was greenish white with sickness as she ran toward her charge. Nausea swamped her again. She clutched the back of a sofa to steady herself and fainted.

"Better get Miss Scofield," said Mark to the steward, bending over the woman.

"She has gone ashore, sir."

"Then bring me some water. And a shot of brandy."

"The bars are closed, sir."

"Oh hell," said Mark, "help me to lift her to the sofa."

"Is Cora dead?" asked Hilary.

III

"Of course not. She's still sick and she thought you were lost. She'll be all right in a few minutes."

The impassiveness with which the child asked the question was strange, and Mark quickly glanced at her. He did not like the expression on Hilary's face. She looked withdrawn, overly calm. She was not Alice in Wonderland now but a little girl who had been touched by shock and fear in real life. Mark repeated that nothing serious was wrong with the nurse and, as he smiled at her, trust came slowly back into Hilary's eyes.

So the elegant Chiltons were also refugees. Mark could not get that situation out of his mind even when he was finally sitting at the bar in the Seashell with a welcome and well-deserved drink before him. They were running away from their dreadful memory and carrying with them their most valuable possession, as refugees always did, tying it up in a bundle, concealing it as far as possible from theft and danger. They were keeping the little girl under wraps and imagining that seclusion and separation would keep her safe.

When the nurse had revived she had insisted that she would be all right, but Mark had gone with her and Hilary to their suite to make sure that she did not collapse again on the way there. He had rung for their room steward and, waiting for him to come, had noted the evidences of luxury that would be commonplace and natural to these people—the space and special décor, the alcove for dining by themselves at will, the spread of books and magazines and newspapers, Hilary's reading matter, with its lore of what went on outside this rich privacy.

Her look of horror remained with him and he could not help detailing the tragedy. Mark imagined the waiting, the hope, the finality—and Hilary had said mutilation. Of course no one would have told Hilary much about that but the word had fallen into her ear from some conversation or servants' gossip and she accepted it without visualization. She had been taught—had it drummed into her—that she must not worry her mother. She had been threatened with that nervous breakdown, another calamity she would not understand.

On the surface now she was docile and obedient. But already she was planning, in her cool, direct, child's way, to escape. To run away. She would probably do that in a few years. Alice in Wonderland would become one of those confused girl escapists who fled from the protection of their families to communal attics, drugs and the streets.

For weeks Mark's thoughts had been dead weights. But not tonight. They were stirring, wakened by a compassion he had not felt in a long time. He had gone to the edge of the jungle and found no story. And here was an obsessive one, stumbled upon in the smoking room of the ship, in the beauty and the future of a child.

"I thought I might find you in here," said Signe Goode.

"Hello. So you're back from your busing."

"You really should have come," she said, adjusting herself on the stool beside him.

"I guess so."

"Did you have a good time in Nairobi?"

"I did not. I haven't had a good time since I last saw you."

"Oh you—" she said.

"And you're looking very handsome tonight."

"You like it?"

"Get that in Capetown?" he asked. "It's your shade of blue. Hold to it."

She ordered a Tom Collins and said again, "You ought to have come. I know you don't like bus trips. But to see all those natives and the way they act. The way they live! It certainly makes you think how lucky we are."

"In what special way, dear?"

"Not living in hovels. With no clothes on the children and hardly any on the grownups."

"It's a warm climate."

"I'm serious," said Signe. "It makes you wish there was something you could do. To change things. To help some way."

"You help," he said rather absently. Not in answer to her wish. But it was true. In the new aquamarine shift that matched the clear blue of her decent, kind eyes, drinking her gin with satisfaction but not relinquishing her new-found concern about Africa, it was tonic to have her simplicity and honesty around. Mark wanted to stop thinking about that look on Hilary Chilton's face when she had asked if her nurse was dead.

The dining room was fairly well filled by the time of the second sitting. As Joan Scofield had said to the Commodore, the passengers were glad to be back. They had piled their souvenirs in their staterooms, occasionally wondering why on earth they had bought some of them, wrapped their color films in foil and labeled the boxes, showered gratefully in their clean, polished bathrooms and had a few drinks.

Alec Goodrich was at his usual table. Dennis had recommended rock oysters because the chef had taken some on at Capetown, and Anatole was opening a bottle of dry white wine. There was a satisfied feeling in Alec tonight about having made a decision which would carry him along for some time. He had not wasted the last two days after sending his cable to Senator O'Brien. He had wangled a flight to Pretoria and taken in the sight and some of the political atmosphere of the administrative capital of South Africa. He had been jarred and impressed. He had introduced himself at the American Embassy, for he knew he could not dig even a little way into the politics of the Transvaal without help, and though he had not asked either for escort or special information, both had been forthcoming. There had been too little time but it was a start and Alec was a quick study. He had felt the intense nationalism, the naïve assurance of the Afrikaners, and he was also convinced that it was only a matter of time until the native black population would boil over its restrictions. He had plenty to think about but it was comfortable to be back on the ship and to know that he would be on his way to a new experience tomorrow. He looked over the dining room to see who else was on hand.

The priest was there, back on the offbeat job that puzzled Alec, for why had an intelligent young cleric been assigned to unimportant work? Mrs. Goode was in her place and so was Claypole. Alec saw Demarest come in, not in the best of tempers to judge by his manner toward his steward and the way he scowled at his girl. Barbara Bancroft was not there. Alec wondered where she was and what she had been doing during these last few days. Not that it was any of his business—not that he cared—but he was conscious that there was a kind of potential between himself and the Bancroft girl. He certainly did not have any intention of developing it but they were both unattached and probably spoke the same social language. He liked her clothes. She was always good to look at, a handsome tableau. And she had herself under control though you never knew how deep that went with any girl.

"Yes, very good, Anatole," he said, tasting the sample of wine offered to him.

It was invigorating to feel organized again. The decision not to go back to Washington to seek that prospective opening had made all the difference between taking things as they came and shaping them to his own wish. The vigor in his mind revived his virility from another angle. Gene Beaufort and Bettina came in and gave Alec a nod and smile as they passed his table. Alec felt a twinge of envy. It must be something to have a girl like that with you on a long journey, have her to talk to, sleep with, wake to. If Cicely were with him—and if she had really wanted to stick with him there was no reason they shouldn't be on a trip like this. . . . Of course she had said she didn't want to break their engagement. But it wouldn't have worked. The thing between them hadn't been uncomplicated as it was with the Beauforts, who were like kids holding hands all the time. With Cicely there had been the whole setup—what she had naturally expected when he was riding high in Washington.

Barbara Bancroft came through the entrance to the dining room. The gilded pillars framed her. She was wearing a white dress tonight, very short and untrimmed, and as usual there was no jewelry clanking on her. Alec liked her clean brown throat. Why was a girl who looked like that traveling by herself? What was she getting away from? More likely who? Howard Demarest rose with a rather fatuous smile to pull back Barbara's chair and seat her. That irritated Alec. Demarest had his own little tart with him. Let him stick to her and leave the Bancroft girl alone. She was out of his class, no matter how much he swaggered around with his money and connections and cocktail parties. But of course any girl who was taking this long journey alone had put herself at the mercy of strangers. And she was probably well able to look out for herself.

Aloysius Duggan also watched Barbara come to her table. He knew the answers to the questions in Alec Goodrich's mind. He too disliked the attentions of Howard Demarest. He was beset by his wish to help Barbara, to heal her wound, to give her peace of mind. He had been able to do that for hundreds of girls and women who had come to him in the confessional and told him of their problems and sufferings. He had sent many of them away restored, ready to take life again.

But he could not do that for Barbara Bancroft and he knew that it was not because of the lack of a dark, curtained stall in a church or because they did not share a faith. It was because he no longer had a sure faith to offer her. That was part of it. And partly it was because when he was with her he did not have the impersonality of a priest. When they talked he could not keep himself on that level.

She had said to him, after that incident with the Zulu children, "Why did you say that perhaps they are the 'people of heaven'?"

"That's what the word *Zulu* means. And primitive people are often closer to things of the spirit than highly civilized men and women. It may look to us like witchcraft or superstition but it's none the less worship. Religion is very important to all the Bantu tribes."

"And the highly civilized tourists corrupt the people of heaven by throwing them money and encouraging that sideshow dancing."

"I don't claim we're highly civilized."

She said, "I wish I were black."

"What would that solve? Do you think you'd be happier?"

"Probably not. But I could be consistent. Boone—the man I knew—became consistent. He's doing his thing. I'm not. I don't even know what my thing is. Not any more."

"It's a period of pause for you. You'll find your thing."

"I wonder. I wonder if I'll ever feel committed to anything again. It's rather ghostly. It's not so awful as it was but it's not like living."

"I know."

"You couldn't know. I don't mean to be rude. Or impudent. But how could a priest, identified with a church and knowing what he believes, realize what it's like to be cast off?"

"Barbara, you don't understand," he began and she took it as reproof and said quickly, "Of course I don't understand your church. But I envy people who believe in things. I've begun to understand Boone. For a while I just resented his destroying what we had and what I wanted to keep."

She still loves that black man. The thought was repellent to the priest. Not because of color but because Boone was a man.

"Such an attractive girl, that Miss Bancroft," said Mrs. Hartley Barton, who was sitting next to Father Duggan tonight. "The one who just came in. At the table in the center. Have you met her, Father?"

"Yes. I've had some conversation with her."

He did not often sit by Mrs. Barton. He was usually at the other end of this table. But tonight the places had been juggled, for there were some guests from shore aboard.

117

"She is traveling quite alone," said Mrs. Barton, "going around the world by herself. In my generation that would have been incredible. But girls today are so very independent."

"It seems to have become necessary."

"She is a college graduate. Of Columbia University, she told me. A very disturbed college, isn't it? But a charming girl like Miss Bancroft seems to have escaped all the turmoil."

She had been gassed. She had told Aloysius that. Her throat still hurt sometimes. She had been put in jail. She loved a young black. She is unhappy because he walked out on her. The facts piled up in his mind as he said, "She shows no trace of turmoil."

"I'm sure she will get a great deal out of the cruise. Travel completes a good education. That's what my father always said. He considered it necessary. But frankly—I don't want to seem intolerant, Father—I sometimes wonder why some of the people you see on voyages today do travel. They could drink and dance—and carry on just as well—in their own communities."

"Mark Claypole, the writer in our midst, says that they travel to escape. That most of our fellow passengers are fugitives."

"Fugitives?" she repeated questioningly.

"Escaping from problems. Difficult situations. Sorrows."

"Well, it's true of many widows of course. And they're so often disappointed. But they don't have the right approach as a rule. So many of them are hoping for new attachments."

"What is the right approach?"

"My father used to say that a person should travel to measure himself against the world. My husband—" she paused for what must have been an affectionate memory—"my husband always said it did not matter where you died and that to hole up in fear of death was animal, not human. To some of my friends and relatives it seems to matter enormously. But I think of what Hartley said when I toddle around on my sticks. There is always something to learn, some place to visit—or revisit. Life is short—you can never do everything you'd like to do. Do you do much traveling, Father?"

"I've had very little opportunity."

"I am always glad when there is a chaplain on the ship. I'm not a Catholic but I have a deep feeling for religion. When I was a girl my father always insisted on our visiting the cathedrals and even without understanding the services one was always uplifted. By the atmosphere."

He did not reply. He knew and loved that atmosphere.

Chapter Nine

There was considerable indignation on board when the announcement was made that *The Seven Seas* would have to bypass Port Victoria because of weather conditions. The previous stop in Lourenço Marques had been short and unexciting in spite of the diligent efforts that the travel lecturer had made to arouse interest in Portuguese East Africa. Leaving the ship at nine o'clock in the morning the passengers had been herded back at three in the afternoon and it had rained lightly through the day, making shopping in the open markets disagreeable. The beaches were deserted and the mosaic-tile sidewalks looked slippery and gruesome.

"It may be the cashew center of the world," said Alida Barnes, "but they can have it. I never have liked cashew nuts anyway. I never serve them at my cocktail parties."

Julia Hayward asked Jim Bates twice about letters for her but there were none. It was a dreary day for almost everyone.

So there was more anticipation than usual about visiting Port Victoria four days later. In the morning the sun was shining over a sparkling sea, its blue decorated by whitecaps here and there. Several tenders were expected to convey passengers from the ship to the island in swift succession and the first one was moored by ropes to the gangplank of *The Seven Seas* shortly after breakfast, on schedule. When it took off those who were watching from the upper decks saw that the brightness of the day had given them an illusion. The ocean was rough and the tender tossed about, diving into troughs as it tried to make headway.

"Get those passengers back on the ship as soon as possible," ordered the Commodore, "and cancel any more shore trips for today."

There were confusion and disappointment. Joan Scofield tele-phoned to the Commodore a half hour later and asked if it would be possible for people to take the trip by tender if they were good sailors.

She said, "For some unknown reason a lot of them were looking forward to this particular shore job."

"I'm sorry but we can't take a chance," said the Commodore. "With a sea like this and probably worse weather before evening we'd have trouble getting the tenders moored to the ship and passengers back on board. If we had some broken bones we'd be blamed for letting people take a chance. Cheer them up, Joan."

"It's not going to be so easy."

"You'll manage. You're the girl who can do it. Run off a party or something tonight. Break out some free champagne. And by the way I've decided that since everyone has to be on board today anyway I'll post a lifeboat drill notice for three o'clock today instead of tomorrow. That will give them something to do."

"It's adding insult to injury, Commodore. A lot of our friends think life drills are unnecessary."

"I'll decide that," he said. "You keep them happy and I'll keep them safe."

He put down the telephone and resumed his conversation with the chief engineer.

"What do you think might be the trouble?"

The chief engineer was a lanky man with an unhurried manner. His pipe gave him a look of leisureliness which the Commodore knew was false. Fred Timmins was quick to see or hear anything that concerned his job. He never neglected anything.

"It's possible that we have a damaged shaft bearing. I may be wrong and of course we can't be sure. It's been too long since this ship was in drydock."

"I know that. But drydocking costs a lot of money. And the company doesn't make any while it's being done." The Com-modore didn't say anything more on that point and he didn't have to. Timmins had told him before this cruise that *The Seven Seas* should be overhauled and inspected in drydock. The Commodore had written the owners to inform them of that opinion and the answer had been the question that he put to the Chief Engineer now.

"There's no immediate danger of trouble?"

"I shouldn't say so. Unless the propeller is bent."

"Even then we could limp along on the other one."

Timmins said, "Unless something should go wrong with that."

"Very unlikely," said the Commodore, inwardly cursing a management which curtailed funds for maintenance. "But when we're in Bombay next week take a close look and have any repairs made that are needed until she goes into drydock. I shall insist on that when this cruise is over."

"I would do that, sir."

But both the Commodore and the engineer knew that little or no attention would be paid to the recommendations or advice of a man who was being retired.

Two notices were posted on all the bulletin boards within the next two hours. The top one was a printed routine one, in which the hour was filled in with crayon: *All Passengers Are Requested To Attend A Lifeboat Drill At 3* P.M. *At Their Assigned Stations.*

The other was gaily crayoned in red on white placard and it read:

MASKED DANCE IN MAIN LOUNGE AT 10 P.M.
BE SOMEONE ELSE FOR A CHANGE!
MASKS WILL BE DISTRIBUTED BY STEWARDS
TO ALL CABINS BEFORE DINNER.
CHAMPAGNE SERVED IN LOUNGE TO DANCERS
AND WATCHERS.

Joan Scofield had figured it out. When she had been prowling about in New York for party supplies, for which there was an allowance in the ship's budget, she had come upon a place that was selling out its stock, and she picked up nearly seven hundred masks for a few cents apiece. She had planned to use them for the last gala on the cruise, but she could find some other gadgets for that occasion in Hawaii, and, since the Commodore wanted her to amuse the passengers in this quasi-emergency, there was hardly any more surefire device than a masked party. It would give them something to talk about even if they didn't like the idea. And if the stewards distributed the masks, people would have to take what was given them. Joan knew that most people like a pig in a poke, especially a free one.

By three in the afternoon the sun had disappeared and the wind had risen. The gray sea was choppy and although there were still complaints about the cancellation of shore trips that the itinerary had promised, nobody really wanted to be in a tender, tossing about as were the few fishing boats in sight. At Lifeboat Station Number Two the assigned passengers gathered, with Jim Bates noting names and faces as they passed him.

Now it was a familiar if not fully friendly group. This was the third lifeboat drill and names were known and individuals placed and rated. The young Beauforts, who danced so beautifully and exclusively every night, were favorites without trying to be, and possibly without knowing they were generally approved. There was general sympathy for Mrs. Hartley Barton, because it was so hard for her to get around and so extraordinary that she did. But she accepted no pity and smiled at the man who held the door to the deck open for her and her canes as if she were conveying a privilege in letting him do it. Julia Hayward was always to be admired but she was nobody's crony. Demarest and Ruby were a continual source of speculation and scandalous enough to be interesting to a good many people.

Alida Barnes crossed the deck to speak to the Julian Chiltons when they appeared with their daughter and her attendant. Hilary looked around searchingly and then managed to maneuver her parents close to the place where Mark Claypole was standing. They spoke to him pleasantly, for of course they had been told the story of Cora's illness and his help and Mrs. Chilton had written him a formal note of appreciation.

Mark winked at Hilary.

"Why is a raven like a writing desk?" he asked her in a tone of confidence.

"I don't know. Why?"

"You must find out for yourself," he said.

Signe Goode knew it was one of Mark's jokes. She smiled at the pretty child but Hilary ignored the smile as if it came from a stranger offering her candy.

"Actually nobody knows," said Mark to Hilary. "They never got the answer at the teaparty."

"What teaparty?"

"You haven't read *Alice in Wonderland*? Too bad."

"Is it a book?"

"One of the best books in the world."

"Will you give it to me?"

"I'll think about that."

Barbara Bancroft and Alec Goodrich reached the door to the boat deck at the same time. There was no choice when they got outside. The crowd of orange-buckled passengers were huddled as close to the door as possible to keep out of the wind, which was not cold but more disorderly because it was warmish. Barbara and the Senator had to make a point of separating or to stand beside each other.

"It's turned out to be a mean sort of day," he said.

"Not a day for romping on tenders."

"I was on the one that made the effort," said Alec. "It was rather fun. Not that I'd recommend it for an outing."

"People were disappointed, I suppose that's the reason for the big treat tonight."

"Masks," he said with distaste.

"You aren't going to wear one?"

"Are you?"

"I don't know. As the poster suggested so cleverly, it is rather tempting to be someone else for a change. I doubt if a mask would do it for me. And you don't usually join in the fun and games, I've noticed."

"Is it so noticeable?"

"Well, you manage to sit in solitary state in the dining room. The rest of us aren't so favored."

"I'd be glad to have you join me," he said, "if your table companions—"

He stopped, feeling that he was saying too much. Perhaps she liked Demarest and those others. But Barbara finished for him, "If my table companions bore me? Probably not more than I bore them. We haven't a lot in common. I certainly haven't much to offer."

She seemed to Alec more beautiful close up. There were highlights in the loose, long hair and it was somehow regulated. The dark lashes were real, even at that length, and she was wearing no makeup except on her lips. They were faintly rose-colored, not scarlet.

"My table might be even more boring," he said, "but I'd be happy to have you try it sometime. Dennis, my steward, is a remarkable character. He plans my meals and is making a gourmet of me. Shall I ask him to set a place for you tonight?"

"Shall we wear masks?"

"Only our usual ones," he said.

She looked at him in surprise, then laughed and said, "Good guess. It really would be fun to talk at dinner instead of making conversation. The only person I ever talk to on the ship is Father Duggan."

"He's an interesting man. I can't figure why they waste him on a post as ship's chaplain. From everything you read about it, the Catholic Church is short on priests. There are a great many dropouts."

"He would never be a dropout. He has too deep a spiritual commitment. I have felt it when I talked to him."

"Are you a Catholic?"

125

"I'm nothing," said Barbara.

"Ladies and gentlemen," the ritual of instructions began on the loudspeaker.

"Is it a date for dinner tonight then?"

She hesitated, obviously between answers, and said, "Thank you. I'd like it."

Aloysius had seen the Senator and Barbara come out together and watched them. He was rather surprised that they knew each other. Barbara had not mentioned Alec Goodrich at any time. But the conversation between them now seemed very alive, almost intimate. The priest liked the former Senator. In their few encounters he had felt that Alec's aloofness was foreign to his character. It was not natural for a man who had been in politics. He had seemed withdrawn and rather sullen at the beginning of the voyage. But at this moment, with Barbara, he apparently was enjoying her company.

Any man would. He himself did. Not only because of her beauty but because she was so responsive. So straightforward. So brave. He wondered how much Alec Goodrich knew about her, if she had told him of her experiences. The priest doubted that she would have done so. But Alec Goodrich would be attracted to her and he was a free man, with no vow of celibacy. Being a celibate had never irked Aloysius. He had never visited a monastery without feeling the charm of complete dedication. But today, glancing again at the couple on the other side of the deck, he had a sense of being imprisoned, cut off from the world.

The masks were of many kinds and sizes. Joan had known as soon as she saw them in the shop that they would make a shipboard party gay. There were half-masks in many colors, plain black ones, grotesque ones that covered the whole face and made one elderly gentleman into a devil and one of the travel escorts into a circus clown. Some passengers had entered into the occasion up to the hilt and had spent hours in changing themselves beyond recognition.

Robert Cayne was wearing a negligee from his wife's trousseau and she was immersed in his pinned-up dinner clothes and had penciled long sideburns and a mustache to show beneath her eye mask. Cayne kept chuckling as they took flashlight pictures of each other and kept saying, "Now I know all about this changing sexes! My Myra Breckinridge!"

Of course there were many who couldn't or wouldn't be disguised. Mrs. Barton, sitting in one of the chairs on the side of the lounge, was very much herself in spite of the cover on her face. The Chiltons, in dinner clothes, had not bothered to bring the masks their steward had delivered to the suite. Mark Claypole wore a death's-head face—until he became bored and went out to the nearest bar for some whiskey to take the taste of champagne out of his mouth. He had danced just once with Signe Goode, who was wearing the gold robe she had bought in Casablanca and a metallic gold wig she had found at the hairdresser's shop on the ship. It was astonishingly becoming.

The Commodore looked in after eleven o'clock. He did not come much farther than the door and was about to escape when the girl in a white lace dress and lace mask—Joan had her own regalia for such parties on shipboard—came to his side and said, "Well, did I do all right?"

"Hello. You put it over. They're having a whale of a time."

"Most of them. Always a few misfits."

"You're looking very lovely."

"This travels with me. You've seen it before. I wore it to the fancy-dress party on the ship last year. And I'll wear it again next year."

"With some other captain to admire it."

"I'll remember that you did," she said quietly.

"Dance with me?"

She lifted her arm toward his and drew it back. "No, I think I'd better not. I'm supposed to be running this show, not enjoying myself. I'll see how the champagne is holding out."

The Commodore moved toward the entrance but not in time to escape Howard Demarest.

"Quite a party, Commodore," said Demarest. "The champagne must run into money."

The criticism from a director was implicit.

"Our passengers have had two disappointments in shore trips," said the Commodore coldly.

"Who decides on giving a blowout like this?"

"The proper ship's officers. In this case I did."

He did not excuse himself. He left and the odor of his contempt lingered. Demarest muttered, "I'll look into this."

"Don't get mad at the Captain, Howie. He's such a doll," said Ruby, who was beside him, holding a glass of champagne.

"You're getting yourself drunk," he told her. "Do that once or twice more and I'll send you back home from the next port."

"I have my own ticket," she said sulkily. "I'm paid for all around the world. Until we get back to New York."

He gave her an ugly look. He had pushed his mask up on the top of his head because he was hot. It was an Indian mask and gave him a doubly savage look, propped over his own angry face. He hit the glass out of her hand. In the hullabaloo nobody noticed.

It had been a bad evening for Demarest. He had a chest pain while he was dressing for dinner. This was the third time it had happened on the voyage. The nitroglycerin took care of the pain but not of his fear of its recurrence. When Ruby telephoned a little later to find out if he was ready for cocktails he told her that he wasn't feeling too well, that the curried shrimps at lunch had disagreed with him. He had never told Ruby of his doctor's warning about a heart condition. Instinctively he felt that to let her know about that would diminish him, make him seem older and less powerful a man.

Ruby said that he ought to lie down and that she didn't mind going to dinner by herself. She would stop in and see him on her way down. But he suspected that she was too willing to do that and wondered if she had her eye on somebody else, maybe that blond boy who was the orchestra leader in the Mayfair Room. She wasn't going to get away with anything like that. So he reassured himself with a highball and when she came in he said he was all right and went with her.

The Bancroft girl was not at the table tonight. He had come to look forward to seeing her. She was a highbrow and resistant but he enjoyed sparring with her, playing her up, partly to make Ruby jealous and partly because he was convinced that if Ruby were not in the picture he could make time with Barbara Bancroft. She was traveling alone. He occasionally thought that perhaps he could do it even with Ruby on his hands.

When he saw her at Alec Goodrich's table he was sharply annoyed. She had no right to go over there. It was way out of line. She should be sitting where she belonged. When Demarest had first come on the ship and talked to the head steward about his place in the dining room he had said, "When you're filling the other places don't load them with old ladies. I have one pretty girl and maybe you can find a couple more."

It had worked out that there were Ruby and himself, the ship's doctor, a Canadian with a presentable wife—that was all right with Demarest, who had looked them up in the *Who's Who* in the ship's library and found that they were people out of the top drawer though they never had much to say—a rather boisterous Texan with an athletic daughter who did not appeal to Demarest, and Barbara Bancroft. She was the pretty girl he had ordered from the chief steward. In a way she was Demarest's property, so he felt. She had not come to his cocktail parties but he decided that was because she didn't want to play second fiddle to Ruby. And there she was tonight, picking up that fellow who had been kicked out of the Senate. Demarest knew the story though he hadn't immediately recognized Goodrich. He had talked it over with several people on the ship after Alec did not show up at his party. Goodrich was a broken-down politician but he evidently still thought he was better than anyone else.

He finished his filet mignon before he did anything about it.

Then he pushed back his chair and walked over to Alec's table.

"Well," he said, trying a jocose approach, "why are you deserting us, Barbara? Were you abducted? Or did you think this gentleman was lonely? You want to be careful when you're with the Senator."

Barbara did not say anything. She turned her head as if to avoid the sight of something unpleasant. But Alec stood up and said in a steely voice, "I invited Miss Bancroft to dine with me tonight."

"Don't make a practice of it. We miss her." Demarest was about to say something else but Alec's expression warned him that it would be dangerous. He turned and lumbered back to his own place.

"I should have knocked him down," said Alec.

Barbara said, "No, don't let him make a production of it. He's been drinking. He's often pretty awful."

"You shouldn't be subjected to that sort of thing. Would you like to get out of here?"

"Why, no, we're going to have crepes suzette. You'd break Dennis's heart."

Aloysius Duggan saw her control the situation. He had known that there was trouble though he could not hear the interchange. But he saw the anger in Alec's face when Demarest intruded himself and knew that he must have been arrogant or insulting. The priest almost rose from his own chair when Alec stood up. If it came to blows he would go over there and stop it or take Barbara out of the brawl.

But it didn't come to that. Barbara watched the waiter prepare the dessert and light the flame of brandy as if it fascinated her. She was very beautiful in black chiffon tonight, with her hair piled high on her head. Alec began to relax and even smiled at something she said. But the priest was tense. Seeing her at the Senator's table tonight had given him a shock. He knew it came from a jealousy to which he had no right. His dinner was tasteless.

At Demarest's table there had been an uncomfortable silence when he came back to it. He broke it, saying defensively, "I thought it was up to me to do something about that situation. Give that politician to understand that Barbara has friends on the ship who are looking after her. She's taking this cruise by herself and she may not know Goodrich's history. He left the Senate under a cloud—wasn't reelected because of being mixed up with a girl."

Nobody answered. It was that way all evening for Demarest. Ruby was willful and difficult. He had been unable to get up an argument with the Commodore. And, though he kept looking for them, he couldn't see that pair anywhere. They weren't dancing. They had disappeared. Demarest brooded over that. They were probably up in Goodrich's cabin.

That was where they were. It was impossible to find a quiet place in any of the public rooms when Barbara and Alec looked for one after dinner. The big lounge was crowded with dancers and spectators. Bridge had been pushed into the smoking room. The library was locked. All the orchestras and combos on the ship were going full blast and even the Seashell offered no privacy. Outside the boat and sport decks were awash, and even on the covered promenade the long, double-jointed chairs had been stripped of their cushions, stowed away out of the penetrating dampness.

"Six hundred and ninety-eight feet of ship and no place to go," said Alec.

"Everybody's staying up tonight. I keep seeing people I've never seen before."

"I've seen people that I never want to see again."

"That Demarest person spoiled your evening. You're not over it yet."

"There are some things you don't get over."

"He's very crude and bossy. But he didn't say anything so very awful."

"It was the implication. I should be used to insinuations like that by this time but coming from that blowhard—along with his possessive attitude toward you—it was a bit much. Shall we go to the movie?"

"I don't think I could take that show again. It's a stupid one."

"We can't climb up and down these velvet stairs all night looking for refuge."

She laughed. "Maybe Mark Claypole had a point."

"Would you come up to my room and have a drink?"

"Yes," said Barbara promptly.

"Thank you very much," he said. "That takes the sting out."

It was a large, comfortable cabin. Jim Bates had opened the bed but everything was orderly and there were two armchairs and a cocktail table at the far end of the room. Alec left the door slightly ajar and rang for service. It was Jim who came.

"On duty tonight, Jim?" Alec asked in surprise.

"Just tonight. My relief was called downstairs. There's a lot going on. A special gala."

"It certainly is. There isn't room to breathe down there. So we came up here for a drink."

"Yes, sir. What can I get you, Miss Bancroft?"

"A gin and tonic, please."

When he had brought it, with an unrequested bowl of nuts, because he was so pleased to see Barbara enjoying herself with a man, he mixed a Scotch and soda for Alec, and left, quietly closing the door. Hearing that click, they exchanged a glance and laughed.

"I love Jim," said Barbara. "He keeps subtly encouraging me to have a fling. He wants me to enjoy the cruise and feels personally responsible for that."

"Are you enjoying it?"

"It's not so bad as I thought it was going to be. It's serving its purpose more or less. I'm seeing things I won't ever forget and I'm learning a lot."

"We seem to be in the same boat as well as in the same ship," he said. "That's exactly the way I feel about it."

"Didn't you want to come?" she asked.

"I had nothing better to do."

"That seems a pretty limp reason."

"It wasn't reason at all. Just impulse."

132

"You said we would wear our usual masks at dinner. I decided not to. Yours slipped off at dinner when we were invaded and it's still off."

"Shall I put it back on?"

"No, don't. I like you better without it. What makes you wear it?"

"Why do I? I suppose to hide my scars."

"Are there scars? They aren't noticeable. You look very healthy and prosperous."

"Don't you read the papers? The political news?"

"I know you lost an election. But is that so disfiguring? It happens to people all the time. Isn't it the chance you take when you go into politics?"

"Losing an election isn't disfiguring. But character assassination is apt to be. You don't look the way you used to look, to yourself or to anyone else. So you cover up the damage with a sour puss."

He said it lightly and didn't look sour. She took out a cigarette and bent forward to the flame he offered.

"Don't they always try character assassination in political campaigns?"

"Quite often. It doesn't always work. But in my case it was remarkably successful."

"I didn't know about it. During the last campaign I was too involved in some of the issues to keep up with all the candidates or read many newspapers. I don't usually believe much of what's in them anyway."

"I wish there were more like you."

"How did they manage to smear you?"

"A girl who worked in my office in Washington was found dead in my apartment."

"Did you kill her?"

"No. I found her and called the police. She had killed herself. But the end result was much what it would have been if I had done it. Except that I'd be behind bars instead of on a ship tonight."

"Why did she do it?"

"It's a very unpleasant story, Barbara."

"Unpleasant stories don't frighten me. I've been living in one."

"Is that why you are traveling all by yourself?"

"I wanted to be by myself. But that isn't relevant. Please go on with the unpleasant story. Did people think you were responsible for her suicide?"

"A great many of them did. The majority of the voters in my state. They assumed I must be. And perhaps in a way I was responsible."

"That needs to be explained. Don't leave it like that."

He considered before he went on. He liked this girl. He rather wanted her to have the facts. Demarest evidently had not yet talked to Barbara about him. But tomorrow he would. He would make a point of doing it.

"I don't want to bore you with my personal history."

"It would interest me."

"All right, I'll tell you how it was. This girl had worked for me in the campaign more than six years ago when I was elected to the Senate. She came from my own state and was interested in politics. She was young—hadn't finished college at that time—and was very idealistic. So when she got out of college a couple of years later she wrote me and asked for a job and I found a place for her in my office. I thought I owed it to her. Before long I knew that was a mistake. But I didn't want to hurt her feelings so I didn't fire her. I thought I was being generous."

"She was in love with you?"

"I wouldn't call it that. It was one of those emotional attachments that grow out of working in a campaign. They are common enough but usually not disastrous. Girls exaggerate their candidates. They get overloyal to a person or to a cause. Do you know what I mean?"

"Yes, I know."

"Anyway she made me too important in her mind. I was going to redeem the world and she would be the disciple who came along.

I tried to cool her off now and then but a man—especially a politician—likes to be flattered. He gets hooked on it. That's why I say I may have been remotely responsible for what happened. I didn't think so at first. It seemed to me that I'd had a very raw deal. But I've had time to do a lot of thinking on this trip."

"What brought her to suicide in the end? Did you finally tell her that you didn't want her to work for you any longer?"

"That's what I should have done. No, she found out that I was going to marry someone else. She saw the item in the newspaper. I hadn't told her. There was no reason why I should. We didn't go about together socially. Once in a while I'd buy her a drink or take her to dinner if we worked late in the day. But she had no reason to believe—and yet she must have had it in her mind—"

"Yes, she undoubtedly did," said Barbara.

"She asked me if it was true and I said it was absolutely true and that I wanted to have her come to the wedding. And thought no more about it. I was very busy. Later—after there was nothing anyone could do about it—one of her friends who lived in the same apartment said that she had been taking pills at both ends of the day —sleeping pills at night and bennies in the morning. Naturally she couldn't think straight. And one afternoon she came over to my apartment. She'd often brought over proofs and papers from the office so the janitor let her in. She told him she would wait for me. And she did. She was full of pills and whiskey and dead."

"Why in your apartment? She must have known what it would do to you politically."

"I don't know why. No one ever will. It might have been a crazy desire to ruin me."

"Or maybe she wanted to be as close to you as she could get."

He turned away. Barbara was remembering the nights when she hadn't wanted to live. "Oh, poor girl," she breathed.

"I warned you that it was a horrid story."

"And you were defenseless, of course. Her friends back home knew that you had given her the Washington job. I can see how easy it was to assassinate your character. And how cruel. Cruel for the girl you were going to marry too. You didn't marry her? Are you going to?"

"No. I'm not going to marry anyone. That's the whole story and don't believe what Demarest will tell you because it won't be true."

"I won't let him tell me anything."

"You're a nice girl. And I'm grateful for this evening. It's broken a kind of suffocating silence to talk to you instead of to myself. Now will you tell me why you are alone?"

"I'd rather not. You've had enough experience with girls who deluded themselves. But it has been a good evening. Very real somehow."

"It's not over. I'm going to ring for Jim and ask him for some refills."

"I'd like one."

He went toward the bell but as he passed her chair he stopped and looked down at her. Then he lifted her face and kissed her.

"Good to be with you," he murmured.

"A stirring of sex," she said.

"Is there anything wrong with that?"

"No. It's bound to happen. But it's not the other thing. It's pleasant and restful and exciting but I don't fool myself. Or you. If it wipes out a little of the frustration and fills a little of the emptiness it's probably good."

Chapter Ten

Signe Goode had been bewildered when she first looked over the land-travel booklet delivered with her ticket for passage, which listed seventy-four tours ashore as *The Seven Seas* circled the world. But by this time she could find her way through its pages. It was impossible to take all the excursions offered for some of them overlapped in time or ran concurrently with others. But to make a choice was an exciting leap in the dark for all the places were strange to Signe and many sounded glamorous.

"You just can't do everything," she said to Mark Claypole, who found her poring over the brochure in her steamer chair. He settled himself on the end of it.

"Fortunately."

"It's so tantalizing to read about all the places you could see and may miss. I can't pronounce the names of half of them. We'll be in Bombay in three days—it says here that's the Gateway to India. I certainly never thought I'd see India! We had some cotton bedspreads once that were supposed to come from India. I got them at Macy's—I used to go into New York from New Jersey once in a while to shop, though Tom always said that you didn't save anything by doing that if you counted the fare and your lunch. But he liked those bedspreads—they were colorful and made up very smoothly—and here I am where they came from—or going to be. Sometimes I think I'll wake up and find this cruise is all a dream."

He pinched her ankle. "Is it?"

"Don't do that—I guess I'm awake all right. I've been reading about the trips in India and what I'll see there. I certainly want to see the tomb of that queen that the lecturer says is the most beautiful sight in the world—you know what I mean—"

"The Taj Mahal."

She repeated the pronunciation carefully. "And Joan Scofield says there's a pink city that is wonderful. Mrs. Barnes and Mrs. Hayward have been there before and Mrs. Barnes says there is a beautiful jewelry store there that sells things to Jackie Kennedy and her sister and to Mrs. Eisenhower—"

"That's playing it fair politically."

"Have you been in India before?"

"No. And I always wanted to see it," he said, dropping the banter for a moment.

"Which trip are you going to take? There's one that goes by train most of the way and I signed up for that. I've always loved trains. You see more than when you fly."

"There's a consensus of opinion on that, dear. But Indian trains may not be like the ones that used to run in the United States."

"It's tour 23—this one. The Englishman in the bureau recommended it."

He took the booklet, scanned the description and said, "He would. It's the most expensive one. But you will see quite a bit of India in five and a half days."

"He says it's quite worth the price."

"Could be," he agreed once more without mockery. For he was reading the tempting description of the journey to Jaipur, Agra, Fatehpur Sikri and Old and New Delhi. He tossed the booklet back to her and said, "You want to be careful about eating salads on your air-conditioned train. And peel the fruit."

"Joan told us that too. What trip are you going to take?"

"None."

"You're just staying in Bombay?"

"I can get free meals on the ship if I do. I'll explore the city. Drink. Find a bookstore."

"You'll miss so much."

"You can tell me about it."

138

"It's not the same as seeing it for yourself."

"I'm well aware of it. But I can't afford the junket. Not while I'm paying alimony to an ex-wife who likes to lunch at The Four Seasons."

He gave his usual uncaring grin and stood up to leave her. Signe said, "Don't go. Sit down just a minute. Please."

He did, protesting. "I can't give you advice on your trip when I've never been in India."

"That's why you should come along, Mark. It would be very educational. And much more fun for me. I'd pay for both of us."

"Oh no." He reached again for the booklet, glanced at the still-open page and said, "It costs three hundred seventy-five minimum for that package trip even for a person taking an upper berth on the train."

"Do you mind upper berths?"

"I wouldn't mind sitting up all night but it's out of the question to let you pay my way."

"They're holding a single-occupancy compartment for me. That's five hundred and fifty dollars. I didn't know anyone else who was going except Mrs. Barnes and Mrs. Hayward so I took the whole thing. It seems selfish—"

"Why shouldn't you?"

"It would be much more fun if you were along. I wouldn't be a nuisance. I don't want to do anything to offend you. But you know that I have a great deal of money and I didn't earn it. It just happened. And you must have worked awfully hard to do your writing and it's a shame that you have to pay your wife. But I suppose there's nothing you can do about that, if it's the law. What I wanted to tell you is that I have a lot of traveler's checks that I can't possibly use up on this cruise. The bank and the travel agent said to take plenty and told me that I should take at least ten thousand extra in case I wanted to buy things. So I did. It seemed crazy but you can always cash in traveler's checks when you get home."

"Not if you pay for trips for impoverished writers."

"Mark, why not? I'd like to. Let me lend you five hundred dollars."

"I don't know when you'd get it back. Or if you would."

"That doesn't matter really."

"I'm not finicky about the sources of money. But I have a few lingering vestigial inhibitions. Let me think about your generosity."

"Please think about it and not as generosity. When the purser's office opens at eleven I'm going down to cash fifteen hundred dollars and that will be plenty to pay for the trip for both of us. If you'll buy me a drink before lunch we'll divide the money. And of course nobody but us will ever know anything about it."

"It sounds as if you had all this figured out."

"I just hoped you'd want to come. But you should go down to the travel office right away and make sure they aren't sold out."

He said again that he would think about it, patted her ankle instead of pinching it this time, and promised to buy her that drink before lunch anyway. As he passed the door of the travel office a half hour later he turned back and went in and inquired about accommodations on tour 23.

"Not much left, if anything," said Cecil Brettingham. "Let me see. I'll have to look at the chart for the train." He spread it out and read, as if to himself, the names penciled in the spaces. "Mr. and Mrs. Chilton—two compartments. Mr. Swett. Mr. and Mrs. Boyle here. Mr. Howard Demarest was in yesterday asking for a compartment and we could only give him a bedroom. Miss Canaday, single bedroom. There are only a few compartments and we've reserved the last available one for Mrs. Goode. Miss Bancroft is in 6. Mrs. Barnes and Mrs. Hayward, upper and lower in 8. Yes, there is one upper left, Mr. Claypole. In 9. Father Duggan has the lower in that room. It's only an upper berth but the train is air-conditioned and we take blankets and pillows from the ship so you should be quite comfortable. Shall I put you down for it?"

"I'll let you know."

The young man in the British sport jacket shook a somewhat arrogant head.

"Sorry, but we can't hold it. It will probably be snapped up in the next half hour. We close reservations for all trips from Bombay at five this afternoon."

"Okay," said Mark, "put me down. I'll come back and settle with you after lunch."

The ship's chaplain was usually offered a complimentary excursion in most of the ports, not on those which included rail or air travel or hotel costs but on the sightseeing bus rides. Father Duggan had found those rides, along with the walks he took by himself on shore, satisfying enough so far. But out of the seventy-four excursions described in the tours book he had marked two that he would pay for himself, the one numbered 23 and a much cheaper one in Ceylon. He had refused the Bishop's offer to continue his pastoral pay while he was traveling and asked that the money be put in the diocesan fund for sick priests. Aloysius had a little money of his own. The residue of an annuity bought by his father had reverted to him, and the quarterly payment of $610 had come in December.

When he had begun to think of leaving the priesthood he had considered the matter of self-support, for he knew this was a serious problem to others who had left and that it was the reason why some discontented priests did not sever the ties which gave them a scant but certain living. Aloysius was fairly sure that he could find a position as a teacher of history or comparative religions in some school or college. If not, he would manage to live on his $2,400 a year. So he had thought until less than two weeks ago when the question of personal celibacy began to stir in his unwilling mind.

He wanted to go to Delhi because he had a friend there whom he had not seen in years but with whom he had always kept up a sporadic correspondence. Sebastian Clarke had been in the seminary with Aloysius and the two young men were as close friends as the rigors of that highly disciplined life permitted. They were both zealous and both dreamers, but while Aloysius wanted to devote his life to increasing the spirituality of American Catholics —at that time his criticisms were directed at the worldliness of laymen—Sebastian's ambitions roamed farther afield. He wanted to be a missionary, to carry the faith to distant places and do his part in trying to blanket the globe with it. He was deeply interested in social and political problems as well as theology and was sometimes demoted for this, as when he wrote a paper on why the Untouchables of Southern India had become Christians in so many cases, and emphasized the fact that there were political motives. The paper was marked C-minus.

After his ordination he had been fortunate in getting the work he wanted. And determined not to be defeated. He became affiliated with the Catholic missions and after miserably difficult posts in Curaçao and other islands in the West Indies he was finally sent to Southeast Asia, to the very province of Travancore about which he had written in his badly graded essay.

Over the years, when there was a change in their residence, Sebastian and Aloysius kept each other informed. A postcard dated months before would come to Father Duggan and the one a year ago had said that Sebastian was in Delhi.

He had written, "Here among the Buddhists and the Hindus I ply my religion. I have a small church and with the help of my Untouchable friends we have put a steeple on it to display the Holy Cross for which the parish is named. How I wish I could talk to you in these troubled times. Yours in Christ, Sebastian."

When he had joined the cruise, Aloysius had been unaware of the ports it would touch or the opportunities for land travel. He had not studied the brochure which had been sent to him. But when he did he realized that if he went to Delhi he could see Sebastian, if he was still there. He did not have the last postcard with him so he did not know the address of his friend, but he remembered about the cross and the steeple and addressed a letter to Sebastian in care of The

Church of the Holy Cross, giving the date and probable time of his arrival in Delhi. He had posted it in Lisbon and knew there would be little chance of a reply. The note might not be delivered but there would not be many Roman Catholic churches in Delhi, and in any case Aloysius would have a day and a half in the city to search for the other priest. He hoped to find him, not only to see what sixteen years had done to the fiery, restless boy of twenty-four but because Sebastian was the one person in the world to whom he perhaps could fully expose his doubts and mental agony.

The train was waiting for passengers from *The Seven Seas* in the Bombay station at nine o'clock on the morning of arrival and it surprised most of them by its modern appearance. It was made of shining steel and the windows of the coaches were large and well polished. The natives in the waiting room were obviously proud of it, as Alec Goodrich noticed. They watched the Americans get aboard, with pleased smiles when they heard or understood words of admiration for what was an Indian achievement. Most of the onlookers had never traveled on the train nor ever would, but it was their train none the less. This Alec understood. He gave them a political wave of appreciation and the pantomime delighted the natives.

There were corridors on the train but the coaches were not connected, so that passage between them was impossible, and a guard ran frantically from one to another, repeating some invisible duty that he could not seem to finish. Stewards from the ship had brought the luggage to the pier and Indian bearers had correctly deposited the suitcases in the compartments which had the names of the passengers inserted in slots on each door. The members of tour 23 had the first coach to themselves, the second was filled with those who were going only to Agra. Behind that one was the dining car, which looked luxurious with white napkins stuck in glass tumblers and flowers on every table. A miscellany of people, brown, black and yellow, were in a fourth coach, which was furnished only with wooden benches. They were evidently headed for various points on the run to Delhi and had brought packages of food.

Alec had walked the length of the train several times before getting on and sized up the various groups. He was sorry that his accommodations were completely segregated from those of the natives. He wanted to study them, not to talk to Julian Chilton about the stock market or to listen to Howard Demarest giving his opinion about India. Alida Barnes had said to Alec on the platform that she had brought along some cocktails and hoped he would have one with her and Julia later in the day. He had thanked her but made no promise. His own flask was filled and Barbara was on the train. He did not know whether he was glad or sorry about that. Or whether she was.

Since the night of intimacy in his cabin they had retreated from each other by undiscussed consent. It had been very satisfying to both of them, Alec believed. He had found her passionate but somehow impersonal, and though there had been admiration and laughter and gratitude there had been no protestations of love between them. He knew that if there was opportunity desire would rise in him again. He was not sure about her. He had seen her name on the door of compartment 6, but the door was closed.

The train rolled impressively away from the station and began to make its incongruous way through the worst slums that Alec had ever seen. He stood in the corridor, grimly observing them. There were consecutive miles of huts and shacks, with roofs made of odd pieces of tin or dirty matting or scraps of canvas. Naked children and emaciated dogs roamed around them. Women squatted beside small fires, cooking in pots. There was a strange look of lethargy.

"Who are these people?" Alec asked the guard.

"Squatters. They come to Bombay from outside."

"What do they do for a living?"

"They steal."

"Only that?"

"Some maybe work a little. Not much. They are very good thieves."

"Aren't they caught? Jailed?"

"The jail is not so bad."

"Why doesn't the government clean up districts like this?"

"If the people are sent away, they come back. They come from the hills, the back country. This is not good part city of Bombay. In Bombay there is plenty fine big buildings, very rich houses."

"And people who live like this."

"They must live," said the guard.

Mark Claypole, moving from another window to where Alec was standing, said, "This somehow disproves that bland statement that when you've seen one slum you've seen them all."

"I've never seen anything like this."

"In the United States we don't expose our ghettoes so frankly to tourists. Not that we don't have plenty. I did a piece on Chicago once that called for some personal investigating and before I was through with it I made my own hair curl."

"There are bad districts in Washington too. But we're working on it, not taking it for granted. Everyone is going to have some kind of an income before too long. According to the guard these people don't have anything except what they can steal. And he implies the government tolerates it."

"India tolerates a lot of things. Caste. Sacred cows. Unbridled breeding."

"You know the country?"

"Only what I've read about it. It should be an interesting trip if they don't make us look at folk dances and ride elephants." And remembering to whom he was indebted for the journey Mark went away to find Signe. To his surprise he was slightly curious about her reactions to her first view of the country in which her bedspreads bought at Macy's had been made.

Julia Hayward had been in India once before. She had come with friends who had a cousin with rank at the American Embassy and had been whisked away from the port in a private automobile, so she had never seen the slums. The horrid sight overwhelmed her and minimized the sense of defeat she had been living with recently. It deafened her to Alida's shopping plans. Alida was sitting by the window on the long plush bench. She had paid for the liquor they had brought and for the taxi from the ship so Julia had insisted that she must take the window seat, though she was not looking out but finding in her notebook the address of two jewelers and a shop which was said to sell the most beautiful saris in Jaipur.

"This is the one," she said. "I made a note, 'beautiful silk saris!' " She glanced outside and said, "How can people live like that?"

" 'Live' is the wrong word," said Julia.

"I can't bear to look at them. They make me itch. Think of the bugs. This is a much better train than the one Fred and I were on when he was alive. I saw that there's quite a clean shower and a couple of toilets at the end of the train. Coeducational ones, I suppose. But you have to put up with it when you travel in these countries. I asked Senator Goodrich to have a cocktail with us before dinner. He said he was afraid he had some work to do—I suppose he's still active politically and sends back dispatches and things, don't you?"

"I wouldn't know. Thank God we're getting into open country," answered Julia. "I see some herons by that stream."

Barbara also was given over to the passing scene, watching with sickened pity the packed, ragged slums. And yet the people seemed to have an ease, even in squalor, that she had not felt in Africa. She wondered if she was imagining that. The ease might be in herself. It could have come—this she knew was possible—from those almost casual hours with Alec Goodrich. She did not regret them. Barbara had not felt that sex was wrong or shameful long before she met Boone. Sex, casual or serious, was a commonplace at Columbia and at all universities, as thousands of pictures and statistical articles proved. Everyone knew it except a few self-blinded parents.

Barbara liked Alec Goodrich. But he needed no more from her than she had given and it was better to leave it alone now. She had told herself again that she would probably never feel for any man what she had felt for Boone, that intense desire for sole possession of a person and for being solely possessed by him. But she was more at peace now. She had taken the first step in accepting her life as it was.

She watched India spreading out before her, little towns with lounging villagers waiting to see the train rush jerkingly by their hamlets of sunburnt mud, windowless cottages. The roads were gray with dust and the piles of cotton beside many farmhouses seemed amazingly white in contrast. Dust was coming through the two window screens now and had already coated the sills. Barbara drew a finger across it. She was liking India and it seemed a long time since she had liked any other place.

Chapter Eleven

Howard Demarest said that the railroad was outrageously inefficient. That was after he found out about the routine for dining-car
service. At half past twelve, when he was having his first drink, the
train stopped and the guard summoned the passengers in the luxury coach to lunch.

"We'll go in after a while," said Demarest.

"Sir, must go now please. Before train starts."

"What's the idea?"

Laboriously the guard explained that it was necessary to get off
the train and walk along the tracks to the dining car and stay there
until another station was reached and the train paused again.

"Maybe one hour."

"That's a hell of a note," said Demarest.

Ruby gulped down the rest of her drink. "We won't get any
lunch unless we go, Howie. And I'm starving!"

During the lunch, which was elaborate, with four courses from
soup to cheese, and beautiful because of the many colors of vegeta-
bles and fruits offered, Demarest criticized the management of the
train, the road bed and the food. He told the priest, who was across
from him at the same table, that he was a director of an American
railroad and it was unnecessary to go through this rigmarole to get
lunch on a train.

"We've set up buffet cars. Dining cars are obsolete. And here you
don't dare eat the salad and this beef is tough as leather."

"I suppose," said Aloysius, "most people in India wouldn't feel
that way about it. Forty percent of them are undernourished."

He spoke sharply. The ride this morning had been emotional as well as interesting to him, for he was seeing the country with Sebastian's eyes, imagining his early encounters with the poverty and insufficiency and habits of this vast country. He had deliberately come among people with most of whom he could not communicate by either faith or language, and he had stayed and put a steeple on a church.

Demarest was trying to catch Barbara's eye. She was sitting with some people called Boyle, a professor from some university and his wife, not interesting or social people. At least she and the lame-duck politician didn't seem to be hitting it off. Demarest waved a hand at Barbara but she apparently did not see it for she made no response. He tried the priest again for conversation and argument.

"How does it feel to be in Hindu country, Father? Sort of out of your bailiwick, I suppose."

"No, I haven't felt that way."

"The Hindus have a stranglehold on India, haven't they, Father?"

"It's the prevailing religion. But there are also strong minority ones—Muslim, Buddhists—and Christians. Many sects."

"I suppose it depends on who is running the country. Politically."

"And on tradition and faith."

"People break away from any religion after a while," said Demarest sententiously. "The Pope seems to be having quite a struggle to hold his people together."

He always spoke loudly as if it added to his authority. Across the aisle Signe Goode and Mark Claypole could hear what he was saying.

Father Duggan did not answer and Demarest persisted.

"It's pretty common knowledge that a lot of the priests and nuns are dropping out. I've read a great many articles on the subject. Substantiated by facts. There doesn't seem to be any doubt about it.

Father Duggan said, "Mr. Demarest, more than six hundred

million of the world's Christians are Roman Catholics. You have read about an infinitesimal percentage of them."

"Maybe so, but it could show the way the wind is blowing. Not that I take sides at all. But I've known some prominent Catholics —in the higher echelons—known them very well—" he did not mention that the Bishop and Monsignor were Katherine's relatives —"and I know that they have their problems like other men in big organizations."

"No doubt," said the priest. He had been trapped when the waiter put Demarest and the girl at the same table with him. He wanted to leave but there was no place to go. Until the train stopped again he must stay in the dining car and listen to this insolence.

Demarest went on. "The way I look at it is this. It is a business-man's point of view who knows about corporations. Now, any big, wealthy organization—and the Roman Catholic Church is one of the biggest and richest that exists—is bound sooner or later to be involved in a power struggle. The younger, modern executives resent the older ones, especially if power and the final say-so are too much concentrated at the top. It's just as true in a church organiza-tion as in one that makes steel. From what I hear a good many bishops and capable Roman Catholic churchmen in the United States—and I guess it's true in Europe too—want a hand in making decisions. Not to have Rome call all the shots. They want to run their own shows or at least have a hand in making policies—isn't that a fact?"

"It is a distortion. And this is a very futile discussion."

"Well, if you feel that way about it—" Demarest stopped talking and renewed his attack on the beef. Then after a minute or two, for he wasn't going to let the priest have the last word, he grinned, not affably, and said, "But I do think the Pope must have got out of bed on the wrong side on the day he made that speech against birth control! Didn't he know that most Catholic women do it anyway, no matter what anyone says?"

Signe said indignantly to Mark, "Did you hear what he said? He shouldn't talk that way to a priest!"

Mark said quietly, "Take it easy, dear. Of course somebody should push his face in. Somebody will before long. But don't start anything now. Not when we're locked in with all this glass and china."

She lowered her voice and said, "I wish he hadn't come on this shore trip with us. Nobody likes him. Except that girl."

"She probably likes him least of all. Knowing him more intimately."

"He's always showing off. Tom used to dislike anyone who showed off in public. He used to say it was because they couldn't do it at home."

"Tom always cut through to the bone," said Mark. He peeled a pear, cut it into sections and layered them with cheese. "Soothe your feelings with this," he told her. "And don't worry about Father Duggan. He's quite able to take care of himself."

At the moment Aloysius could not. He was filled with revulsion because there was a horrid likeness in what Demarest said to some of the things he himself had thought and criticized. He had questioned the power of the Pope over the bishops and the procedure for nominating the higher clergy. He often felt it was a self-recruiting oligarchy whose views were slanted against modernity and would not move with the times. He had told the Bishop that Catholic women would disobey the ruling of the Pope on contraception. And it was true that many priests and nuns were breaking their vows and that the number of ordinations was lessening almost catastrophically.

But his concern came out of love for the soul of the Church, its Sacraments, out of a deep and mystic faith in God. Demarest's comments were drawn from no comprehension of religion. With violent though silent denial Aloysius rejected the statement that the Church was one more big corporation. He had promised not to be drawn into arguments about the problems of the Church, but, even if he had not, Aloysius knew that it would be useless and degrading to try to explain to Demarest that though the Church might be rich that was not its strength. The teaching of the greatest churchmen had been always to have less rather than more. Its strength was in humility and self-denial. In thousands of places priests struggled incessantly to meet the costs and needs of their parishes. It would be idle to tell that to the worldly, probably corrupt man across from him, who was reddening with wine. He wouldn't believe that the foundations of the Church were what they had been from the beginning, suffering, love of man and trust in eternity. That it had been kept alive through all the centuries not by acquisitions of wealth and power but by love. By the mystery of grace. And by loyalty? The question came to the priest cruelly.

The train shuddered to a slow stop. Aloysius did not offer any farewell to his companions but left them immediately. He walked for a few minutes on the edge of the track to calm his feelings and then swung on the train and went back to the little room he shared with Mark Claypole. The writer was not there and the priest closed the door. He watched the strange country glide by outside his window and wondered if he would be able to find Sebastian. To him Aloysius could confess his doubts and disloyalties—perhaps even his still unadmitted desires.

The Seven Seas dwarfed the warehouses on the dock in Bombay to which she was moored. Her decks were deserted and her public rooms empty. In the space that had accommodated nearly six hundred passengers and an even larger number of crew members there were less than a hundred people by noon. A skeleton crew remained for maintenance and safety but most of the stewards and sailors had been given leave for the day.

Mrs. Hartley Barton was on board. For yesterday morning she had fallen in her cabin and her forehead and one eye were badly bruised. She could not remember the fall and was not sure how long the blackout had lasted.

"Was it a stroke?" she had asked the doctor calmly when he had been summoned and had examined and bandaged her face.

He hesitated and she prodded him. "I have had a small one before."

"If this was a stroke it was also a small one. There's no paralysis and very frequently people have occasional blackouts as they grow older. I think this is nothing serious but we must keep you quiet for a bit. Our little hospital on the ship is pleasant and there is always a nurse on duty even when we are in port."

"I had intended to go to Agra. Perhaps I'll be able to go tomorrow even if I look rather odd?"

"No, it would be very inadvisable. You've never seen the Taj?"

"Oh yes, a number of times."

"Well, then I'm not so sorry for you," he said. "It would really be out of the question for you to leave the ship tomorrow."

So Mrs. Barton lay in the narrow hospital bed, with the railings pulled up around it. She knew that precaution was because the doctor thought she might black out again. And sooner or later she would—probably sooner than later. But, as Hartley said, it did not matter where you died. She thought of her will and of the labels she had placed under the most valuable pieces of furniture, disposing of them to the various grandchildren who she hoped would treasure them. She thought of the Sevres china and the Waterford glass and the collection of rare double-lipped fingerbowls of all colors which she and Hartley had assembled during journeys through Ireland and Wales. Then she finished her mental housekeeping and began to travel in the past, since it was impossible to travel on shore today. She recalled the first time she had seen the Taj Mahal. She was with her very young and handsome husband. They had waited for sunrise, which gave the white marble mausoleum a delicate flush and a look of being almost afloat in the air. They had watched it with delight and she had said, "Imagine any man caring that much for a woman." And Hartley had said, "I can imagine it, Sara." She had always remembered his saying that. Mrs. Barton half smiled under her blackened eye.

The chief engineer had considerable acquaintance with men in various ports who understood the mechanism and construction of ships, and before they docked he had summoned by ship-to-shore telephone a man in Bombay whose expertise he trusted. He was an Indian who spoke little English, but his gestures were fluent and he and the chief engineer could understand each other well enough.

The Indian had been asked to bring a diver with him, for the engineer wanted to have the stabilizers below the water line looked at and the two men had come on board in the morning. They had been working ever since. They were inspecting the oil-fired boilers, the steam-driven turbines, which drove the electric generators that ran the power system of the ship, its essential motors, lights and navigational system and the luxuries like air-conditioning, and they did it with the skill and concentration of surgeons examining before diagnosis. The Indian would bend close to a machine and listen as if for a heartbeat.

Many of the passengers had visited the navigating bridge, for the Commodore permitted groups to come there at special hours on stated days and very often showed them the equipment himself, explaining its functions in simple and nontechnical terms. They were impressed by the shining efficiency of the machinery, the master gyrocompass, the radar installation, the automatic pilot control. Unless they were engineers few of the passengers thoroughly understood the intricate mechanism, although some, like Howard Demarest, who had asked to be shown around by himself instead of with a group, pretended to more comprehension than they had. The bluff of the company's director had been obvious to the Commodore.

"He knows that a twin-screw ship has two propellers and that's about all," the Commodore told the engineer. "With people like that in control no wonder they didn't know she should be dry-docked."

The Indian who was working with the engineer did know.

"Is many small things," he said, "some no matter much, some need fix now."

The engineer tapped the main shaft that worried him.

"You think we might have trouble with this?"

"Cannot tell. Must be—" he sought for the word and the engineer gave it to him.

"I know—the shafts must be in perfect alignment or they whip. But the other propeller is okay, I'm sure."

"Is danger only."

The Commodore appeared in the engine room and shook hands with the Indian.

"Find anything wrong?" he asked.

The engineer answered, "He doesn't know any more than I do. There's a funny sound—he heard it too. But we haven't the time to tear down the propeller." He spoke to the Indian, "How long would it take? To fix good?"

"May need new part. Two—three weeks—"

The Commodore shook his head. "Can't be done. Not with six hundred prepaid passengers who expect to leave here Saturday after they've made their rounds on shore. Did you find anything else wrong?"

"Nothing that can't be taken care of while we're here. He's going to do some work on the boiler that's hooked up to the shaft we're sure of. We can't have a flareback there. With that cheap fuel oil there's always a danger of that. It's a minor repair and there's a little work to be done on the reduction gears."

"Have him get on with it. And I'll speak my piece about cheap oil before I retire," said the Commodore. "Tell them they'll have to allow more funds for maintenance or tie the ship up. Did you get a diver to look at the stabilizers?"

"He's still down under—here he comes now."

The thin brown diver spoke no English. He had put on khaki pants but no shirt and was barefoot. He stood in the doorway until the other Indian beckoned him in. They talked in a rapid dialect and the diver pointed to the right.

"Well?" asked the Commodore.

"He say—" he also pointed—"that one not good."

155

"The starboard fin—"

"Is bad rust. He say not loose, maybe go all right. Not if typhoon."

"Then we'd better not run into a typhoon," said the Commodore. "But stabilizers don't worry me too much. We used to get along all right without them. People are getting not to expect any more motion on the sea than they do at home in a bathtub." He said to the Indian, "Thank you, sir, good to have you on board. Do your best for us."

But his face was grim as he went back to his quarters. He smoked a cigarette, then called Joan Scofield on the telephone.

"I wanted to take you to dinner on shore, Joan," he said, "but I think I'd better stick around. We're having some repairs made and something might come up. Will you stay aboard and eat with me up here?"

"I'd love to. I hope there's nothing seriously wrong."

"I don't think so," said the Commodore.

Chapter Twelve

Constantly mocking at himself for being enmeshed in the patterns and schedules of tourism, Mark Claypole did the best he could to go along with them in Jaipur. He would not admit to himself that he owed Signe companionship and escort because she had financed the Indian trip, but he stayed negligently close to her as they visited the Palace of the Winds and from a balcony looked beyond it to the rugged hills that were crowned with forts.

"Very good city planning," he said. "It could teach Chicago something."

"Everything is such a lovely pink," Signe marveled. "It all matches."

"It's pink paint on the buildings here. In Agra the buildings are actually made of pink sandstone."

"How do you know that?"

"I read about it in a book. Have you had enough palace?"

She consulted the printed schedule that members of the tour had been given on the train. "It's about time to go to lunch at the hotel. This afternoon they take us in private cars to a place called Amber and we ride on elephants up to another palace. That will certainly be an experience!"

"I'm sure it will be."

"You think it's silly?" she asked, conscious of the note of cynicism.

"Not for you, dear."

He looked depressed. But he joined her at the communal lunch after a couple of fortifying drinks at the hotel bar, and then submitted to the hot automobile ride to Amber, where the elephants waited in a hangdog row.

"Take the one on the left," he advised Signe. "He seems to have a little life left in him."

"They put four people on each elephant. We can have the front seats."

"Not for me. I'll walk up the hill. See you when you get back."

Walking up the rocky hill, Mark tried to figure out his distaste for these expeditions. He liked to travel. He knew that strangers needed guides and direction in foreign countries. And the professionals were doing as good a job as seemed possible for the passengers on *The Seven Seas.* Was it snobbishness that made him dislike being with the group? Personal conceit? Or was it basically frustration because they were shown only the obvious things?

He wandered through the seventeenth-century palace, thinking of the kind of life for which it had been built, admiring the inlay which had glowed on the walls for hundreds of years, then walked down the hill and saw that Signe was safely back, still sitting her elephant and smiling down at someone who was taking a picture of her. She was a very pretty sight.

He gave her a hand down.

"You looked very handsome on your elephant. You should have been an empress."

"You should have had that ride, Mark. You really missed something."

"I'm always missing things. It's my nature."

"Sometimes I think you don't like sightseeing."

"It makes me feel a little like a Peeping Tom."

"What on earth do you mean by that?"

"It's like looking in the windows of places where people live when you don't know the people. For a quick thrill."

"Oh, Mark, you don't mean that."

"Probably not. But can I skip some of the rest of the routine without seeming an ingrate?"

"Why, of course! Do what you please."

"Thank you, dear."

He had absented himself from a performance of Indian folk dances arranged especially for the members of tour 23 at the hotel where they dined. He had skipped the group dinner and taken a bicycle rickshaw to the old part of the city, then paid it off and merged on foot with the native life. Sacred cows roamed the streets and camels and elephants were beasts of burden, not treats for tourists. Beggars were everywhere, though there seemed no one who would have anything to give them. It was dirty and confused, natural and ancient in its manners.

He felt again the stir to write, not of the sights around him but of his own feeling of contact here with the core of India and the curious pleasure of anonymity, for no one stared at him or seemed to find his presence strange. He gave some coins to an old man without legs and bought small bananas and sweets at an open food stall when he was hungry. It was dark when he sought another rickshaw, and he had to walk a long mile before he found one to take him back to the train.

The plan for the next morning was for the party to be wakened before dawn and driven to the Taj Mahal to see it at sunrise. Mark wanted to see it by himself, if at all. He did not want to hear the comments. Signe would be certain to say that she wished Tom could see the tomb. He wasn't sure that he really wanted to see it. Millions of the glances of tourists, millions of photographs had made it commonplace. He managed to slip away from the group when the automobiles reached Agra and again on foot he found a hotel, where he had bacon and eggs. He refused to let himself feel guilty. Signe had staked him and he owed her companionship. But not today. He would take a day off.

Mark spent some of Signe's money for a room and bath in a hotel which was not the day's headquarters for the members of his tour —he had checked the mimeographed program to make sure of that —and there he tried to record his experience of the night before on the single sheet of soiled letter paper that he found in the drawer of a table. He failed. It would not come into words. He tore up the paper and tried to sleep. Failing also in that he went out to walk among the monotone of pink sandstone buildings that was Agra. It was late in the afternoon when he finally came upon the Taj Mahal, and he realized at once that he would have been childish and churlish to miss seeing it.

He marveled at its perfection. There was no interruption of background, for the wide river flowed behind it. There was no distraction of tourists with cameras, for at this hour almost all the people who were walking amid the paths and lagoons before the tomb were Indians, many of them women wearing multicolored saris. They added to the validity of the picture.

Mark wondered who had conceived this faultlessness, what poet of a man—or more probably men. The travel brochure described it as a love story in marble but he doubted that. It hardly checked with the facts. The Empress Mumtaz Mahall had borne fifteen children before she died in giving birth to the last one, and her husband had other wives and concubines. He was a Moslem but his astrologer told him he would have to marry a Hindu to get an heir, and Mumtaz had given him a son—a son who later imprisoned his father so that he could not build a black mausoleum for himself across the river from the white beauty. Was this passion for mauso-leums a defiance of death rather than mourning for a woman who must have been well worn out with childbearing?

He was wandering toward the steps leading to the shrine of the tomb when he saw the Chiltons, without the nurse for once. They were sitting on a marble bench with Hilary between them. When the girl saw Mark she lifted her arms in a greeting of surprise and happiness. She wore a dress that ended in a frill and a round comb to hold her straight hair back and she was very much Alice today.

Mark stopped to speak to them.

"They don't exaggerate it," he said. "Have you gone through it?"

"No," said Mr. Chilton, "we have a problem. Hilary doesn't want to."

160

"Why not, Hilary?"

She shook her head.

"This is the most beautiful thing you'll see," said Mark.

"Come, Hilary," urged her mother, "what's the matter?"

Hilary looked at Mark and told him. "There's someone dead in there. I don't like cemeteries."

Her mother shuddered and put her hands before her mouth as if to repress a cry.

"That's not what it is," said Mark. "This was built to keep someone alive. Nobody can forget her. She was the Empress Mumtaz Mahall. Come, let's see what it's like inside."

"All right," she said. "I'll go with you."

"Okay?" Mark asked Mr. Chilton.

"We'll be very grateful. We'll follow along," said Mr. Chilton, and to his wife, "Take it easy, dear. She just had a notion."

Mark took Hilary's hand and she came willingly, with a little skip, her stubbornness broken.

"What I should do," said Mark, "is to throw you into the pool with a mouse, a duck, a Dodo and an eaglet."

"Why? With those animals?"

"Because you are getting a bad habit of wanting your own way."

"But I really don't like cemeteries," she said. "My brother—"

"We won't go into that," he answered firmly. "You look pretty today."

"They say I will be beautiful when I am older. They often say that about me."

"Perhaps," he said, "it's possible. But not if you run away."

"I will take myself with me," she said practically.

"You would get dirty. Inside and out. Your hair would snarl. You would smell bad."

"Why?"

"It would be inevitable. Now forget your future and let's go into the house that was built for the Empress."

Delhi would be the last stop. They would arrive in the morning and after thirty-six hours there return on the train to the ship in Bombay. The train jolted badly on the night run to Delhi. Most of those who had brought liquor with them had run out of it and were whittled down to the wine available in the dining car. The dust in the compartments seemed irremovable and the floor of the shower had become very dank.

Alida Barnes had spent several hundred dollars on an aquamarine bracelet in Jaipur and one of the semiprecious stones had already fallen out of its setting. This annoyance and the feeling she had been defrauded held the center of her thoughts tonight and Julia was tired of telling her that it could be properly reset when she got home and that she had bought a treasure.

Ruby Canaday fondled Demarest as if she meant it. She wanted to be necessary to him at least until she had shopped in Hong Kong, where the clothes were marvelous. She had the name of a tailor there and wanted several costumes and a dress of silver paillettes like one she had once modeled. It had a Hong Kong label.

The journey had been pleasant for Alec Goodrich. During the days he had learned more and more about India, and on the third night on the train, after telling himself why not, he had knocked softly on Barbara's door and she had opened it. When he left her several hours later he had met the priest in the corridor coming back from the toilets but he was fairly sure that in the dim light Father Duggan would not identify the door from which he emerged. In any case a priest must know what went on in the world.

Aloysius had known whose door it was. He could not be certain of anything more than that. They might have been only talking, enjoying late drinks, playing one of those interminable games of gin rummy which had gone on during the journey. Possibly Barbara had been taking Goodrich into her confidence. Perhaps it had not been enough to tell himself her story. He believed none of this but he needed the doubts and clung to them.

He did not try to deceive himself during the rest of the sleepless night or pretend to only paternalism or protectiveness in his feeling for Barbara. This was stinging jealousy, personal desire of a woman. And it was sin until he openly renounced his vow of celibacy and was released from it. He should leave this cruise, fly back from Delhi instead of returning to the ship, and tell the Bishop that his decision was made. He should confess frankly that he no longer had the right to perform the duties of a priest of the Church. But he did not have enough money to do that. And if he did he would never see Barbara again, most certainly lose her.

It had been a foolish, wasteful thing to come to Delhi. There was little chance that he could find Sebastian. Priests were moved from missions after brief assignments. And now Aloysius no longer felt that his friend might help him. Perhaps he would not even try to locate him.

He was the last passenger to leave the train in the morning. Breakfast was to be provided at a hotel in the city but he had no appetite for it and the thought of facing Goodrich and Barbara sickened him.

"Coming along?" asked Mark Claypole, after he had finished his shave before the washstand mirror. "Ready to go, Father?"

"Not quite. Don't wait for me."

Mark suspected that there was probably a necessary prayer that Father Duggan was obliged to say and left him to it. The priest lingered until the guard called, "All leave for hotel please, ladies and gentlemen!"

Aloysius stepped down from the vestibule and saw his companions going toward the waiting automobiles. But as he was about to follow them he noticed a man scanning the doors of the rear coaches and trying to look through the dirty windows. He stopped short, caught a glimpse of the profile of the tall thin man wearing a cassock. "My God," said Aloysius and it was not profanity but thankfulness for a miracle. "It's you, Sebastian! I was going to try to find you—how did you know I'd be on this train?"

"It figured—and I didn't want to waste a minute. I've been counting the days since I had your letter. Ah, this is good, very very good! Now—you have no obligation to stay with these people, have you?"

"Not until tomorrow."

"Then we'll go home," said Sebastian. "Believe it or not I have a cottage of my own. Give me your bag. It's only a short walk to where we pick up the bus. If you wish you can say your Mass in my church and then we'll have breakfast."

Aloysius had said Mass every morning in the theater of the ship with all the reverence he could summon up, and the Bishop had told him that he might consider that obligation dispensed with if at some time in the journey there was no proper accommodation for the service. On the train it had been impossible.

But he said in the bus, after they had studied each other for signs of age and change and joked and laughed with the pleasure of reunion, "I shall need absolution before I say Mass, Sebastian. And you may not give it to me."

Sebastian's smile vanished at the somber words. He said quietly, "I shall hope to. You do not look depraved. Perhaps a bit weary and tense. Shall we go immediately to the church?"

"I would like to."

Sebastian's church was very small. It was made of wood, painted very white but the wall boards were rough timber. The little steeple, topped by a gilded cross, looked venturesome and out of place in a neighborhood of Indian huts, where women were washing clothes on the stones of a stream behind the chapel.

Sebastian told him, "This is the old city. There are several handsome Catholic churches in the new city, for many of the diplomats and the foreign businessmen established there are Catholics. But mine is a mission. In New Delhi the cows are no longer allowed to roam the streets. Here they are tolerated, for they are still considered sacred by many of my neighbors if not by my parishioners."

The windows of the chapel were set high and had no glass. They

164

were barred with iron. Sebastian unlocked the single door. "This is necessary, unfortunately," he explained.

Inside it was clean and bare. There were no statues and the pews were a few rows of wooden benches. But the altar was a table of white marble and there were polished brass candlesticks on either side of the tabernacle. Before it lay a rug which gleamed with color even in the dim light. Through the bars of the window behind it the hot pink blossoms of flowering trees could be seen.

"I almost always have flowers for my altar, you see," said Sebastian. "Your bag will be safe here behind the door."

He genuflected and went on, "If your need for absolution is urgent, my dear friend, there is my box over to the right. If you lift the curtain beside it you will find a place to kneel.

He entered the confessional and Aloysius knelt on the low, shaky bench behind the curtain. Their conversation had begun. It went on for nearly half an hour before Sebastian said the words of forgiveness and dismissal of sin. Then, in borrowed vestments, with his friend serving him at the altar, Aloysius offered his Mass and felt washed clean in that half hour.

But the problems remained. Aloysius could not let them alone now that he was free to talk to someone, and he found that Sebastian was as aware of what was happening within the Church and as concerned about it as he himself was. There were digressions from that dialogue. Sebastian explained the disastrous results of cow worship, which meant that thousands of half-starved cattle roamed around unmolested, devouring crops, and the peacocks were also holy and could not be killed though they used up thousands of tons of grain. Aloysius told of the church with the statues of black saints that he had seen in Africa. They reminisced about life in the seminary. But always their talk returned to the problems and dangers faced by Catholicism.

"If I am critical and dissident it is not because I have lost faith in God. Nor in the Sacraments. It is my faith in the judgment and infallibility of the institution which is slipping away."

165

"I know. There are times when it is difficult for one to go along with doctrines that seem outworn. And harder for you than for me because you are more involved."

"We're both priests. Why should it be harder for me?"

"Because I'm a missionary. The Church allows us more leeway, more rope, so much that sometimes it would be easy to hang yourself. Its authority binds us of course but it is accepted that a missionary has to yield to the customs of the countries to which he is sent and make exceptions to some rules. I chose the missions partly because I was curious about the world and eager to see as much of it as possible—thoroughly selfish motives—but also I had a hunch that I might feel trapped in a diocese—even more selfish a reason. As it is, in my very unimportant way I can be personally ecumenical. Perhaps that feeling of being trapped is one reason why so many priests are dropping out."

"That's part of it. But the main reason is that they are forced to preach in support of rulings which they do not believe are right. The rule against contraception. The stand against divorce. The one against abortion, even if a girl is raped. Do you think that such blanket prohibitions are reasonable? That they make sense in the world as it is today?"

"No."

"What do you do about it?" asked Aloysius.

"I try to explain the rules as best I can. To give reasons for them."

"And when you know they are broken? Do you overlook that?"

"It's possible to extenuate—"

"Excuse guilt—or what you have declared is guilt—because of circumstances?"

"That's what it gets down to quite often."

"But it's hypocritical. If you can't go along with the doctrines and decisions of Rome you should stand up and be counted."

"Counted as what? As a priest who is more concerned with sex relations than in doing his own job?"

"What do you think his real job is?"

"Maintaining religion in the world," said Sebastian. "Without it there's no hope for man. He will destroy himself. My job is to maintain Christianity. And the job of the Hindu priest is to maintain his religion. And the Mohammedan likewise. We're all in trouble, not just the Catholics. Basically priests of all religions are trying to do the same thing. Read the Koran or the teachings of Buddha. They uphold almost the identical virtues of Christianity during life and they believe that the soul does not die with the flesh. That's the great fear of man—it always has been. And the only hope. No, I don't think my priestly duty is first and foremost to fight a battle for the use of the pill. Of course I don't have the problem you do because in India it's difficult to get the native women to use it."

"Don't you think they should in an overpopulated country?"

Sebastian said with a wry look, "Of course I think so."

"And you consider yourself a priest of the Church?"

"Oh yes. I baptize children. I go to the edge of death with people who need me to help them over the gap. I give them the Blessed Sacrament and teach them that it is not a cookie but the body of Christ." He walked up and down the little sitting room which allowed him only half a dozen paces, and his face was intense with feeling.

He sat down again and said, "The way I see it, we're getting off the track. Religious doctrine shouldn't be concerning itself so much with sex. Sex isn't spiritual. It's a function of nature. Love and sacrifice can ennoble it and make it spiritual. But from what I read —" he swung his hand toward the corner where books and magazines were piled high—"love is being discarded. The relation between the sexes is becoming something like a bowel movement. Our business, Aloysius, is not to argue in the contemporary foul lingo about the act but to build up tenderness and compassion and devotion between men and women."

They talked in the cottage and while they walked about in what Sebastian ironically called his parish. Sebastian took his guest to the open-air Moti Mahal, the most famous dining place in the old city, and they watched their lunch being cooked in the clay urns heated with charcoal. They visited a Hindu temple, whose priest seemed to be a warm friend of Sebastian and gave Aloysius his blessing. For dinner they had a chicken brushed with spices and a delicious vegetable curry prepared by the old woman who took care of the meager housekeeping. There was wine. Sebastian said that when he bought it for the altar he stocked up a little for himself. The day vanished and dusk had come long ago but there were still many things they had not discussed.

Aloysius asked, out of a companionable silence that had lasted for a few minutes, "Do you think priests should be allowed to marry?"

Sebastian said, "Well, a priest who finds celibacy too difficult or too frustrating should marry. But I personally think he diminishes his usefulness to his vocation if he does. It's entirely possible that in the present frame of change the marriage of priests may become optional or that those who do marry will be given honorable duties as deacons and laymen with some clerical duties."

"But you wouldn't approve of that—"

"God knows it's not a matter for me to approve or disapprove. But I look at it from my experience and I see more reasons against it than for it. Quite practically a priest hasn't time for marriage, to give a woman the devotion she has a right to. I think a conflict of devotion is almost inevitable. You cannot worship God and a wife any more than you can worship God and Mammon."

"Love for a woman is quite different from love of wealth."

"Of course. But it's even more absorbing."

"It's a man-made rule again. In the early centuries bishops and Popes did marry."

"And it did not improve the morals of the Church. I think there is a deep, rather intangible reason for celibacy. A good priest— there are bound to be plenty of lapses—a good priest cannot give too much of himself to one individual or to one family. He sets himself apart by his abnegation of many pleasures and, because he gives his life principally to God, people feel that he can link them with God. His celibacy makes him a secret person and his parishioners are able and willing to come to him with their sins and secrets. A good priest has to be something of a monk. You always had the temperament of a monk, Aloysius. Self-denial came easily to you—so did solitude. I think," he added slowly, "that the desire you felt—may feel again—for this girl is more acute because it goes against your nature."

"Have you ever had such desires, Sebastian?"

"Oh, yes, God forgive me."

The old woman had spread blankets on a worn leather couch for Sebastian. He had insisted that Aloysius should have the narrow bed. Long after midnight they reluctantly agreed that they must have sleep.

"Goodnight," said Aloysius, "it's been a grand day. There are no words to tell you how much it has meant to me."

"And to me. I shall hope and pray that you will not leave the Church. I know you are suffering and that it will be a difficult decision. But—in this time of crisis—the Church needs men who will accept discipline and set that example. This unhappy world needs discipline, subconsciously craves it. And beyond that I am quite sure that you love the priesthood more than you could ever love life outside it. More than you could love any woman. Your Bishop may release you but I do not believe you could ever release yourself. Goodnight. God bless you, Father."

In the hotel Barbara had gone to the newsstand to buy cigarettes. As she waited for change she saw a copy of the *New York Times* on the counter, and glanced at it carelessly, not intending to buy it, for she did not want to be distracted or drawn out of the atmosphere of India. But a picture on the front page suddenly sent her into shock. It was one of three candid press photographs and the caption above them read BLACK TERRORISTS ARRESTED AFTER BOMBING ATROCITY.

"The newspaper too," she said in a numb way to the girl behind the counter.

She must hide somewhere to read this. She saw Alec Goodrich coming through the lobby, and as the door of an automatic elevator nearby opened and some men came out of it Barbara went quickly into the cage and pushed the button for the ninth floor. The hall into which she emerged was empty and there was a red exit sign at the end of it. On the fire escape outside she read about Boone.

The picture of him showed a defiant, angry face. The expression was one of contempt and resentment. He was still handsome—even that quickly flashed picture showed the splendid molding of his head—but he looked like a hard, reckless character. That was what Boone Champion had become. He and his companions had manufactured bombs. Without being detected they had planted several in office buildings, and eighteen people had been blown to pieces. Yesterday a department store had been bombed, and the police had found the trail to the place where the bombs were made. The city was outraged—the department store had been full of women and the count of the dead was not yet complete. Turn to page 18.

On page 18 there was a picture of the place where the explosives had been made. It was a shabby tenement with overflowing garbage cans in front of it. There was also a picture of a girl who was suspected of being an accessory. She had disappeared. She was a black girl. The picture had been taken from her college yearbook, the paper stated. She was said to have been living with Boone Champion.

"No," said Barbara aloud, "not Boone."

She stared at the ugly picture and remembered how Boone used to look. She had seen and met him first at a mass meeting when students had been protesting that there was discrimination against the colored help in the dining room and dormitories. Boone had talked eloquently, talked of justice and true democracy, urged them to work for it. He had seemed so noble—he was noble.

She imagined almost visually the reaction of her parents when they read about this and saw the picture of Boone on the front page, as of course they must have done. They would shudder at it, be very glad she was in India.

They would say, "She won't know anything about this."

On the fire escape of a New Delhi hotel whose name she had forgotten Barbara knew all about it. Far more than her parents or the reporters knew. She had seen him change. She knew that a crusader had become a criminal, but that Boone had once wanted and believed in making a better world, not in destroying the one he lived in. Through the haze of her horror she wondered if she could have prevented this. He had rejected her love, thrown her out of his life, told her to keep out, he had found another woman—what could she have done? Was there some way she could have kept him from this madness? If she had never had anything to do with him would he have come to this? It was after they had decided to marry that he had begun to turn against her and to hate all whites.

The newspaper was several days old. At the time that the police had been surrounding that dreadful house, handcuffing Boone, she had been on the train watching cotton fields and strange animals, liking India because it did not seem so angry as Africa and did not remind her so much of Boone. She had been expecting that Alec Goodrich would seek her out. As he had.

They would put Boone and the others to death. The newspapers said there would be no question about that, no defense possible under the new law to punish those who caused death by bombing. The public was aroused and frightened. They would kill Boone and there would be nothing of him left, none of that brilliance and eloquence and hope.

Far below in the street she saw cars moving, diminished people walking. She felt dizzy as she looked, tempted. It would be easy and quick. She did not want to return to those strangers with whom she had been traveling, carrying this hideous knowledge. She could never tell Alec Goodrich of her connection with the criminal he had probably read about this morning. She had found it impossible to tell him anything about Boone, feeling that he would not understand.

But Father Duggan knew. Perhaps if she showed him this paper he would tell her if she was to blame. He would know. He was a priest. She would try to find him, tell him, ask him. She went inside and rang for the elevator.

When Howard Demarest announced at breakfast in the hotel that he was going to the American Embassy because he had promised to present his letter of introduction to the Ambassador, Alec Goodrich decided not to go there. It had been vaguely in his mind to do so and he needed no letters, for he had met the present Ambassador several times in Washington. He was a close friend of Senator Marcus O'Brien. But Alec did not want to be drawn into companionship with Demarest and witness more of his pushing arrogance, and that would certainly happen. He told himself that making the call was unimportant. He would visit the House of Parliament later in the day and leave the Embassy to Demarest. Ruby had been sloughed off this morning. She stood idly in the lobby, glancing at a showcase of jewels, but she was not so intent upon them that she failed to smile invitingly at Alec as he passed, on the chance that he might be interested in her solitude. He walked by quickly.

Alec had also met the Prime Minister when she had visited Washington. It was at a private dinner, for protocol would not have allowed him an invitation to the White House banquet in her honor. But he had been included in the small affair because he was one of the most sought-after bachelor Senators in the capital. He was not yet engaged to Cicely. He had been able to talk to the Prime Minister as the guests assembled before dinner, and though the conversation was brief he had never forgotten it or her. He had been charmed by her beauty but even more impressed by the grace and simplicity with which she carried the weight of power. Since then he had followed her career closely and taken personal interest in her publicized political battles.

The intricacy of the political structure of India appalled Alec as he studied it. That of his own country seemed simple and orderly in contrast. In India there were innumerable factions, many of them deeply rooted in religion and separated by differences in habits and languages, which had to be somehow blended by the government. The heavy problems of poverty and overpopulation hung over the whole country, but along with them rose the obvious efforts for reform and change and the ambition for beauty, wealth and sophisticated living. The contrast between Old and New Delhi astonished Alec today as he saw first the crowded, picturesque squalor of most of the old city and then the almost exhibitionist modernity of the broad streets, mansions and public buildings in the adjoining new section.

He bought some newspapers and read them as he lunched in an Indian restaurant. The New Delhi paper, printed in English, was full of political news and comment. The Prime Minister was having very immediate problems, and factionalism within the Congress seemed at a boiling point. Alec hoped the great lady could keep control. Then he looked at the *New York Times* and read the account of the bombings with anger and shame that this story of incredible crime would be spread all over the world and disgrace the United States. Violence was out of hand in his own country. They had caught these murderers but others would certainly imitate their crimes unless the government took action to prevent the spread of lawless force. If he were in the Senate today he would demand action—but he was not in the Senate. That shamed and depressed him.

The House of Parliament in Delhi was reminiscent of all buildings conceived and built for the dignity of law making. There was no session going on and the guard allowed Alec to enter. He went down a wide hall, splendid with marble and mosaic. Several distinguished-looking Indians in native dress passed him, and a tall English-man in a frock coat. Then Alec saw the Prime Minister. She came through a door held by an attendant and, followed by another, she walked swiftly toward some other chamber in the house of government.

There was no way for Alec to avoid meeting her in the hall. But he knew she would not notice or recognize him and he gave himself the pleasure of observing the concentrated, calm face. Her eyes lifted and, seeing him, a look of surprise and puzzlement came over her face. She smiled and stopped, close to him.

"Ah, Senator Goodrich," she said, "I am glad to see you. Are you visiting India?"

He bowed over her hand. "Very briefly. I am very honored to have you remember me, Madam Prime Minister."

"I remember our conversation in Washington. I have often quoted what you said about the inevitability of a basic income for everyone in your country. From what I read you are making progress, Senator."

"Unfortunately I am not involved in the progress. I am no longer a Senator."

"No?"

"I was defeated for reelection last November."

"I am sorry to hear that. But it happens to very useful men. This I know well. And there is always another election to win. You will try again, of course."

He heard himself say, "Of course."

"Shall you be long in India?"

"Only overnight."

"I would have liked to have a visit with you. But it is very busy for me today. I wish you success next time, Mr. Goodrich."

Chapter Thirteen

The lecturer told his audience that there was a legend that God had given Ceylon to Adam and Eve to console them for the loss of Paradise, and that when they saw the island and went to Colombo and Kandy they would probably think that it was as close to Paradise as any place could be. There were not so many people listening to him in the theater this morning as usual. Many other events were competing with his talk. There was the final golf game of the tournament on the sports deck. In the lounge Joan Scofield was giving a lesson on the draping of saris, demonstrating the winding of one on her slim figure, though she was well aware that when most of the women tried it they would tie themselves in knots. A Late Risers' breakfast was now featured on the Lido deck and was extremely popular because so many passengers wanted to sleep late on the days between ports. As Robert Cayne said, people did not come on a cruise to go back home worn out, and some of the shore trips were murder. He was taking fewer pictures and did not have his camera with him this morning because his last bill at the purser's office had included seventy-four dollars for film in spite of all he had brought with him.

Mr. Cayne did not hear the story that the sharp-coned mountain in Ceylon had a foot-shaped impression in the rock at its top and that the Moslems believed it was the footprint of Adam, but the Buddhists claimed it was a print made by Buddha on his last trip to Ceylon, and Eastern Christians held that it was made by Saint Thomas, the doubter. Mr. Cayne was having breakfast on the deck where he could see the ocean—if he cared to look—but he had his back to it for he said he had seen enough ocean—while he had his orange juice, freshly squeezed, and bacon and eggs and crisp rolls from a hot aluminum container which was wheeled to his side. He wore only shorts and sandals, for it was hot outside the air-conditioned rooms. On the Lido deck almost everyone was partially naked. Paunches protruding from shorts and sagging breasts under thin shifts were a commonplace sight and embarrassed nobody, and Bettina Beaufort and Ruby Canaday were at their most beautiful in bikinis.

The luxury of *The Seven Seas* had become customary to many of the passengers by this time. They took it for granted. Some were so spoiled by it that they complained at any slightest flaw. Mrs. Robert Cayne, who before her marriage had usually breakfasted on canned orange juice and instant coffee, standing at the counter in her Pullman kitchen, was petulant this morning because there were no English muffins left and she had to settle for a Danish roll.

"Considering what we're paying for this cruise you'd really think we could get what we want to eat instead of having them skimp on food," she said.

There were sausages and ham and Canadian bacon and kippers on the shining hot trays, biscuits, rolls, toast, a dozen kinds of jam and marmalade, eggs cooked in all fashions, grapefruit and oranges with their sections carefully loosened from their rinds, baskets of choice bananas and plums. Mrs. Cayne sat at a small table with her husband, sheltered from too much sun by a gaily striped umbrella. The napkins were linen. The ocean sparkled. But there were no more English muffins.

Robert Cayne said, "It's a shame, darling. I'll speak to the steward about it."

Signe Goode enjoyed every minute of those breakfasts on deck, especially if Mark woke up before noon and came to join her. He had not appeared yet this morning and, although she would not dream of saying anything about it to him, she wished that he would drink less. And write more. She had gone to the ship's library and found the book there which Mark had written. Signe had read it, marveling. To know that much about people, what they thought as well as what they did, and put it all down was amazing. Mark was a wonderful person. He was kind in spite of the remarks he made sometimes. Signe was sure that he talked that way because he was discouraged about his writing. And worried about money.

In a corner of the lower promenade Father Duggan, who had breakfasted hours before, stopped by Mrs. Barton's chair to ask if she was feeling better. He didn't believe her when she said that indeed she was. The bruises were fading and yellowing but her face was gaunt. Her hair was held neatly in a gray hairnet and her lips were pale and looked old.

"Another day that the Lord has made, Father," she said smiling.

"Indeed it is. And how good to hear you say that."

"It's the way I feel. Few things are more pleasant than a fine day on the ocean."

Jim Bates in a very clean white coat came up to the priest and waited respectfully until he turned. He held out a note.

"Miss Bancroft asked me to give you this, Father."

"Thank you, Jim." He took the envelope from the steward and said to Mrs. Barton, "I must go along. Have a good day."

The note disturbed him. He had not seen Barbara since the last day on the train in India. He was not sure that he wanted to see her or what feeling would arise beyond his own control. She had not appeared at lunch or dinner since they had sailed from Bombay twenty-four hours ago, and he had tried to keep his thoughts away from her. He went into an empty writing room and opened the envelope which held a single sheet of paper. On it was written,

Dear Father Duggan,

I have had some very bad news and would like to talk to you. Would you be able to see me in my cabin sometime today at your convenience? I would be very grateful. I shall be there all day.

Sincerely,
Barbara Bancroft.

Father Duggan went into the nearest public room and sat down to think it over. The television in the front of the lounge was turned on and a number of people were concentrating on the pictures and information. He did not listen but it offered cover for his thoughts, for no one would start a conversation. Knowing what he did about the girl, guessing what he did, vulnerable as he was to her beauty and charm, should he expose himself to temptation? Walk into the occasion of sin, mental sin at least? Listen to any further confession she might have in mind? It would probably be the wiser thing to ignore the note and to tell her when he saw her again casually that he was sorry but he had been preoccupied all day with other obligations. Bad news? What could it be? If she was grieving, was it his duty?

The picture of an avalanche in Switzerland faded and a sharp staccato voice announced that this was the morning stock-market report. Robert Cayne in the front row of viewers took out a ballpoint pen and an envelope. This bear market was getting on his nerves though he assured his wife every day that it couldn't go on much longer. It would bottom out.

Behind him Julia Hayward sat and her handsome face did not betray the panic she was feeling. She knew her small portfolio of stocks well and had been aghast when, in Delhi, she had seen in the New York paper that one of the stocks she owned had omitted its dividend for the quarter. That meant a loss of two thousand dollars, and the gloomy comment in the financial news said that some tobacco companies were in bad shape and might be forced to liquidate. And this unfeeling voice was stating now that another of her holdings had lost ten points, and might also pass its dividend. If that happened and she lost thirty-five hundred dollars a quarter during the rest of the year how could she live? Nobody could live on twelve thousand a year in New York and that would be about all she could count on. She moistened her lips as the weather report began, and swiftly left the room.

It was a beautiful day, perfect for pleasure on shipboard, but Commodore James, the Chief Officer Karl Van Sant, and Fred Timmins were not relaxing. They were in conference. Timmins had reported that the fin on the right stabilizer did not seem to be performing properly, and the Commodore, after checking on the navigational bridge, was inclined to agree with him though the deviation from normal was small.

"Of course on a sea like this the passengers wouldn't feel it," Timmins said.

"The weather's going to stay like this for a while," said the Commodore. "It's perfect in Colombo, from what we hear on the radio, and the long-range reports look as if it would stay pretty much that way until we reach Hong Kong."

"We'll be all right in Hong Kong," said Timmins, "and we'll have a long enough time there to fix the fin. But by rights the ship should be put into drydock there until we see if anything is wrong with the screw."

"And feed the passengers for two weeks at the Peninsula?" asked Van Sant. He was a man of fifty-odd, practical and unexcitable. He had been executive officer on a submarine chaser during the Second World War and was less a seaman than a manager. The Commodore had been too old for active duty in that war and always said he had just run a ferryboat for the fighting men. Fred Timmins had been building ships in the United States while the war lasted.

"Fly them back from Hong Kong," said Timmins jocularly.

"We'd have a hundred lawsuits on our hands."

"But we're protected by the terms of the passage. It's on the ticket that the company isn't responsible in emergencies for changes of schedule."

"Passengers don't read fine print," said Van Sant. "A lot of them would sue. And it would ruin the reputation of *The Seven Seas.* People don't expect a ship like this one to have trouble."

The Commodore said, "We haven't had any trouble yet. And we couldn't drydock in Hong Kong, Fred. You know as well as I do

that the port is too crowded and we couldn't get proper accommodations. But we certainly must get the stabilizers fixed there. All
these decks on the ship may increase the fun and games but they
make her topheavy, and if we ran into a bad storm or a typhoon
there might possibly be some slight danger of capsizing."

"There sure might be," said Fred.

"Keep your cool, Fred," Van Sant advised him amiably, "we'll
get back to New York with her all right."

"To San Francisco at any rate," said the Commodore, "and then
we'd have less of a problem. If she did have to have extensive repairs
there, we'd be on the home ground. And more than half of our
passengers leave the ship for good at Honolulu and San Francisco
so a lot of them would be out of the way and we could delay or even
cancel the rest of the trip around Panama and back to New York."

"We won't have to," said Van Sant confidently.

"I don't think so either," the Commodore said, "but our first
responsibility is to get the people who've paid for the cruise and our
crew back safely. And they're going to be taken care of. Now the
least said about this, even among the staff, the better. Things leak
out and I'd hate to have Demarest know that there might be a
problem or he'd start telling us what to do about it."

Father Duggan asked Jim Bates, "What is the number of Miss
Bancroft's cabin, Jim?"

He knew what it was for he had inquired at the Chief Steward's
office. But to ask Jim made his visit out in the open and not surrepti-
tious.

"Miss Bancroft is in 9, Father."

The priest thanked him and knocked lightly on the door.

Barbara opened it immediately, as if she had been listening for
the knock. She said, "Come in, Father. This is very good of you.
Won't you sit down?"

She did not try to smile. Nor did he, after one glance at her face.
He took the small armchair, noted the pile of half-smoked cigarettes

in the tray on the table beside it, and waited.

Barbara said, "I've been wanting to talk to you ever since that first morning in Delhi. But I couldn't find you."

"I was staying in Old Delhi with a friend. He met me at the train and we went to his place. What did you do in Delhi?"

"I don't remember—I walked around—I was by myself—I had to be. . . . Father did you see the New York paper in Delhi?"

"No, I didn't. We got to talking and doing a bit of sightseeing."

"That morning I went to the newsstand. And I just happened to see this—"

She was sitting on the chair before the desk and she lifted a newspaper from it and gave it to Aloysius. It was wrinkled and limp.

"There on the first page. About the bombings."

He read it and turned to page eighteen and read that also. He studied the pictures. Then he looked at Barbara.

"That's the one," she said. "Boone. The man I told you about."

"It's a terrible thing, Barbara."

"Ever since I read it, I've been thinking. Thinking back. Remembering. He wasn't like that, Father. Not when I knew him. He didn't want to kill. He was just like the rest of us—wanting to change things that were unjust and rotten—especially for black people. But he didn't want to kill anyone—Boone was friendly. Popular! He loved people and wanted them to have a fair chance —not to be discriminated against—"

"He must have changed greatly."

"He did. He wasn't the same person. I told you that."

"Did he take drugs?"

"I don't know—oh, we all tried pot once in a while and some people got hooked on the other things but Boone never did—I'm sure of that. Heroin wouldn't make him violent anyway. It was his black friends who believe in total racial revenge."

"It's tragic," said the priest.

"I can't bear to think of it but I can't think of anything else.

181

Father, could it have been my fault in some way? That's what I keep wondering. It haunts me. Could I have been to blame?"

"It's possible," said the priest.

Her eyes widened. Then she laughed.

"Why do you laugh?"

"Because I just realized that I expected you to tell me that I wasn't. I wanted to hear you say it! That was probably the reason I wanted to see you! To have you clear me and you don't!"

He said, "You mustn't allow yourself to become hysterical, Barbara. I said that it was possible because you told me that this man came to feel that his love for you made him a traitor to the people of his own color. Love is very close to hate—love that frustrates itself can become hate. His love for you turned to dislike and distrust—then he hated all white people—then it became hate for the world, desire for destruction—do you understand what I mean?"

"That if I had never had anything to do with him he might not have become a murderer?"

"I don't know that. You don't know it. And it's futile to speculate on what might have been. You have to face what has happened."

"Yes," she said more calmly, "that's what I have to do. I must go back and stand by him. Through the trial. I can be a character witness."

"He wouldn't welcome you, Barbara. He'd resent you. So would the men who were his companions in this crime."

"You think so?"

"I'm sure of it. And there would be scandal and publicity. The newspapers would dig out the facts about your previous relationship and publish them. He would hate that. And you'd crucify your parents."

"They never understood. I know what they are saying now."

"But you don't know what they are feeling. Or seem to care, when you suggest identifying yourself with this horrible crime."

"But you say I may have been responsible."

"You couldn't atone for that by further exhibitionism."

"Exhibitionism!"

"It was probably more or less that from the beginning. You wanted to be one of the far-out people—a rebel in public—rejecting convention—you still want to."

"No—it's not that."

"Do you love this man now?"

She shuddered. "But I did," she whispered.

"You were determined to. You clung when he tried to get rid of you. As he did finally. You bolster your pride by thinking that you can never love anyone else. That's false. You probably never really loved him. He was your possession. In your own lingo, he was your thing."

He spoke firmly, without emotion. The personal desire he had felt for this girl had left him. He saw her as she was, one of the confused young people in the contemporary world. She was brave. She meant well. She deceived herself more than anyone else. He wanted, with deep compassion, to help her now, even more than he had before.

"They will execute him," she said.

"Perhaps. But before that happens he may save his soul." He thought for a grave moment and then said with decision, "I shall try to help him, Barbara. When I go back to New York I shall arrange to see Boone."

"You will?"

"I promise that."

"Will you tell him I am sorry? For many things."

"No. I shall not speak of you to him. I shall try to make him believe that there is a God who will forgive any crime that is truly repented."

She shook her head. "He doesn't believe in God."

"He may change."

"None of us believed in any religion. We thought all the old institutions should be abolished. But it wasn't just exhibitionism."

"I know that. There were noble impulses."

"We thought the rules we were supposed to obey were wrong. Out of date. That if we protested hard enough openly enough they would be changed. We wanted to stand up and be counted. You know what I mean?"

He had heard himself echoed. "Yes," he said, "many of us wanted to do that."

"I still do. But how? Not by blowing up people."

"You'll find out how to do it. So shall I. Barbara, you're very tired. If you could say a prayer, I think you could rest."

"Say it for me, Father."

"I shall. Tonight and again in the morning. Every morning."

He went out and meeting Jim Bates in the corridor he said, "Miss Bancroft is rather tired, Jim."

"I didn't think she'd been feeling well since we left Bombay."

"She's better. Bring her some coffee. And a chicken sandwich."

"And a martini?" asked Jim. "That's what she likes to drink."

"Bring her one of those too," said Father Duggan.

So far it had been a good trip for the excursion staff, without too many tangles. The stay in Ceylon presented no problems. Practically all the passengers would spend the first afternoon sightseeing in Colombo and on the next day they would go in a fleet of automobiles to Kandy, the town high in the green hills which always delighted tourists. The weather promised to be fine and the guides in Ceylon were exceptional. Most of them were schoolteachers, moonlighting as guides when they had a chance, for the pleasure of contact with foreigners as well as extra money.

"The shopping district in Colombo is called The Fort," Joan Scofield told the women grouped around her in the lounge, "and you'll see an absolutely priceless assortment of jewels—sapphires, rubies, emeralds. It's one of the biggest gem markets in the world. Just to look at them is fun and if you didn't spend all your money in Jaipur you'll have a chance to do it tomorrow. And if you want

another sari the Ceylon ones are clear aquamarine and hot pink—
they are beautiful in this setting. You will love Colombo but the big
treat will be Kandy. I won't spoil it for you with my feeble description. You must see it for yourselves."

Signe Goode rarely missed one of Joan's informative hours. But
she listened this morning with a feeling that she would not enjoy
Ceylon no matter how beautiful it was. And it was her own fault.
She had only herself to blame. She should have known better than
to talk to Mark about his writing. It was none of her business and
he had a right to resent it, to be sore at her, sick of seeing her. So
she told herself, worrying at the same time about what he was
doing. Probably he was drinking in his cabin.

It was on the train as they were returning from Delhi that she
had said, "Now we have four days at sea. You can get on with your
writing."

"Is that a command?" he asked and she knew she had said the
wrong thing. She had sounded bossy, as if she had a right to tell him
what to do.

"Of course not. I just meant you'd have time to settle down to
it."

"Zola—he was a French writer and a very good one—when he
was lazy his mistress used to lock him in a room until he started
writing. It's an idea, dear."

He had left her blushing furiously at that word *mistress.* He had
not mocked her that way before. She had not seen him since. For
the last days he had not even appeared for meals. She wanted to
telephone his room just to make sure he was all right but she did
not dare to do it. For he had a right to feel insulted. She had given
him that money and then acted as if she owned him.

She did not see him during the afternoon in Colombo. But the
next morning as she was going through the foyer on the main deck
on her way to the tender which would take them to the island again
she heard Mark's voice and turned. He was asking the purser if
airmail went out from Colombo and he did not notice Signe in the

thick flock of excursionists. Signe hesitated—perhaps she should go right over to him and apologize again—but Jim Hicks touched her arm and said, "I've been looking for you, Mrs. Goode. The tender is about to leave and you'd better go down immediately. We've reserved a place for you in the third car that will be waiting on the island."

Barbara Bancroft had also been assigned to the third car. She took the seat beside the driver to leave more room in the back seat. Julia Hayward was the other person in the car, and unhappily, feeling completely unwanted, Signe climbed in beside her.

It was a small, old car, well shined up but its loose parts rattled. The driver was a handsome young man who spoke cultivated English. When Barbara introduced herself and asked his name he said, "In Sinhalese my name is difficult to pronounce. Please call me Joe."

He had an infectious smile. He seemed so happy to be driving the three unhappy women, so interested in them and eager for their interest in his own country, that they had to respond. What part of the United States did they come from? My English is good? Thank you. I have spent one year at the University of London, after I graduated in the University of Ceylon.

They drove through rice fields and tea plantations, and at times there were glimpses of the raw green of the jungle. Small communities of natives dotted the route swarming with children who were naked and gay, waving at the travelers. They waved in return and Joe blasted his horn in salute. But he shook his head and said, "In Ceylon there are too many children. Many are always hungry. Many die."

Barbara asked, "Could we stop in one of the villages?"

"They would be honored."

They stopped in one that was set beside a stream where the children were bathing. They rushed to the car and girls and women came out of the huts to see the strangers. Everyone smiled.

"They're so friendly!" exclaimed Barbara.

Joe said that Ceylon was a friendly country. He took his passengers into one of the huts, making courteous explanations to all the people who lived there, and the visitors saw the lack of almost everything but shelter. A girl came close to Julia and touched the gay chiffon scarf she was wearing with a kind of reverence.

"You like it?" asked Julia, smiling, and she took off the scarf and put it around the girl's neck, gesturing that she was to have it. Everyone was delighted, none more than Joe, who was proud of his generous Americans.

Back in the car Barbara asked what the natives did for a living.

"The men work in the rice fields. Many women work in the tea fields because their touch is gentler on the tea leaves. Rice is their living and their life. They eat rice in the morning and at night—there is never enough for all. Too many children," he repeated.

"No birth control?"

"We try to teach the women about that. It is very difficult."

"You're a teacher, Joe?"

"Oh yes. In Kandy I will show you my school. Also many of us work outside the school, teach in the villages. What you call extension classes, field work. We teach very practical things, how to plant other crops than rice, how to limit the family. But Ceylon needs more teachers—that is the great problem."

In the back seat of the noisy car Julia and Signe had fallen into conversation. The gift of the scarf had made Signe feel that the aloof and fashionable Mrs. Hayward was really a warm-hearted woman. Now that she liked her, talk came easily.

"How can they possibly live on four or five hundred dollars a year?" Julia asked. "Joe says that's what the average income amounts to, in our money."

"It seems very little," said Signe, "but Tom—my husband—used to say that people could always get along if they cut their cloth according to what they had to live on."

"That's not always easy."

"I know. I can remember when we were first married. My

husband was just learning how to be an accountant. That was more than twenty years ago and his salary was a hundred dollars a month. I had to watch every penny. We had only one room—that was long before we bought our house and his mother came to live with us."

"And you could manage on that?"

Signe laughed. "I had to. It was fun in a way. We didn't starve and I learned never to waste anything, not a spoonful of gravy. We had a good time. We always went to concerts in the park and the free things. I sometimes think we were just as happy in those days as we were when Tom was making ten thousand dollars and we could have everything we wanted."

"Everything you wanted on ten thousand dollars?"

"Oh, yes. Naturally we didn't think of taking a trip like this."

"But you're doing it now."

"I can now." Signe did not explain further. She said, "I only wish that my husband could have had a cruise around the world. Tom always enjoyed looking at pictures of other countries on television." She went back to the point where they had started. "It's too bad that they have so many children if they can't feed them properly. When there are people who never had any, like me. We both wanted a family, a boy and a girl. Have you any children?"

"I have a son," said Julia, "and a grandson."

"How wonderful for you!" said Signe.

It seemed to Barbara all day that she was lifting the brightly decorated cover off tourism and seeing what lay beneath it. Joe had become her friend. While the passengers from *The Seven Seas* were entertained by the Kandyan dancers on the lawn of the guest house, Joe took her to see his school and then to the university campus. He introduced her to other teachers and she heard more talk of the struggle to persuade the natives to limit their families, and of the shortage of teachers.

She told Joe, "I had some courses in education. When I first went to Columbia I thought of becoming a teacher."

188

"But you decided not to?"

"I became interested in other things."

"It is unfortunate that the teaching profession lost you."

"I might go back to it. If I could teach in a place like this. Could I get a job here, Joe?"

"It is too bad but there is no money to spend for American teachers."

"Suppose I did not ask for money?"

He laughed at the joke. "That indeed would be the miracle."

Later at the guest house Father Duggan found her. She was alone in a chair on the terrace, watching the sunset. Joe had gone to the Temple of the Tooth to collect the other women who would go back to the dock in Colombo in his car.

"It's very beautiful here," said the priest. "It would have been very generous of God to send Adam and Eve here after they had sinned."

"After they had sinned," she repeated. "I wish I could be sent here. I would like to come back to Ceylon. It might be the answer."

She had Joe's Sinhalese name, and his address, written in beautiful script on a card in her handbag.

Commodore James was in a jewelry store in Colombo in the late afternoon that day, inspecting a tray of gems, looking for the one that would suit her, that she could always wear. And that he could afford. The manager of the shop hovered respectfully, pointing out the beauty of this emerald or that ruby, but not pressing too hard, for he instinctively knew that this tall man in his splendid uniform of authority was not a person to be cajoled into buying.

"That sapphire ring," said the Commodore finally. He could see it on her long, slim finger.

"Very beautiful."

"The price?" the Commodore asked and when the merchant named it he raised his eyebrows and shook his head.

"But for the Commodore I would be willing to make a sacrifice."

"It would have to be a very considerable one," said the Commodore.

The price came down step by step. The manager sighed and yielded, mentioning at last a sum which was little more than what the gem had cost him. He put the ring in a small blue satin box and the Commodore paid him and went out with the box in his pocket. He was annoyed at meeting Howard Demarest and Ruby Canaday just outside the door, and he heard the girl say coaxingly, "I just want you to see how beautiful it is. I don't expect you to buy it!"

The Commodore gave them a spare, unsmiling greeting.

"Find something for the lady?" asked Demarest with an insolent grin.

There was no reply but the Commodore's muscles grew tense. He strode down the street, thanking God that Joan was not with him. But the implication stung. This was what he had been determined must not happen. There must be no slur on Joan's reputation nor on his own behavior as master of *The Seven Seas.* Of course even if Demarest in his nasty, prying way wheedled information from the shopkeeper about what the Commodore had bought there was no way in which he could discover for whom the ring was intended.

But he felt stained by association by also being a man buying a jewel for a woman whose relation to him was and could not be publicly acknowledged. The Commodore knew well enough that there were plenty of illicit affairs on shipboard during a long cruise. He had not considered it any of his business when Demarest brought along his little tramp and protected himself by putting her in a separate cabin. The Commodore had seen that sort of thing too often to be surprised. He knew that the travel agents and even some of his own staff couldn't be prevented from having a dip into sex with a pretty girl or provocative woman. He himself liked to see good-looking girls on his ship, and flatter them casually at his dinners.

His feeling for Joan Scofield was no longer casual. It had been growing for a long time and on the night when they had dinner in his quarters on the ship in Bombay it had matured. They both knew now. Since then they had been more than careful to conceal the knowledge from everyone else. This afternoon he had had an impulse to bring her to choose a jewel for herself but he had not yielded to it. And they had decided that there must be no more dinners by themselves on board the ship. Once was all right. Twice, and the steward who served them might begin to gossip.

The Commodore felt that he must talk to Joan. He had made some personal decisions and wanted her to know what they were. He wanted to be alone with her, have the feeling at least once more that they belonged together even if they were thwarted. And time was running out. On the run to Hong Kong both of them were sure to be besieged with responsibilities. In Hong Kong his full attention must be given to the repairs to the ship. So he had asked Joan to dine with him tonight at a hotel a few miles out of Colombo, which overlooked the Indian Ocean. It was too small to have been chosen as the destination of any shore excursion and it was unlikely that any passengers from the ship would be there.

"The sunset is sure to be splendid," he told Joan. "I'll meet you on the dock about six. The launch will run me in."

"No," said Joan, "I'll go in on the tender earlier and take a taxi to the hotel. It's much better that way."

He knew that it was better but it did not make the arrangement satisfying. He was not a man who liked ruses. But after he left the jeweler's shop he called a taxi for himself and was waiting at the hotel when she arrived. He had reserved a table beside a window overlooking the ocean, which was turning slowly from red to copper color. It was very beautiful and so was Joan tonight. She was wearing a dress of white cotton lace and he told her she looked like a bride. Then he wished he had not said that.

"I do my best," said Joan. "I'm not a bride but I'm certainly looking at a man I'd like to marry."

"Don't make it too tough, Joan."

"You look a little tired. Is anything wrong?"

"We've had a few problems with the ship. But I'm not worried."

"Nothing serious could go wrong with *The Seven Seas.*"

The Commodore said, "There's no ship ever built that can boast of that. All ships are man made and oceans and weather are forces of nature. We're undoubtedly safe enough on this one but things were not done that should have been done before we made this cruise. Penny wise, pound foolish—the owners may find that out when they get *The Seven Seas* into drydock."

"If that man Demarest is a sample of the owners—"

"I don't know. There may be better men in the company."

"It's not fair. You should own the ship."

"I'll be lucky if I own a rowboat."

"Rudolph, you mustn't let yourself be wasted. What are you going to do?"

"I've given it a lot of thought. I don't think I'll do what I told you the other night—sit around and whittle. I might get a job with some shipbuilding company—maybe even the Navy could use me. Not in any big way—but I'm prepared for that."

"You're not going to live in that place where you have a house?"

"No. And that's what I wanted to tell you tonight. I'm not going to live in that place or that house."

"You'll sell it and go somewhere else?"

"I'm going to give it to my wife," said the Commodore, "and I'm going to ask her to give me a divorce."

Joan put down her glass and her eyes asked him to tell her more.

"I think she will do it. I think she may be glad to be rid of me. When I was younger and used to come home from voyages here and there it was different. She rather liked to show me off."

"I'll bet she did."

"But now I'd be in the way all the time. The house is fairly valuable—a nice piece of property. She can live in it—take someone to live with her—it wouldn't be the first time—or she can sell it and go to live with her sister. But that's neither here nor there. All I wanted to tell you, Joan, is that if I can't live with you I'm not going to live with anyone else."

There were tears in Joan's eyes but she did not speak.

"Yes," said the Commodore, "you can bring the dinner now."

It was brought and praised and tasted. He tried the wine, accepted it and when both glasses were filled raised his toward her.

"But if you get a divorce," began Joan.

"That doesn't obligate you in any way," he said quickly. "I've thought about that too. I'm an old man and you're a young, beautiful woman. You should marry someone of your own age. And have children."

"I can't have children," Joan said.

"I didn't know that. I'm sorry, Joan."

"And since my husband died I've never known or seen anyone I wanted to live with except you."

"It will happen. And aside from age we couldn't marry because I may not have any way to take care of you. I can't be sure I'll get a job."

"I can work. And you'll have a pension. Or Social Security."

"That wouldn't do at all, to have you work and me loaf. I couldn't live like that, Joan. But I'll always remember that we have lived together in a way. On the ship. We've had our dinners—in Casablanca, Capetown, in my quarters, tonight. I'll remember each one of them as if it were still happening. There's something else." He took the satin box out of his pocket. "I bought this for you today because maybe when you wear it you'll remember the times we were together."

She opened the box and looked at the jewel.

"How beautiful!" she said.

"You like it?"

Joan slipped it from the velvet nook and put it on her finger, looked at it for minutes and then held it up for him to see.

"You said I looked like a bride. Maybe I really will be one someday. But anyway I'm engaged to be married."

Chapter Fourteen

The days were full to the brim on the run from Ceylon to Hong Kong. There had been a half-day stop in Singapore, unsatisfactory for either sightseeing or shopping, and, although Bangkok was usually one of the ports of call, it had been scratched from the schedule before the cruise started, because the political situation in Thailand made it potentially dangerous for tourists. So for almost ten days *The Seven Seas* was on the ocean, invariably near the coast and with unsurpassed good weather. The cruise director and his assistants, the hostesses, the travel lecturer and the bridge teacher, as well as the members of the orchestras, had a harder time than normal because there was such a long time between shore breaks. The young men in the travel bureau had it easier than usual.

Joan tried to arouse some interest in folk dancing but could not. The appetite for entertainment was too avid for that simplicity. She persuaded the cruise director to have music for tea dancing at four in the afternoon, for the older women and men who always had tea and cakes at that time liked to watch the few who would dance as they themselves munched and sipped. Especially good movies were rerun. And all day long there were competitive games going on with cards or tennis rackets or shuffleboard shovels.

After the dinner sittings there were Bingo games and horse races to be gambled on in the big rooms, and one night Alida Barnes persuaded the Chiltons to allow Hilary to draw the numbers which paced the wooden horses around the track. Hilary was very excited and dramatized herself as she passed the numbers to the announcer. Noticing her as he passed through the lounge on his way to the Seashell, Mark Claypole scowled.

Nearly every night the clocks were set ahead an hour. But before that the lavish midnight buffet was always set out on a long table at the head of the great staircase. There were whole turkeys and hams, salads, cheeses and sweets. There were replicas in ice of temples that had been seen by the passengers in India, or animals that had been seen in Africa, decorating the ends of the table, and sometimes the chef would dress roasted partridges in their own feathers as a special feature. The same people usually gathered around the feast and after four highballs it was almost inevitable that Robert Cayne would forget his noonday worry about the stock-market report of slipping values and start to sing the ballads of the barbershop. His early manhood dated from the time they were popular and nearly always there were enough men of his own generation at the buffet to join him in the off-key choruses.

In the cabins below there were always some men and women who had passed out and some who were quarreling and some who were making love. Some wrote letters, on the airmail letter paper with the picture of *The Seven Seas* in color on it, or figured what they had spent and how they were going to come out financially at the end of the trip. A few studied the heavens on the open deck aft, for there was a professor of astronomy on board. One or two people usually walked on the boat deck for late exercise. Alec Goodrich always did that.

Jim Bates came out for a change of air from the chill air-conditioned corridors.

"They're at it pretty late tonight, Jim," said Alec.

"It's quite different on our transatlantic passages, Mr. Goodrich," said Jim. "There's more people on serious business on the ship then. And a lot of people in the second class that don't have much money, crossing the ocean to visit their relatives or immigrating to the United States."

"You like those trips better, Jim?"

"They're different, sir. I think maybe I do. But of course you don't see the world like you do on a cruise like this one."

"Yes, you see more of the world than I thought I would when I first came aboard." Alec lit a cigarette and said, "I haven't seen Miss Bancroft around lately. I hope she's feeling all right."

"She seemed a bit under the weather when we left Bombay, sir. But she has been more like herself the last two days."

"I haven't seen her in the dining room."

"Miss Bancroft has been having her meals in her cabin. It gets like that sometimes, sir. Passengers get tired of the big menus and just want a snack."

"I suppose so." Alec started to walk away and felt his foot slide toward the railing. He steadied himself and asked, "Jim, is the ship rolling a bit? She doesn't seem as steady as usual."

"I've noticed that myself, sir."

"Funny. There's a little wind but not much of a sea."

"It could be there's a little trouble with the stabilizers. They'll soon put it to rights. Mr. Timmins, the chief engineer, never allows anything to be out of order. Not for any length of time. If one of the elevators stalls or something goes wrong with the air-conditioning he gets his men after it right away. They tell me that Mr. Timmins is one of the top men in his line of work, very experienced—"

"Yes, I've talked to him and he seems very able. You certainly need a wizard of an engineer on a ship like this with all its complicated machinery."

"No one has to worry about the machinery with Mr. Timmins in charge, sir."

There was a slight tremor to be felt as Alec walked the deck. But Alec paid no more attention to it. His thoughts were on Barbara, wondering if he had anything to do with her sequestering herself this way. She didn't seem like the kind of girl who would have regrets, or get suddenly morbid about an affair which both of them had entered into like two healthy adults who were attracted to each other. Had he said something to offend her? More likely she was avoiding Demarest in not coming to meals downstairs. Perhaps

Demarest had been annoying her, trying something. She might need help in that situation. Alec went back to his cabin and telephoned to her. It was only eleven o'clock.

"Did I wake you up?"

"No, I was reading."

"How are you? I've been missing you. What have you been doing with yourself?"

"I haven't been doing much of anything. I went on the trip to Kandy in Ceylon."

"I finessed that one. I haven't seen you since we had breakfast in the hotel in Delhi."

"I know."

"I looked for you that morning but you seemed to have disappeared."

"That morning—"

"Barbara, is something wrong? Did I do anything to hurt you?"

"No, it's nothing to do with you."

"Will you come up and have a nightcap with me? It's not too late."

"Alec—things have happened since I saw you—"

"I can tell that by your voice. Barbara, has Demarest been making a nuisance of himself?"

"I haven't seen him in days. I haven't been at the table."

"I know that. It's been worrying me. If you won't come up here, let me come to your cabin."

"No, I'm sorry but I'd rather you didn't."

"You're in some sort of trouble. Let me come. I won't stay a minute longer than you want me to."

There was a pause. Then she said, "Don't worry about me. All right, I'll come up and have a drink. But, Alec, things are different. I'm not in the mood—you know. I can't be. There are things on my mind."

"That's all right. I just want to see you."

She was wearing black linen pants and a white blouse. Though she couldn't be pale because of her deep tan she seemed to have no color under it. She looked thinner.

He had a drink waiting for her. She took it gratefully and sat back in the armchair as if trying to relax.

"What is it, Barbara?"

She shook her head. "It's hard to talk about this."

"Then don't. I'm afraid I let you down in some way."

"No. I'll tell you, so you won't think you had anything to do with the way I feel, so you'll understand why I can't—not now—"

"You're sorry?"

"Not for that. Alec, did you see the New York papers in Delhi?"

"Yes, I saw the *Times* and an ancient *Wall Street Journal.*"

"Did you read about the bombings in New York?"

"I certainly did. Thank the Lord they caught those criminals. The electric chair is too good for them. Blacks like that, crazy militants, are not only killing people and destroying property but they are ruining the chances of decent integration for their own people. It's wicked. Very depressing. Is that what got on your nerves?"

"Yes. I think of the people in those offices—and I see the ones in the department store. Some woman trying on a new dress, feeling happy, someone buying a present, a crowd facing forward in the elevator—good people doing a little shopping—and then blown to bits—"

"It was a vicious business. But you mustn't take it so hard personally. Did you know anyone who was killed?"

"I may have. I don't know. The list was incomplete. But I did know one of the men who planted the bombs. Who made them."

"You did?"

"Yes, I was going to marry him, I thought I was, six months ago."

"Good God—"

"So you see—"

"Have you dreamed this up? It doesn't sound possible."

"It was possible until he ganged up with the violent blacks."

"And then you got rid of him?"

"He got rid of me."

"That's incredible."

"But true. Alec, you told me that you felt that you might have been responsible for the suicide of that girl in your apartment. Not directly. Remotely, without knowing what you were doing. That's what's been haunting me. That's what I feel about one of the men who did the bombing."

What she said gave Alec a bad jolt. This girl and a black. He was not naïve enough to think that such attractions didn't exist. They were defended by liberal philosophers, shown on the stage, were the subject of dozens of books, invaded social life and politics at high levels. Alec thought, when cases came to his attention, that it was the business of those involved, not for him to judge. But he did not like to think of Barbara in that picture. The affair had been broken off—she was probably exaggerating in saying that the black had been the one to do it—but now she was blaming herself because he had become a criminal. That was fantasy unless— Had she led him on, let him believe that things were possible which were not possible? Alec remembered very well how he had been tortured by the death of the girl in his apartment. Beneath his anger and sense of outrage there had been the accusing doubt. Had he let her come to Washington because her hero worship flattered him?

Barbara said in a dreary way, "I keep thinking that if I'd had nothing to do with him it might have been different—that he over-reacted in a dreadful disappointment, disillusion—that's why he broke off with me."

"I think you are building this up," said Alec, "blaming yourself unreasonably. I did the same thing so I know how you feel. But you have to fight it. Did you come on this cruise to get away from the whole mess?"

"I had to get away."

"So did I. And it is doing me a lot of good. I'm getting things, especially myself, in better perspective."

"I was too, until I read that newspaper in Delhi."

"I had a letter in Capetown suggesting that I go back to Washington at once—fly back. I pretty nearly did. Then the thing here— the journey—pulled at me. I didn't want to leave. And not because I'm running away as Claypole said most of us were doing. I just wanted to run on for a while."

"I don't want to go back at all."

"That would certainly prove his theory."

"Do you dislike Mark Claypole?"

"Oddly enough I don't. I think that cynical manner is defensive. And he's certainly brightening the life of Mrs. Goode. You have to hand it to him for that."

Barbara laughed and said, "I rather like her. She's so unremarkable."

"Which makes her remarkable," said Alec. "Shall I freshen your drink?"

"No, I'm going to bed."

"And to sleep?"

"I think maybe I am."

"Make it a promise."

He took her to the door of her cabin, pushed her hair back from her face and kissed her lightly.

The ship's doctor was very busy on the day before *The Seven Seas* was due to arrive in Hong Kong. His office hours were between ten and one o'clock and this morning every chair in the small waiting room was taken. The nurse listed the names of the would-be patients and Dr. Sedgwick told her which ones to admit, but not in the order in which they arrived. There were always hypochondriacs on board and people who wanted free medical attention. They would tell him their ailments, ask his advice and then talk about the remarkable doctors who took care of them at home. There were always some who wanted sleeping pills and others suffering from hangovers which they personally diagnosed as symptoms of serious illness. This morning there were some seasick passengers both in the office and calling from their cabins, because the stabilizers were not working and though the sea was not at all rough their stomachs could not stand even the slight rolling of the ship. Or they imagined so.

Yesterday a notice had been posted on the bulletin board stating that the stabilizers were turned off because one was in need of small repair. This would be taken care of in Hong Kong and the weather ahead until then would be so good that there would be little discomfort. None the less some was claimed.

Dr. Sedgwick said, "I'll see Mrs. Beaufort first."

Bettina Beaufort, looking like a child in her shorts and jumper, came in and sat down by the desk. She looked excited and scared as he took out the folder with her name on it.

He smiled at her and she asked, "Am I?"

"Yes, you are. You're elected."

"Oh," she gave a little gasp and said, "We didn't intend to—right away."

"Nature usually knows best. You'll be fine. And sometimes putting it off means disappointment in the end."

"Well—we talked it over last night and Gene said that if it was true that I'm pregnant he'd be glad. He'll be a wonderful father."

"You'll probably make a pretty good mother."

"I don't know—I hope so. Now what do I have to do?"

"Nothing for the time being."

"I wondered—is it all right to dance?"

"Oh yes. Later on you won't feel like it."

"That's wonderful—it's such fun on board ship."

"All right. Just go on as usual and if you have any worries give me a call. I'm right here."

"Thank you so much, Dr. Sedgwick. I'll always remember that I found out on *The Seven Seas.*"

"Good girl," said the doctor and told the nurse to bring in Mrs. Barton.

She came in slowly, managing her sticks, and as he said good morning he saw the difference, the failing.

"How are you feeling?"

"Oh, much better."

He made the examinations, put down a few notes on her record and said, "I hope you're resting a good deal."

"I'm resting up for Hong Kong."

He frowned slightly and said, "You want to go ashore?"

"I can, can't I?"

The doctor said, "It might be better if you just stay quiet."

"But I don't want to miss Hong Kong. I've had such good times there."

The doctor said to himself that one more time might not make any difference.

"Well, if you don't overdo. Where are you staying?"

"At the Peninsula. We always did."

"They'll take good care of you there. Don't run around shopping."

"I don't shop. Not any more. In the early days we always had big wicker hampers and we'd fill them to the brim with things to take home. But now—"

The telephone rang again and the nurse answered. "The doctor is with a patient right now—yes, Mr. Demarest—just a minute, I'll see if he can talk to you. Doctor, it's Mr. Demarest."

Dr. Sedgwick weighed the reminiscences of Mrs. Barton against a conversation with Howard Demarest, a table companion whom he disliked. But he was a director of the Line. And certainly not a well man.

"I'd like to see you, Doctor," said Demarest. "Can you come up right away? The Mandarin suite, you know."

"I've an office full of patients, Howard. What seems to be the matter?"

"I didn't sleep well. I've had a kind of heart flutter."

"I'll be up," said the doctor. He hung up, looked at the list and said to the nurse, "Inquire which of those people are feeling seasick and take them in rotation. You know what to give them. I'll be back in a few minutes."

He went out through the private door and up to the Mandarin suite. Howard Demarest was in bed wearing white silk pajamas. The girl had been here. The doctor could smell her perfume and there was a tray of lipsticked cigarettes and several glasses beside the bed. He made a cursory examination. There was nothing new. Howard Demarest wasn't doing much to improve his heart condition. He was hung over and in a bad temper.

"Couldn't sleep, with the ship rolling. They've cut off the stabilizers."

"The ship's pretty steady without them."

"Damned inefficient," said Demarest. "Things ought to work properly on a ship like this."

The doctor said, "They'll get the stabilizers fixed in Hong Kong."

"And run up a bill for the company to pay."

"I'll give you a tranquilizer," said the doctor, "and stay where you are for the rest of the day. I suppose you'll want to go ashore in Hong Kong."

"I have to. I'm meeting some very important people at the Peninsula Hotel for dinner. It's all set up."

"Well, take it as easy as you can." The doctor had no doubt that Demarest would destroy himself sooner or later, but except for his heart trouble he was strong as an ox and with proper medication men like that could go on for a long time. He gave Demarest a powerful tranquilizer and went back to his office.

Demarest fell asleep. It was a heavy, complete sleep and Ruby Canaday, coming in quietly, noted that. He didn't stir as she watched him thoughtfully, thinking not of him but of the Mikimoto pearls she wanted to buy in Hong Kong. There were some in the locked case in the shop on the ship and she had priced them longingly. On the ship, even duty free, they cost four hundred dollars, but she had been told they were cheaper in Hong Kong.

She knew that he had cashed traveler's checks yesterday. He had been very mean lately. He would not buy the bracelet she wanted in Ceylon. In Hong Kong he had promised to buy her some clothes but he would balk at the pearls. Old stingy gut, she said to herself, looking at him as he snored on the bed she had shared. Noiselessly she moved over the thick carpet and took his wallet out of the dinner coat he had worn last night. A few hundred dollars—she certainly had it coming to her. She replaced the wallet carefully and went from the bedroom to the sitting room, closing the door between them. She rang for the steward and when he came she said that Mr. Demarest was not feeling well and must not be disturbed. Jim Bates said coldly that he would see to it. Ruby wrapped her yellow coat around her yellow bikini and went out to the swimming pool after stopping a few minutes in her cabin to hide the money. She rehearsed what she would say. "I looked in and Jim Bates was in your sitting room."

Nearly a year ago the travel agents had reserved rooms at the Peninsula Hotel for the passengers on this cruise. Not for all of the five hundred and seventy-six, of course, but for the ones who were paying most for their passage. At the time they made the reservations they did not know the names of the people who would occupy the rooms but they booked forty, knowing that at least that many would be in demand. They were assigned to the Chiltons, Alida Barnes and a rather reluctant Julia Hayward, to Howard Demarest —"he'll want one for the girl too"—to Signe Goode, for they had found out she was made of money, to Mrs. Barton because she said with polite firmness that she always stayed there, and to various other passengers who deserved the favor of the most renowned hotel in Hong Kong. Mark Claypole was given a far less expensive lodging, and Robert Cayne said to his wife, "I asked what a double room would cost and you could have knocked me for a loop. I said they could count us out. We can be just as comfortable somewhere else and we can go to the Peninsula for a drink and look around. I'm beginning to itch to get back home where they don't rook you every minute."

"You want to get a handmade suit," said his wife. "Everybody does in Hong Kong. You can get a silk suit for half what it costs in New York. And I want a few things. Then I won't have to buy any clothes this spring."

"All right," said Cayne, "I suppose they'll take a check on a New York bank. But I tell you I'm not going to give a fortune to these stewards, when we get back to New York. That's what runs up the cost of a trip like this, these tips."

The great ship sailed into Victoria Harbor among junks, freighters, sampans and warships. It looked like the floating palace it was advertised to be and, as it approached the dock with its flags flying, many people on the smaller craft stared and waved and wondered what it would be like to travel on the huge American liner.

On board the loudspeaker was calling the name of Mr. Mark Claypole. "Please go to the radio office for a telephone call, Mr. Mark Claypole."

Signe Goode heard the summons and thought it meant that Mark had friends in Hong Kong. She wouldn't see anything of him but she hadn't expected that she would. He didn't want to be bored with her any more. She knew that it was wonderful to be about to see Hong Kong but the ring of barren mountains, the strange, crowded harbor and the long plaza of shops on the dockside did not seem to welcome her. She hoped that Mark would have a good time in the city. She wondered if he had money enough for a good time.

Mark went to the radio office because they were certainly calling his name. But he couldn't figure it. There was no one he knew in Hong Kong, though his first book had had a small sale there. It couldn't be a call from New York. Milt Knott would have the manuscript he had mailed from Colombo by this time but Milt would never spend the money on a call to Hong Kong.

"New York calling, Mr. Claypole. You can take it in the booth."

Suzanne might be in a jam. This was the sort of thing she would do.

"Hello—Claypole here—"

The voice was distant but clear. "Hi, Mark, this is Milt. Having a good trip?"

"Good enough."

"I wanted to catch you before you landed in Hong Kong because I didn't know where you were going to stay there and I thought you'd like some news."

"What news?"

"Your piece came and I shot it right over to Phil Prentiss. He's nuts about it."

" 'Pictures I Took Myself '?" asked Mark unbelievingly.

"The title's a knockout. And the vignettes are great. Phil is going to feature it."

"Well—that's a pleasant surprise. What's he paying?"

"Twenty-five hundred. But I didn't call about that peanuts. The big news is that Giant is buying *Bird of Passage.* They want some changes and to have you go to Hollywood and work on the film with them as soon as you get back."

"You're not kidding?"

"I'm not kidding when I telephone you on the other side of the world."

"Well, thanks, Milt. That's wonderful. You're sure it will go through?"

"It's gone through. I always had faith in that story. And 'Pictures I Took Myself ' is really great. Been taking pep pills?"

"It's the sea air. Well, I'll hang up and not waste any more of your money—or is it mine that pays for this? I'll try to believe it and thanks a million for the call."

He put down the receiver and looked at the instrument as if to prove it was really there. He'd put it over. He thought of what he had written—vignettes that were imaginary but stemmed from the

206

truth of what he had seen on this voyage, word pictures he had taken himself—and they would be published. He wanted to tell somebody. He wanted to tell Signe Goode. He went down and pushed through the groups on deck until he found her, alone, looking at the nearing city.

"All set to go ashore?"

She started when she saw him, looked a little afraid and said yes.

"We're going to have a grand time in Hong Kong. We're going to celebrate."

"Celebrate what?"

"What you did for me."

"I don't know what you're talking about."

"You told me that I had four days to work. That I should stop whining and get at it. And I did. I worked four days in that nasty cabin, without leaving it. I mailed the piece in Colombo and they just called me from New York and they like it. They're going to use it—print it, you know."

"That's wonderful," said Signe. "I'm so glad!"

"And because you somehow shamed me into getting to work, I thought you'd like to know that it paid off."

"I thought you were mad at me," said Signe. "I thought you were sick and tired of me."

"Never, dear. But after I mailed the thing I didn't want to talk about it. It's like that. When you're working on a piece it feels good but when it's done you don't think it has a chance. I kept out of sight because I didn't want to sponge on you any more and I was a little short of money. But now I can pay you back—if you'll wait until we get to New York."

Howard Demarest said angrily to the purser, "You remember I cashed eight hundred dollars in traveler's checks yesterday."

"We cashed a great many checks yesterday. Let me look at the record. Yes. Eight hundred."

"And three hundred dollars was stolen from my cabin."

"That's a very serious accusation, Mr. Demarest. You probably just mislaid the money."

"It was not mislaid. It was stolen. And I know who did it. The room steward."

"Our stewards are all honest, Mr. Demarest."

"One of them isn't. Jim Bates was in my cabin while I was asleep. Under sedation. The money was in my wallet when I hung up my coat after dinner because I checked it. It wasn't there when I started to pack my things an hour ago to go ashore. I want to have Bates searched and his quarters searched."

A calmer voice behind him spoke. "You can't do that legally," said Alec Goodrich. He went on, speaking to the purser and ignoring Demarest, "I came down to speak to you about the same thing. Jim Bates came to me very much distressed and insulted. Mr. Demarest accused him of taking this money. I am confident that he did not."

"What right have you to horn in on this?" snarled Demarest.

"I told Jim that I would be glad to represent him as his lawyer if any action was taken."

"It will be taken."

"Think twice about that," said Alec coldly. "I don't know if you are familiar with the laws of libel but possibly—quite certainly because Jim is innocent—you might lose a great deal more than three hundred dollars."

"Gentlemen," said the purser, "nothing can be done about this at the moment. We are about to disembark and this office is always closed while we are in port."

Alec walked away as the purser closed the window. There was no doubt in his mind as to who had taken the money. Jim had told him that Miss Canaday had been in the room and said that Demarest must not be disturbed. But to accuse the girl was embarrassing and she was probably tricky enough to throw the money overboard if she knew she was suspected. He had reassured Jim, telling him

208

that the money would turn up, and said that he would take care of the situation personally if Demarest made any more trouble.

The passengers from *The Seven Seas* were not given guided tours in Hong Kong. They went their separate ways. To tailors. To floating restaurants on the bay. To ride the ferry. To take the trolley car to the top of Victoria Peak. Mrs. Barton did none of those things. She was weaker than she had thought she would be and she hoped she would not fall again. She went at once to the Peninsula Hotel. From her room she called the housekeeper, who remembered her well. A small procession of special courtesies began. A floor waiter brought Mrs. Barton a vase with a single exotic orchid. Another came with a bowl of fruit. A third carried in a tray with fragrant tea and thin sweet cakes. Mrs. Barton was sipping the tea when the housekeeper came to greet her personally. If she was shocked at the sight of Mrs. Barton's worn face and her lameness she concealed it perfectly.

"It is good to have you with us again."

"It's been ten years since we were here," said Mrs. Barton. "The hotel is greatly changed. I miss the big mahogany armoires."

"They were too big when we lowered the ceilings because of the air-conditioning. All the rooms have been done over. But I think you'll find we have kept the atmosphere of the Peninsula."

"Yes," said Mrs. Barton, looking at the orchid, "you have."

Howard Demarest was impressed by the hotel. He had been in bigger ones but this place had class. He felt it as he always recognized distinction even when it was out of his reach. He had calmed down after his anger at losing the money. When he went back to the ship he would take care of Bates. He would see that the Commodore did something about the thieving steward. Now he must telephone the people to whom he had introductions and make some appointments. Ruby could look out for herself. He told her tolerantly to pick out some clothes and put them on his bill.

Ruby lost no time in looking after herself. Within an hour she had found the shop in the arcade which sold Mikimoto pearls. The quiet deference of the salesman was a little awesome, so she put on her air of hauteur. She looked at the beautiful cultured pearls on their black velvet cushions and hesitated as if they were not good enough. But she desired them almost with love. Finally she bought a string of a hundred pearls for exactly three hundred dollars. They were not the largest ones but they were perfectly matched and the clasp was set with a small diamond. The salesman then wrote a careful guarantee that they were genuine Mikimoto pearls, describing the length of the string, the diameter of the pearls, the price and date of sale. Ruby put it in her handbag. It was one of the happiest moments she had ever known, certainly the best one on this journey.

"If you are staying in the hotel we will put it on your bill, Madam."

"No, I'll pay cash," said Ruby.

Mark and Signe had lunch at Gaddi's and he told her that it was one of the ten best restaurants in the world. He ordered Coburger ham with melon, a cheese soufflé and coffee. He paid for it himself.

"Not today, dear," he had said as she suggested giving him some money before they came to the restaurant. "It may clean me out but I'll have money when I get to New York."

"What is the story you wrote about?" she asked over the coffee.

"It is just word pictures of people. Candid shots in words."

"What people?"

"A child who's known too much reality and had too little fancy. A worried priest. A rejected politician. And an elderly lady who lives in the past, not because she was left behind but because she likes it better than the present."

"It's about people on the ship?"

"Yes. You're in it. So is Tom."

"Tom?"

"Your late husband."

"But you never knew him!"

"I know him very well. He wasn't on this cruise until I put him on the ship. I know just how he'd feel about a jaunt like this, how he'd hate the cost and manage to get his money's worth."

She stared across the table in amazement. "He would," she said.

Mark laughed. "Let's find a bookstore. I want a copy of *Alice in Wonderland*. There should be one in Hong Kong."

Alec Goodrich had hired a car and driver and called Barbara's room.

"Wouldn't you like to drive to the border of Red China?"

"I'd like to see it. But I'm not very good company, Alec."

"Please come. You don't have to talk. It should be interesting and rather exciting."

They drove through the chaotic city and into the country, where the small gardens were cultivated in old traditional ways, watered by pails slung on a rope over each shoulder of the gardener. Then to the hills and the driver stopped at one peak to point out the coves behind the harbor.

He said, "During the typhoons the people who live on the junks in the harbor put their boats in the coves, and live in the huts— many families in each one—until the storm is gone."

"They wouldn't be safe in the harbor?"

"They would be destroyed. A typhoon could wreck a great ship like you came on."

The low mountains of Red China looked sullen and ominous. The driver borrowed field glasses for them at the inspection point and they left the car and walked as far as was allowed. Through the glasses they could see the barbed wire and sentinel posts and the small settlement behind them.

"That's our ultimate problem," said Alec. "If we can't solve it politically, the jig is up."

She asked, "You're going to stay in politics, aren't you?"

"Well, a lady in India said I should try again."

"She was right."

"I've been thinking about it. I could try for the House. It would be a tough assignment. I'd have to make pretty much of a door-to-door campaign in my home district. The incumbent is going to retire next year. Of course it's a comedown—somewhat humiliating even if I got elected. But I'd have my foot in the door. Be in business again."

Barbara said, "Humiliation isn't the worst thing that can happen to a person. You can take it. You can live with rejection. But you can't live with bitterness and hate. They're like acid. They eat into you, they'll destroy you."

Chapter Fifteen

The Seven Seas was due to sail at two in the afternoon on Wednesday and the passengers had been told that they must be on board by one o'clock. Most of them returned laden with packages or followed by Chinese boys carrying their packages as far as the gangplank. Nearly all of them were exhausted after two days of continuous sightseeing and choosing and fitting duty-free clothes.

Father Duggan and Mrs. Barton were among the exceptions who came back refreshed. She had spent all her time in the hotel, sitting for hours in the great hall lounge where the East had met the West for many years. To Mrs. Barton it was not so dramatic as it used to be when a rajah might arrive with a retinue of servants in native dress and ladies wore hats and veils. But the flavor of travel on the grand scale was still here and Mrs. Barton had enjoyed it as she did the daily fresh flowers in her room and her afternoon jasmine tea. Father Duggan had found a church in which he was permitted to say his Mass each morning and he had gone on a kind of retreat, contemplating not his problems but his God. He had of course not stayed at the Peninsula Hotel, but the Y.M.C.A. had been clean and comfortable and extremely cheap.

Howard Demarest came on board before noon, for it was a hot day and he was tired. He left Ruby wandering among the shops in the plaza on the dock, warning her not to forget the time when she should be on board. He showered, dressed in fresh clothes and at one o'clock called Ruby's room. The bands were beginning to play on the long pier in honor of the ship's departure. There was no answer and he went down the corridor to her cabin. She opened the door, wrapped in a bath towel and said she had been in the tub and had not heard the telephone ring.

"Go ahead and finish your bath," he said, "and hurry up for there's quite a show on the dock. When you're ready we'll go down and see the takeoff."

He lit a cigar and moved her open handbag to give himself more room on the sofa bed. A small folder fell out of it and he picked it up to put it back in the bag, glancing at it carelessly. On the white cover was printed in black letters:

THE ORIGINAL CULTURED PEARLS
MIKIMOTO
GUARANTEE

Idly he opened the folder and on the first page he read: THIS PORTION OF THE GUARANTEE MUST BE COMPLETED AT THE TIME OF THE PURCHASE. Beneath were small labeled oblongs with inked entries beside them. He saw NUMBER OF PEARLS and in ink *100 (one hundred)*. LENGTH, *25 inches*. DIAMETER OF PEARLS *7.04 mm*. PRICE *$300*. DATE SOLD—and the date was Monday, two days ago. The salesman had signed his name under the facts and figures.

Turning the page over he saw a picture of Mikimoto, the Cultured Pearl King, and a description of how the pearls were made. He did not read it. He was fitting the facts together. There could be no possible doubt. Ruby was the one who had stolen his money. That was the exact amount. She had been smart enough to accuse the steward and he had been fool enough to believe her. In a gust of anger he started toward the bathroom door but a sharp pain gripped him. He felt for his box of pills and remembered that he had left them on his bedside table when he changed his clothes. He must get back to his suite. If he could make it. The pain had never been quite so bad before.

A light went on in the steward's room and Jim Bates looked at the indicator. He was wanted in the Mandarin suite. His usually pleasant face became grim. He wasn't going to take any more abuse from Demarest. He wouldn't answer. Let him ring his head off.

For five minutes he tried to make the decision stick but he couldn't. He was on duty, it was his job. Mr. Goodrich had said, "Keep your cool, Jim. Just do your job and pay no attention to anything he says."

He went slowly to the Mandarin suite and knocked. There was no answer but he heard a sound like a groan inside. He opened the door and saw Howard Demarest on the floor.

"Pills," gasped Demarest, "box by bed."

Jim rushed to get them, knelt down by Demarest.

"Here they are, sir. I'll call the doctor."

He opened the box and Demarest managed to put the pill under his tongue. He lay slack, looking deathlike. "Don't go," he whispered.

Jim picked up the telephone and said to the operator, "Get the doctor to come to the Mandarin suite on the boat deck. Mr. Demarest is sick."

He brought a glass of water and put a pillow under the man's head.

"I'd just lie there for a bit. You're going to be all right, sir."

"Good boy. You didn't take the money. Found it. Sorry."

"That's all right, sir. I'm very glad you found it."

"I'll tell the purser. Goodrich too. If I get by."

Jim asked, "Would you like me to ring Miss Canaday, sir?"

"No." Demarest opened his eyes and looked straight at Jim. He didn't have to say anything more. Jim knew that Demarest had found out who had taken the money.

Ruby was dressed and waiting restlessly for Demarest to come back. She was slightly worried. When she came out of the bathroom he was gone and that guarantee thing was lying on the floor. But even if he had looked at it, it wouldn't mean anything to him. None the less she tore it in small pieces and flushed it down the toilet. If he mentioned it, she'd say that it was just an ad she had picked up. And if he ever noticed the pearls she would tell him it was only an old string of beads that she'd had for ages. Maybe he had tired of waiting and gone down to hear the bands. She looked at herself again and went down to the crowded deck.

Leaving Kowloon and Hong Kong was always an exciting sailing. The beautiful white ship had its largest audience here, a kaleidoscope of people of all colors waving from the dock and the freighters and sampans saluting, except for those silent ones which flew the flag with the Red Star.

Standing as always on the top officers' deck, surrounded by some of his staff but taller and always seeming to dominate them, the Commodore was an image of control and good organization. But leaving each port on this cruise was a special wrench. He would not see that circle of mountains again. Fragrant Harbor it was called by the Chinese. They always joked about that when they passed the sampans. He said a silent farewell to the Fragrant Harbor and began to consider the problems that might come up between here and San Francisco. It was one thing to cruise along the coast of Africa or run between Bombay and Singapore and quite another thing to strike across the middle of the Pacific Ocean. The great ship moved with dignity and beauty out of the harbor. The tug was gone. The wind was coming up.

Fred Timmins was dead tired. He left his assistant in charge and went to bed. He had been having a harassing two days. He had been able to get divers to work on the stabilizers but he could not get the new parts he had hoped for, and though the men were competent they had done only a repair, not a replacement job. It would probably be all right now, hold up for the rest of the voyage. There was a slight sea now but the ship was perfectly steady. Timmins fell asleep.

Chapter Sixteen

"This is a very funny book," said Hilary.

She had it in her hand and when she saw Mark she escaped from the chair where she had been sitting beside her nurse and ran to him. Under a blue bandeau her hair flew back in the wind. It was a very breezy morning and she wore a coat that matched her eyes and the hair ribbon.

"It made you laugh?"

"No, not that kind of funny. I mean it is crazy."

"Why?"

"Because none of these things could happen. But of course it was just a dream."

"Not just that. Did you enjoy reading it?"

"Yes, I did. I like dreams. People who take drugs have wonderful dreams."

"People who don't take drugs have better dreams. What part did you like best?"

She thought, deciding. "I think the Mad Hatter's tea party. With all the people and animals who didn't belong together and were always interrupting each other."

"Yes," said Mark, "it is very like the makeup of the tables in the dining room on the ship."

She laughed. "They are all Mad Hatter's tea parties. Mark, it is such a funny book."

"So you said before. Without amusement."

"You don't ever know what is coming next. But it feels like it is happening to you. My father said it was written to make fun of England and queens."

"People have had many opinions about why it was written for the last hundred years and more."

"Why do you think it was?"

"To show the wonders of a young mind. Maybe to match the confusions of dreams against the confusions of reality."

"It's fun to hear you talk, Mark. But I never understand it all."

"Better that you don't, said the Dodo."

"Are you the Dodo?"

"Sometimes when I make an effort to think."

"He said Alice must give out the prizes. She gave them comfits. What are comfits?"

"Assorted Lifesavers—lemon and orange and cherry flavors."

"If you're the Dodo, I'll be Alice."

Cora came up to them. She said, "You mustn't bother Mr. Claypole, Hilary."

"I do not bother him," said Hilary coldly.

"Not at all," said Mark.

"Your mother said you must come inside when it got colder. And now the sun's gone. We'll go into the lounge and listen to the music until it's time for the lifeboat drill."

Hilary looked at Mark. "Off with her head," she said.

"Hey, you're not the Red Queen. You're Alice. Better go along. I'll see you at the drill."

He was pleased that she had caught the spirit of Lewis Carroll's fantasy. It proved, as he had guessed, that she had an imagination which could break through her stylized environment. When she ran away—as she surely would—it might be in the right direction. What was the right direction? Some of the signs at crossroads had been torn down, some deliberately misplaced. Mark began to feel a story stirring under a title. He rounded the corner of the deck at the end of the covered promenade and the wind almost pushed him back again.

They had been at sea four days since leaving Hong Kong and now the breakfasts for late risers on the Lido deck and the lazy luncheons by the outside swimming pool had been given up. It made for a good deal of monotony, and drinking had increased at all the bars. The wind was too high for anyone to play Ping-pong on the sports deck where the tables were set up. Passengers who were determined to exercise still played shuffleboard or swam in the indoor pool deep in the ship on D deck. A very few used the gymnasium, but the hairdressers and the doctor and his nurses found it difficult to meet the demands on their time.

The semi-confinement created restlessness and the cruise director and the hostesses were constantly trying to allay it. On the program of the day's events which was slipped under every cabin's door in the early morning Joan had FORMAL DRESS SUGGESTED printed in the upper left-hand corner nearly every day. It gave those women who still wanted to compete with each other's elegance an outlet, and many of them wanted to try out the clothes they had bought in Hong Kong. But the suggestion was often ignored.

She had planned the customary white-elephant sale for tomorrow. A long banquet top had been placed on one of the tables in the largest lounge and tomorrow it would be a counter to which passengers brought the articles they were sorry they had bought and might like to exchange for something another person had chosen, or sell for ready money. It was always a very popular sale. Mrs. Cayne intended to rid herself of two expensive beaded bags which she had bought in too much of a hurry in Singapore, and Alida Barnes had found that there would be no room in her luggage for the brass and copper trays she had bought in Casablanca. There would be bookends, cigarette boxes which did not close well, animal skins purchased impetuously in Africa, and saris that women realized on reflection they would never wear at home. Signe Goode had thought at first she would put something up for sale, but when she looked over her souvenirs she remembered so clearly where she had bought each of them and what pleasure she had when she did that she decided to keep everything. She would go to the sale and perhaps see something else she would like to buy.

Today there was little routine entertainment and the notice of another lifeboat drill had been posted. There was some complaining about that, for the day had become gusty and unpleasant. But it was well known that several passengers who had evaded one of the drills had been called upon by the Chief Officer and asked to explain why they had not attended. This could be very embarrassing and the bells at three o'clock this afternoon were obeyed by almost everyone in spite of the carping. With coats and sweaters under their lifebelts making them look clumsier than ever the group at Station Two assembled. They said repetitiously that the sea was getting rough and facetiously that if it didn't let up they might really need those lifeboats.

Her steward said to Mrs. Barton, "I'm sure you would be excused, Madam."

"No indeed," she said, "I always attend lifeboat drills unless I am really ill. My husband always said it was inexcusable not to."

Jim Bates hastened to help her to the deck when she came out of the elevator, and now she was braced against the wall of the ship with Gene and Bettina Beaufort on either side of her. Demarest came out by himself today. Ruby Canaday appeared later and asked the ship's officer who was in charge at this station if she had her life preserver on right. It was not right and he retied it for her. Demarest did not look her way. That had been noticeable for some days and aroused considerable speculation. Alida Barnes said to Julia Hayward, "You can see that something's happened to that affair. Look." Julia did not look. She said, "Of course. And who could possibly care?"

Alec Goodrich stood by the rail with Barbara, watching the angering waves. Hilary managed to be beside Mark, asking questions. Watching them, Signe Goode thought it was a pity he had no children. Father Duggan's sensitivity made him conscious of the bleak mood of the passengers and he knew he was committing a sin of omission in not being more of a pastor to these people. But he stood alone.

The familiar instructions were repeated and the bells rang for dismissal. As the passengers hurried from the deck to get out of the wind the motion of the ship, to which they were adjusting with the sway of their own bodies as they walked, suddenly seemed to change. There was a curious jerk as if the ship had balked in its thrust against the waves. The Beauforts, who were taking Mrs. Barton to the elevator, instinctively reached for her arms above the canes as they steadied her and themselves.

"Seemed almost as if we hit something."

"Big roller, I guess."

"It felt the way it does on an airplane when the pilot changes too quickly from automatic to manual steering."

"I almost tipped over!" exclaimed Hilary with excitement.

"Curiouser and curiouser, wasn't it, Alice?" said Mark casually. And then as Cora diligently reclaimed her charge he asked Signe to come down and have a drink before they were shipwrecked. She laughed and said that wasn't going to happen but she'd like the drink anyway.

Fred Timmins had been playing a game of gin rummy in the alley outside the engine room with one of his assistant engineers. As the weather had worsened he had stayed down there a good deal of the time. He heard a faint grinding noise, dropped his cards and jumped to his feet to feel and recognize the shudder which meant the ship had lost a propeller blade.

Within the first minute of his inspection he heard the voice of the Commodore through the communications system, calm and unruffled.

"Commodore here. What is it, Fred?"

"Screw gone bad, sir. Shaft bearing. Can't be anything else, sir."

"Turbine 1?"

"Yes, sir."

"Turbine 2 all right?"

"Seems to be, sir."

"Build up more steam on 2 and we'll count on her to do the job."

"It's all we can do now, sir."

"Everyone in your crew down there knows what's happened?"

"I expect so, sir."

"There's no need for panic of any kind. But no one is to give answers or explanations to questions from passengers or to members of the crew outside the engine room. No passengers are to be allowed below for any reason. Those are orders."

"I'll see to them, sir."

"Have boiler 2 watched with extreme care. Build up steam but don't overdo it. Check the reduction gear continually. When you have things fully under control come up here, Fred. We're a bit concerned about the weather ahead and I want you to sit in on any emergency plans."

By five o'clock every table and stool was taken in the Seashell bar. The Skyroom and the Mayfair were less crowded than usual. Their orchestras had begun to play but no one could dance with pleasure or even safety. No one tried. In the little Seashell the storm seemed more remote though everyone talked about the weather.

"The ship's moving smoothly again."

"I wouldn't call it too smoothly. My glass slides away the minute I put it down on the bar."

"Probably thinks you've had enough."

"It could be right but in weather like this what else can you do?"

"They're putting velvet ropes up in the corridors and on the stairs and in the lounges, for people to hang on to when they walk."

"That's always done when it gets a bit rough. It's insurance against lawsuits. They don't want anyone traveling on *The Seven Seas* to break a leg or a hip and sue the Line for half a million. That right, Howard?"

"They'd have a hard time collecting it," said Demarest from his end of the bar. He did not usually patronize what he called "this little dump" but he did not like the service in the Sky Room and

222

when he looked in at the Mayfair he had seen Ruby. He was teaching her a lesson by avoidance. Let someone else buy her drinks from now on.

"Do you think we're in for trouble?"

"Not if the officers know their business," Demarest said, as if he had reservations about that.

"I'm sure they do," said Alec Goodrich, who was also at the bar with Barbara. "It's a very competent staff at all levels."

The remark made its point. Demarest had grudgingly admitted to Alec that he had mislaid the money that he had accused Jim Bates of taking. The humiliation still stung.

"The barometer keeps falling," he said shortly.

Inevitably someone said, "Well, you're a lot safer on a big ship than you would be on a plane over the Pacific in weather like this."

"You certainly are. And this ship is unsinkable," said a cheerful drinker.

"That was what they said about the *Titanic.*"

"The situation was quite different. We're not in an iceberg area."

"The *Andrea Doria* went down. I knew a couple who were on that ship. Good friends of mine. She was saved but she never got over it."

"*The Seven Seas* is in a class by itself. This ship has every safety arrangement. Thirty sliding watertight doors and they can be operated from the bridge electrically, and there are sirens that can be heard for nine miles."

Mrs. Cayne, who was sitting at a table with her husband, said audibly, "I think that the officers ought to come around and talk to us. Explain that bump. Tell us if anything is wrong. The way the captains of airplanes do."

The men from the travel bureau, in a group at the next table, exchanged glances of irony and distaste. Cecil Brettingham half turned toward Mrs. Cayne and in his elegant British accent reduced her remark to its ignorance and insolence. He said, "I imagine the officers are quite fully occupied at the moment."

"Without baby-sitting the passengers," said Mark Claypole less politely.

He and Signe Goode were at the bar where they could hear the talk from the nearby tables.

Some woman was worrying, "If it's as stormy as this tomorrow they might cancel the white-elephant sale."

"Oh, I hope not. There are always things in those sales at the end of a voyage that you can get for half you'd pay if you bought in the ports. And things you meant to buy and missed. I wanted to get a piece of jade in Singapore—I had the name of a wonderful shop —but there wasn't time. The whole trouble with this cruise is that they don't give you enough time to shop."

Mark said to Signe, "Let's hope it's the whole trouble with the cruise."

"Are you worried about the storm, Mark?"

"I don't worry, dear."

"Do you think there's something wrong with the ship?"

He shrugged. "I wouldn't know. But there's uneasiness in this room. The refugees are huddling together."

A man who had won the big swimming contest on the ship came in looking for a place. Finding none, he stood at the bar. His hair was blown about and he looked as if he had been out on deck.

"It's really fierce outside," he announced. "I went out to have a look. The wind is getting much worse. I could hardly open and close the door from the deck. This isn't just a rainy day."

As he finished speaking, as if in proof, the ship rolled violently. Tables lurched even though they were screwed to the floor, bottles toppled on the shelves behind the bar and one that the barman had been using to refill glasses fell forward and flooded the laps and legs of the nearest customers, one of whom was Howard Demarest.

"Let's get out of here," Alec said to Barbara.

"What do you suppose happened?"

"My guess is that one of the stabilizers is gone again and in a storm it's a poor time to have that happen. We're due for some rolling but let's face it in a place that doesn't reek of whiskey."

Demarest mopped the liquor from his pants and kicked away the bar stool.

"Hell," he exclaimed, "I'm going up to see if those fellows are on the job!"

He rang for all the elevators and finally one came up and he pushed the button inside for the navigation bridge deck. Aft on that deck was the Sky Room, where Demarest never got good service for the steward in charge was a man who did not like brusque or peremptory orders. All the rest of the space on the deck was reserved for the mess hall and bedrooms of the officers and pilots. The Commodore's private suite was at the bow end. The officers' quarters were fenced in and signs reading OFFICERS ONLY were on every entrance to them. Demarest ignored the signs and went through to the Commodore's sitting room. The Commodore was sitting in an armchair, looking grave but quite calm. The Chief Officer was talking on the telephone. One of the pilots was standing by as if waiting for orders. Chief Officer Van Sant turned from the telephone, stared at Demarest and spoke to the Commodore.

He said, "Mr. Timmins has cut off both stabilizers. The one that failed was the one repaired in Hong Kong and he says it was a patch-up job that didn't last."

"He told me at the time that he didn't think it would in bad weather," said the Commodore, and then as if he had just noticed Demarest he spoke to him. "If you will excuse us, we are in conference, Mr. Demarest."

"I'll join the conference, if you don't mind. As a director of the Line I may as well tell you frankly that I am expected by the holding company to report on conditions on this ship and on its handling by the officers and crew. I had intended to do this quietly, acting only as an observer. But under the present circumstances—"

"I have been quite aware of your observations, Mr. Demarest."

"What's wrong with the ship? It sounded as if she were breaking to pieces a few minutes ago."

"No, the ship is not breaking to pieces," said the Commodore icily. "But there is a wind of almost hurricane force. One of the stabilizers was damaged and has become useless. For your information, there are two fins, on either side of the hull below the water-line, operated by an electric hydraulic system, and the fin motions are controlled by two gyroscopes. The fins are now inoperative."

"What's being done about it? Things were flying around in the bar."

"We shall have to adjust to some discomfort. Instructions have been given to rope off heavy furniture such as pianos. Ropes have been strung in the public rooms and on the staircases to assist passengers if they move about. We are going to advise all passengers to stay in their cabins after dining and to stow away breakables in their lockers. All heavy luggage in the baggage room has been tied down and secured. We are taking all possible precautions against personal injury. I am sure that you will be comfortable in your suite and cooperate with us by taking no unnecessary risks. All stewards will be on duty continuously tonight."

"How long is this storm going to last? You must have a weather report."

"We do not know how long it will last. We will try to bypass the eye of the storm if possible. At present we cannot be confident of that."

"Have you contacted other ships in this area?"

"We know the position of some of them at this time. But none will be able to help us without endangering their own ships if this storm gathers strength. Radar can work badly at times like this and we are having some electrical trouble."

"These things should have been seen to before the cruise began."

"You are quite correct," said the Commodore.

"You seem rather indifferent to the damage that might be done to the ship. Or has already been done from lack of foresight. I shall hold you personally responsible for damage to a twenty-million-dollar investment by my company."

The Commodore rose to his feet. He was the taller man and at the moment he seemed to tower over Demarest.

"I hold you personally responsible, Mr. Demarest—you and the directors of your company—for the safety of my passengers—you and your penny-pinching group whose only interest is in your profits and who are apparently ignorant of what is essential to your variegated holdings. This is not a chocolate-cream factory. This is a ship built for long and unpredictable voyages. I urged months ago that *The Seven Seas* be put into drydock, thoroughly inspected and that all advisable repairs and replacements be made. The answer I received from your company was a query as to whether the ship was in good enough condition for this cruise. I could not say that it would not stand the cruise. I simply did not know.

"The situation at present is that we have lost a propeller and are operating on one screw, which is possible but always has an element of danger. The electrical system is failing for some reason and in my letter I pointed out that it too needed a complete overhaul. We have run into a near hurricane. The piling-up of problems is due to the fact that your directors would not spend the money to make *The Seven Seas* completely seaworthy under all circumstances. My personal fault was in not refusing to retain command of the ship unless she was drydocked. I am going to do my best with the aid of these gentlemen and the rest of my staff to come safely through this emergency and protect my passengers, you among them. Now get out of my quarters and stay out for the remainder of the voyage. Get out!"

Demarest looked from the Commodore to his Chief Officer and then at the pilot. He saw the same cold accusation in each face. They said a propeller was gone. Demarest did not like the sound of that. He remembered now that there had been a letter suggesting that the ship be drydocked. Seven or eight months ago—the

227

meeting at which it had come up flashed through his memory. There had been objections to doing that. The cost of the cruise would have to be raised to pay for drydocking, and it couldn't be done at the time because the price had been announced and some people were already booked on that basis. The general opinion had been that the Commander of the ship was probably bellyaching—someone had suggested he might get a kickback on repairs. He was an old fellow, about to be retired. The decision had been—James was right about that—to write him and ask if it was really necessary, pointing out that in his own letter he had not stated that anything had broken down on the ship. And the consensus was that another year, if the company decided it was worthwhile to stay in the passenger-ship business, they would have to raise the rates and cut the costs.

The Commodore did not look like an old fellow now. He was giving orders. The ship rolled violently again but the stance of the officers was firm. It was Demarest who grabbed at the edge of the sitting-room door and went out.

Commodore James made no comment on Demarest's intrusion. He said to his Chief Officer, "I'm going to study the course a little more. It might be possible to weave around the storm. If we can skirt around it during the night the worst would be over. A blow like this can't last. But I want every lifeboat rechecked."

"Getting the boats into the sea and away from the ship would be tough in this sea," said the Chief Officer.

"They're good heavy boats. The builders didn't skimp on them. And we have skilled seamen to handle them. They've been thoroughly drilled. What we'd have to worry about is getting the passengers into them. I don't think it will come to that but before too long it may be a fifty-fifty chance. A skeleton crew will have to stay with us on the ship in any case to do what we can to save her even if the second propeller fails and she becomes no better than a raft."

Fred Timmins came in.

"How's it going, Fred?"

"We're doing all right. Making only about ten knots but we're moving."

"You said something about trouble with the electrical system."

"I don't think it's the generator. The failures are spotty. The men are working on it but we have better than a hundred and fifty miles of wiring on the ship and to locate the trouble takes time. We have the emergency diesel if we get a power failure."

"That will take care of the gyroscopic compass and the steering system."

"And the navigational lights and fire pumps."

"If the lights go out the passengers might panic."

"We can't allow that," said the Commodore. "I'll ask Joan to circulate among the women with the other hostess girls, and keep them calm. She'd better come up and I'll have a word with her about what to say to the passengers." He had a second's lift at the thought of seeing her, then said to Van Sant, "I wish you'd make that announcement about people staying in their cabins after dinner. If they go to dinner. A lot of them are probably seasick. The doc will have his hands full."

Father Duggan also had his hands full. During the lifeboat drill in the afternoon he had sensed the rising nervousness of the passengers. After the shocks caused by the loss of the propeller and the stabilizers he knew he must do something to help. He had posted a notice on all the bulletin boards that he would have a service of Benediction at five-thirty o'clock, and when it was over he would hear confessions for the following hour. Mass would be offered at seven tomorrow morning. He added the final announcement as reassurance that he expected the shipboard life to proceed in its usual way tomorrow.

With the ship pitching and rolling he had expected a very small attendance in the theater, if any at all. But if even a few of these people wanted the opportunity of prayer and penance he must give it to them.

He had been astonished. Not only were most of the few Catholics on board at the service but the whole theater was almost filled. For the first time on the voyage Father Duggan felt the theater was his church. The ceiling lights were dim—there was obviously trouble with the electricity—but it made the candles on his makeshift altar seem brighter. He lit two and battened down the holders with heavy ashtrays.

The service was unfamiliar to many of those present, but it was a simple one and could not be misunderstood. He intoned the hymn in English, blessed the congregation with the Host and knelt on the swaying platform for the prayer.

"Blessed be God. Blessed be His Holy Name."

They repeated the words after him. Finally he lifted his voice and sang the Recessional, which people of all faiths knew:

"Holy God, we praise Thy Name,
Lord of all, we bow before Thee,"

and the chorus rose as if it were relieving the anxiety.

He sat behind a screen and heard confessions, better ones than he had heard before on the ship, digging deeper into faults and failures and with more remorse.

"Father, there is one thing I have never confessed—I was always too embarrassed—probably I had no right to receive communion but I did—now, if anything should happen I want to confess—"

"Father, I'm really a fallen-away Catholic. But I still believe in the Church. It's just that I couldn't go along with its stand on birth control—"

"Father, I'm so glad we have a priest on board. For I want to confess—"

When he was through with the hour of confession he went back to his cabin. Jim Bates was looking for him. He said, "Father Duggan, a lot of people have been calling your room and asking where they could find you. They want you to come to their cabins. I guess they're scared as well as seasick. I don't think you can see all of them but I took down the names."

"Oh, yes, I can see them all. It may take a little time."

"They took Mrs. Barton to the ship's hospital. She said to the nurse that she'd like to see you."

"I'll go there first."

"You'll miss your dinner if you make all those calls."

"That's all right."

"There's coffee in the stewards' pantry on this deck. And Danish. I'll bring you some right away."

The railings were up around Mrs. Barton's bed and she looked very frail.

"Thank you for coming, Father."

"I was glad to come."

"I won't keep you. But I wanted to speak to a man of God though I'm not a Catholic."

"We are both Christians."

"And you believe in immortality?"

"Yes."

"It takes great faith. I am sure the doctor does not believe in it. He is kind but he thinks I'm just an old bag of bones falling to pieces. I am sure the pleasant nurses think that too. That there's nothing more."

"There is immortality no matter what they think."

"I'm glad to hear you say that. I'm on the edge of it. Is the storm very bad?"

"The weather is very rough."

"I hope the ship comes through. It does not matter to me. But I've been lying here and thinking of these people on the ship who should go on. Young Mrs. Beaufort. She is going to have a child. They were so happy about it. I hope she is all right. Give her help if you see her."

"I shall if I can."

"And I think of Barbara Bancroft, who is traveling alone."

"She has great courage," said the priest.

231

"Some of these people I have liked so much. Some I disliked. But if the Good Lord would take only me and spare the rest of the people on the ship—"

"Leave that to Him," said Father Duggan, "but I'm afraid the Good Lord does not make that kind of bargain. I believe He will take care of all of us. Would you like me to say a blessing?"

The Commodore had given orders that no information about the problems and calamities of the ship should be given out by the officers and engineers. None the less the word soon went around that the stabilizers, which had steadied the ship with their fins, had either been broken or washed away. The electrical situation was apparent. The lights flickered on and off for a few hours, then most of them went out. The elevators were not running. There was no television news and personal radios only squawked. The air-conditioning was not working. Joan Scofield and her assistants explained that electricity was being conserved, that the electricians were working and the lights might come on in full brilliance at any time. In the meantime the emergency generators were quite able to take care of the navigational needs. But as the night went on and *The Seven Seas* shuddered and rolled, lifted now by the waves and flung back into their depths, reassurance took less hold. Rumors spread through the ship. She was off course. The fire doors were inoperative. Alec Goodrich, holding fast to the window ledge in his high cabin, saw towers of white spray fly a hundred feet into the air above him.

"In a way it's magnificent," he said to Barbara, whom he had asked to stay with him. They could watch the storm through the windows and they did, not talking much, drinking a little tastelessly.

In other cabins passengers clung to their bedsteads. A few slept, having taken extra sleeping pills. A few were drunk though all the bars had been ordered closed at ten o'clock.

Signe Goode and Mark Claypole were in a corner of the smoking room, sitting on a sofa that was screwed deeply into the floor. He fell asleep and she was glad that he did. She sat quietly, with him leaning against her, thinking of what an odd end it was to something that had begun when she read a column in a newspaper. She told herself that she wasn't sorry, no matter what might happen. All those places she had seen, all the things she had learned—she began to make lists of them in her mind as Mark snored slightly.

On the bridge the Commodore had been debating with himself, asking advice from Timmins and Van Sant, watching the course and the barometer.

"We can't take a chance," he said at three in the morning. "We're pretty badly battered and the passengers need a little time to get to their stations. It will begin to be dawn within two hours and that will make it easier to get the lifeboats off, if we must. I'm going to talk to them. Ring the bells, Mr. Van Sant."

The bells rang and over the immediate shock and terror which permeated the ship the Commodore's voice came calm, deliberate and with complete authority.

"This is Commodore James speaking. I regret waking you and I do not wish to alarm you unduly. We are not in desperate straits but we are in a difficult and possibly dangerous nautical situation. It is a time for self-control and cooperation with your ship's officers. I am requesting all passengers to proceed to their lifeboat stations. The wind is brisk on the boat deck but with due caution there need be no accidents. Wear your warmest coats, hoods, or caps. Put on your lifebelts and proceed immediately to your station. It is possible that we need not take to the boats but it is wiser to be ready to do so. Thank you for your cooperation."

To be on the safe side Jim Bates knocked at the cabin doors of all the passengers for whom he was responsible. He was courteous but very firm. Alida Barnes was crying but Julia Hayward was calm and he left her to take care of the frightened woman. Father Duggan was the first man on the deck. Alec Goodrich and Barbara Bancroft came together and Jim was glad of that.

233

"Miss Canaday," he called through her door, "the orders are to go to your station."

"I won't do it."

He unlocked the door with his pass key and found her lifebelt.

"That sweater isn't warm enough, Miss Canaday."

"But it's the warmest thing I have except my white mink coat, and I won't wear my mink coat out on a night like this."

He almost laughed. Then he took the white mink from its hanger and wrapped it around her.

"I'm not going out there," she declared flatly.

Jim left her standing in her defiance. He knocked at Howard Demarest's door and the director of the Line immediately appeared, looking very serious and wearing his lifebelt.

"Please use your influence with Miss Canaday," said Jim. "She is refusing to go on deck because she doesn't want to get her fur coat wet."

"The little fool," muttered Demarest. "All right, Jim. I'll get her out."

"And don't forget your pills, sir."

"My God, I would have," said Demarest.

The people gathering at Station Two, their figures distorted by the lifebelts, their heads tied in scarves or with caps pulled down over their ears, looked grotesque in the weak light that glimmered from a few bulbs connected with the emergency system on the walls, but there was nothing comical about the sight. Heavy ropes had been fastened from the railing to huge hooks on the side of the ship so that there was something to hold on to on the wet decks. It was a much larger group than the usual one at the passengers' drills, for members of the crew were here as well as some from the service staffs. Alec Goodrich saw Pat, the bartender from the Sea-shell, and Anatole, the wine waiter, wearing a heavy sweater and no golden chain tonight. Joan Scofield was there and her face, framed in a white angora hood, was very deliberately calm. She carried a flashlight and helped people to place themselves along the ropes as she watched for signs of hysteria and severely told the hairdresser who had objected to the drills that she must be quiet.

Robert Cayne, unshaven, looked the age he really was instead of the one he pretended to be to match the youth of his wife. She was very frightened, clutching his arm and saying, "Oh, no, Bob! They couldn't expect us to get in that awful boat on a night like this!"

"Chin up," he said. "We're together. They'll have to get us out of this. It's their responsibility."

Bettina and Gene Beaufort said nothing. With clasped hands they watched the young officer checking the list of those assigned to the long boat which had been lowered to the railing of the deck.

The Chiltons appeared, with Hilary between her parents and the maid following with a look of horror. Hilary said, "There's Mark. I want to go over there. I want to be with Mark."

"Stand back against the wall, Hilary."

"No, please—"

Julian Chilton moved cautiously on the wet deck with his wife and child to where Mark Claypole was standing beside Signe Goode.

"Will you take her hand?" Mr. Chilton asked Claypole. "It will make her feel safer in this crowd."

"Of course." Mark tucked the child under his long arm and felt her shivering against him.

"Are we going to drown, Mark? Cora says so."

He looked down at Hilary and saw the same shock and withdrawal that there had been when she had asked if Cora was dead and when she had refused to go into the Taj Mahal because it was a cemetery.

"Of course we aren't going to drown," he said cheerfully, "unless you start crying. Remember how Alice nearly drowned in a pool of her tears?"

Someone heard that and tried to laugh.

The door to the deck opened and very carefully a nurse and Jim Bates propelled a wheelchair through it, in which Mrs. Barton sat with her usual composure. She was wrapped in an old-fashioned mink coat, its collar dangling mink tails. She wore a hat and to make it secure had put a black lace mantilla over it and tied it under her chin.

"Thank you, Jim," she said. "I've put the brake of the chair down so I'll be all right now."

Everybody stared at her. Her voice, her manner, the mere fact that she had managed to get on deck gave general reassurance. If she could do it—

Julia Hayward moved toward the chair with several others to be ready in case its brakes did not hold.

Mrs. Barton said, "Quite a bad storm, isn't it? I remember that once when we were crossing the Tasman Sea we had to take to the boats. There are ferocious storms on that little sea and lifeboats weren't equipped the way they are today."

Demarest was watching. He said to Father Duggan, who was near him, "You have to hand it to the old lady. She's certainly got guts."

"She has faith," said the priest, "so she is fearless."

"Whatever it is that keeps her going, I admire her for it."

Again, as on the train in Asia, Demarest had Father Duggan in a place where he could not get away immediately. And the priest's sensitiveness told him that Demarest needed companionship very badly. He did not seem frightened of the storm but very alone. Demarest could feel no personal importance tonight but only human helplessness.

He spoke again, as if he had been considering the priest's statement.

"My wife used to talk about faith. She wanted me to go along with her religion. She is a Catholic, and she's bringing up my boy and girl that way. In Ireland. But I don't know. I never could catch on to it—what you call faith, I mean."

He was explaining a great deal to the priest, including the arrogance and the tawdry girl.

"It's a good thing to have in a tight situation like this, I guess," Demarest said.

"Yes."

"I don't mind telling you, Father, that when you think time may be running out you wish you'd done a few things differently. Or not done them."

From where she stood, holding to a rope, Signe Goode said aloud, "I wish Father Duggan would say a prayer. It would make us feel better."

There was a murmur of agreement, a pause of expectation as the priest moved from his place by Demarest to the railing of the ship. He did not hold on to it but somehow balanced himself and said in a clear voice that could be heard over the pounding of the waves:

"Dear God, we pray to you tonight, those of us who believe in you and those whom you care for even in their unbelief. We pray that all those on this ship may come safely through this storm. We ask that you will give us calm and courage if we must venture on the ocean in this lifeboat. We ask that you will forgive our sins of commission and omission and give us true contrition for them. Let this angry sea and this tempest bring us closer to you and also reveal us more clearly to ourselves. Give us faith in God, for that is the imperishable lifeboat which can carry man from this life to eternity. Now let us accept His will without fear and with hope and say together, Our Father—"

"That was a work of art," said Mark to Signe. "Glad you thought of it."

"The priest isn't scared at all," said Hilary.

Most of the group were silent now. Alida Barnes was crying softly and Julia put her arm around her friend with more affection than she had ever felt before.

Ruby Canaday whimpered to the French hairdresser, "I was a fool to come on this trip."

"After this terrible tonight I work no more again on any ship," answered the hairdresser violently.

Joan Scofield's lips moved. Under her breath she was praying, "Dear God, save his ship. Save his ship."

The minutes passed, built up to nearly an hour. Hilary slept, leaning against Mark. There were sighs, occasional bursts of sobs, murmurs of encouragement. The spray still lashed as high as the boat deck now and then but the ship seemed to shake and tremble less. Or was it their exhaustion?

"I think," Alec told Barbara, "that it's a bit better out there now."

"You think so? It hasn't been quite so terrible here on the deck since that wonderful prayer. You remember that he said 'even in unbelief'? He surrounded everybody with a kind of comfort, no matter what. I love Father Duggan," said Barbara.

There was suddenly—and unexpectedly—a flicker of bright light. It went out and then came on again, this time staying steady. The lights that usually strung the decks illuminated everything. For an instant people looked bewildered and then they began to exclaim and talk.

"Evidently they've got the power fixed," said Cayne. "I should hope so! Sweetie-pie, it's going to be all right."

"Ladies and gentlemen," said the ship's officer in charge, "you must remain on deck until further orders."

They waited, obedient and tense. Then at last came the voice of authority.

"Good morning. This is Commodore James speaking. Electric facilities have been restored on the ship. We believe we have bypassed the eye of the storm and with God's help we shall ride it out in a few hours. You may return to your cabins, exercising great caution in moving about until the weather is calmer. Thank you very much for your courage and cooperation."

Chapter Seventeen

The launch that brought the customs officers aboard in San Francisco brought also mail and newspapers, and the people aboard *The Seven Seas* found that the ship's arrival was headline news. During the brief stop in Honolulu—only long enough to replace the fins of the stabilizers, recheck all the wiring and decide that it was not taking too much of a chance to proceed to San Francisco with one propeller—the magnitude of the storm they had endured had become common knowledge to the passengers. The ship's officers had known the next morning how disastrous it was, through radio communication. Trawlers had gone down—"all night I wondered when we'd collide with one of those trawlers," said the Chief Officer. Two small cargo ships had disappeared and were being searched for by navy planes.

These facts had been kept from the passengers and crew until they reached Hawaii so that no further fears would be excited. From the islands there would still be six days before the ship would reach the great landlocked harbor of San Francisco. Then all passengers who had not disembarked at Honolulu for a longer stay and who had intended to continue with the cruise through Panama would be flown back to their destinations in the United States. There were many communications between the Commodore and officials of the Line before plans were complete. Howard Demarest sent his own cables and received a number in return.

But in San Francisco the passengers found out that the eyes of the world had been upon the peril of *The Seven Seas.* It was the worst storm on the Pacific for many years. Some reports called it a stray typhoon, for typhoons usually occurred only in the China

239

Seas and the Indies. Some analyzed it as a hurricane due to a new fault in the depths of the ocean. It was certainly to be a chapter in the history of storms on the seas.

In the newspapers brought by the launch the passengers read about themselves as they waited for the line to form which would take them to the officials who would examine their passports. Alec Goodrich picked up a couple of newspapers and gave one to Barbara, who was standing with him in the lobby. He glanced at the one he held and groaned.

Barbara laughed. "You and the Commodore and Mark Claypole seem to be the big news."

"One more black mark for me. 'Defeated Senator on luxury liner.'" But Alec sounded more amused than angry.

There was a spread of pictures. A very handsome one of the Commodore, a youthful one of Mark Claypole and one which had been frequently used in Alec Goodrich's last campaign. The headlines read:

LINER SURVIVES WORST STORM IN 30 YEARS
ARRIVED IN SAN FRANCISCO TODAY WITH MANY
WELL-KNOWN AMERICANS ABOARD

Among the well-known ones listed were Mrs. Hartley Barton of Philadelphia, Mr. and Mrs. Eugene Beaufort, who were on their wedding trip, Mr. and Mrs. Julian Chilton of New York City, and Mrs. Alida Barnes of New York and Palm Beach. Mr. Caspar LeGrue, the Nobel prize winner, was also on board. The reporters had matched the passenger list with *Who's Who* and *The Social Register.*

"Who on earth was Mr. LeGrue?" asked Mrs. Cayne, reading the names and feeling let down because Mr. and Mrs. Robert Cayne were not mentioned.

"I think he was the little gray-bearded fellow who gave astronomy lessons. If I'd known he was a Nobel prize winner I'd have gone to them. But you can't know everybody on a cruise like this."

"That picture of Howard Demarest must have been taken years ago," said Mrs. Cayne.

It was at the top of a separate column whose headline was FINANCIER DIES AT SEA. There was a story about his career and his many holdings and one of the pictures which had been used years before in *Fortune.*

Looking at the picture of a younger Demarest, Barbara said, "I never liked him. He could be obnoxious. But it was a pretty desolate way to die. I heard that it happened hours before Jim found him."

"The doctor wasn't sure how long it was. He died in his sleep. But Demarest knew his number was up. He told me so himself."

"It must have been a shock for poor Jim."

"Demarest made up to Jim for any shock he gave him."

"How?"

"It's a curious story. I don't think there's any harm in telling you, though these things are usually kept confidential until an estate is probated. But you like Jim, so this will please you, and I know you'll keep it to yourself. It was the day after the big blow and we were limping along toward Honolulu when Demarest rang me up in my cabin. He asked if I'd come up to his suite. I liked him a lot less than you did and I was going to brush him off, but he said it was a legal matter that concerned Jim Bates and he knew I was a lawyer. I went up prepared to make trouble if he was going to accuse Jim of anything again. But there was none of that. He gave me a drink and then he told me that he had a heart condition and that it was more or less touch and go for him. During the storm he had been worried because he hadn't done what he was thinking of doing for Jim and he didn't want to take a chance on waiting until he got back to New York. Just in case. He said to me, 'That boy saved my life twice and I wouldn't have blamed him if he hadn't done it the first time.' Anyway he wanted me to draw up a codicil to his will and he's left Jim ten thousand dollars."

"What a lot of money! What a windfall for Jim!"

"That's what I thought. I said it was quite a bundle. But he had a reason for it. I gathered that after that money row he had talked to Jim quite a bit and found out that Jim's great ambition was to take a course in hotel management and work into that. There are colleges that offer that training and Jim was tired of the sea—or maybe of the people on cruises. He's been on ships since he was sixteen. This money will see him through a three-year course and give him a profession."

"It's wonderful for him. But I'm astonished that such a man would do it."

"There was something to Demarest under all that bombast. He was smart enough of course or he wouldn't have made all that money. But he was always trying to prove something, have everyone know he was the big shot and could have everything he wanted. And yet he knew there were things he couldn't get. Like the night he made an ass of himself at my table. My guess is that the storm shook him up. There he was, no better than the rest of us, good only for a seat in a lifeboat. He couldn't demand his own life and he couldn't run the ship. And that was something else I'll tell you about," said Alec. "I said I'd draw up the codicil and get witnesses and bring it up for his signature—he was in bed, I think he must have had some sort of attack before he called me—anyway, he said there was another thing I could do for him.

"He had come on this cruise, he told me, partly for his health—and I suppose for fun and games with the little bitch who stole his money—but also as an observer and maybe a hatchet man for the holding company which owns the American Republic Line. He was supposed to report back to them about conditions on the ship, possible changes and economies and whether passenger service on this scale was a good investment."

"He was always criticizing something. The food. The ship's officers."

"He had his comeuppance on that from the Commodore. Well,

he had made a report and had the ship's stenographer run off a few copies. He wanted me to take two of them and—just in case anything should happen to him before the end of the voyage—to give one personally to the Commodore and mail one on landing to the chairman of the board of the Republic Line.

"He was obviously a bit panicked," Alec said, "kept saying that all this was just a precaution. But he didn't look good and once he stopped and took a pill—I suppose it was heart medicine. But he told me that he didn't want his report to be lost by accident or delayed by a lot of formalities, 'just in case' again. That made sense, for such things do happen between death and probate. He wanted me to read the report so I'd see what he was getting at. I didn't want to read it—it wasn't any of my business and I told him so, but he persisted and I didn't want to push him into another heart attack. So I looked it over."

"I suppose it was sour, all criticism."

"No. That was what surprised me. It amounted to a recommendation that this ship be put into drydock in San Francisco or New York, whichever was more feasible—and would cost less. It also recommended that Commodore James oversee the job and suggested that he be retained past the usual date of retirement at the discretion of the directors of the holding company. This, he said in the memorandum, was because the Commodore had done an exceptional job of seamanship which saved the lives of those aboard ship and a very valuable property of the company. There were other notes about ocean travel and cruises that were rather interesting, evidently relating to questions that had been brought up in previous discussions. He said that there were always people who would want to travel by ship and that cruises should be promoted with more advertising. He thought they could be more profitable, that prices could be raised, and costs cut." Alec chuckled. "He even suggested special economies. Did you know that *The Seven Seas* on this trip carried a thousand pounds of caviar and thirty-five tons of filet mignon, prime ribs of beef and steak?"

"Not really—"

"Yes, there was quite a lot of data. Demarest had nosed around and knew where the waste was. Looking at that midnight supper I think maybe he had a point. Anyway it was quite a document. I delivered one to the Commodore after Demarest's death and I'll mail the other to New York in the morning."

"Will the recommendation be important to the Commodore?"

"I should imagine so. It certainly surprised him. When I called on him and said I had a paper which Mr. Demarest had asked me to deliver in person he took it and looked at it as if it were a poisoned pill. I was on my way out of his quarters as he was reading it and he called me back. He looked astonished and said, 'Is there some monkey business about this?' I said I was only doing what I had been asked to do and he said, 'My God, I kicked him out of here!' I guess I wasn't the only one who had a run-in with Demarest."

"Will that mean the Commodore won't have to retire?"

"I don't know. I'm not on the board of this conglomerate that owns the ship. I imagine he doesn't want to retire. The age cut-off is an automatic thing and hard to take for a still very vigorous man like James. But Demarest should wield a good deal of influence even with a dead hand."

"Strange that he would ask to have him kept on if they had a row."

"I don't know. He paid the Commodore off for saving his life and preserving a property in which he had a stake. But also that report let Demarest set himself up as an authority on seamanship—he was the one who knew that the master of the ship had done an exceptional job and he was the person who knew caviar was being wasted. He was showing off as usual—but it was all to the good, for once. And he couldn't help being the kind of person he was."

"Perhaps he was different when he was young. People change."

Alec knew that she was not thinking only of Demarest as she said that. He looked down at her thoughtful, beautiful face and forgot the dead man.

"Barbara, haven't you changed your mind this morning?"

"No."

"But you will keep it open? Not slam the door on the possibility?"

"I won't slam the door. Or lock it. But it has to be closed for now. So that we will be by ourselves to think things out. And try to work them out."

Last night in his cabin he had tried to persuade her. She had been tender as well as more responsive than ever before. Then they had talked, not in argument but in explanation of themselves.

"Why don't we go on together, Barbara? Get married? I think we could make something of it."

"Alec, I'm not right for you."

"I think you are. The other night, when we were first conscious that the storm was going to be dangerous and later on when I was with you on the deck, I had a lot of thoughts. I was glad you weren't alone, that I was there with you—not that there was anything I could do to protect you."

"Oh, yes, you did something. I wasn't facing the storm by myself."

"That was it. I remember thinking that if we should have to take to the boat I was going to stay as close to you as possible. I was proud that you weren't making a fuss but taking it as it came. I thought that you were the kind of person I would like to die with —and then suddenly I found myself thinking or live with."

"I like hearing that."

"Then will you take the chance and marry me? Right now I haven't a great deal to offer—"

"More than I would have to bring you."

"Don't say that. You were wonderful tonight."

"That's not marriage."

"It's basic to it."

"I think so. But there has to be more. That isn't enough to keep two people together in the days as well as the nights. Through all the things that happen, are bound to happen. Two people who marry should not just want each other but the same thing for the world, share the whole job. I don't think you and I would, Alec."

"Why not? I want a better world too."

"Not so impatiently. And with more hope." She smiled but not happily as she admitted that. "I'm a dissident. You're not. I believe in replacement instead of repair, if I believe in anything. I'm a girl without a country and you're a patriot. Don't you see why it would be all wrong?"

"You'll come back to your country."

"I may one day. But as it is I'd be a very bad wife for you. Alec, I wish you so well and I believe that it will be well for you. You were terribly hurt when you lost the job you liked so much. You're going to get that job back in one way or another, sooner or later, even if it means fighting it out from a new beginning. It may be tough but you're different now from the man who hated everybody at the bar on that first night."

"If I am, that's your work."

"Not much of it. Anyway, I'd be no help to a man in politics. I think campaigns are false and degrading."

"I wouldn't ask you to campaign."

"Wives have to go along. Alec, I like you so much that I almost love you. But I couldn't marry you. For your sake more than mine."

"What do you plan to do?"

"Immediately? I'm going to stay with my parents for a little while. You know—I'm going to try to please them, not frighten them. I've worried and terrified them for the last two years and they've been pretty brave. They deserve a break."

"You're not going to try to see that man?"

"Boone? No. He wouldn't want to see me. Father Duggan is sure of that and I think he is right. I can't help Boone because he would know I was being loyal to the person he was, not the one he is now. And he would resent me because he has shed that person with contempt. But Father Duggan will see him and perhaps he can get through. If anyone can."

"I don't think you'll get much satisfaction out of being a dutiful daughter, Barbara. I don't like your plans."

"But you haven't heard all of them. I'll stay in what isn't really home any more only for a little while. Then I think I'll go back to Asia. Maybe to Kandy. They need teachers and I would pay my way. I had a curious feeling of being in a place that was right for me when I was in Kandy. Maybe the feeling would come back again. And when my unfinished business here is over—I want to know what will happen to Boone for I'll have to live with that— then I'd like to go back. Perhaps it won't work out but I can give it a try."

"Will you keep in touch with me?"

She thought about that.

He said, "I won't bother you. Just a word now and then. So I'll know where you are and how you are. And so I can tell you what's happening to me—you're closer to me than any woman has ever been, Barbara."

Barbara said, "I would like that very much. It will be like being on the deck that night—neither of us will be alone to face the possibilities."

Father Duggan had said his early Mass and had his early breakfast. He was packed and ready to go. To go back, as he was writing to his friend Sebastian. He described the storm in some detail and went on:

I didn't think at one point the ship would survive the storm. But it did. And I found out—I had begun to find it out before then as my relations with various people on the ship developed—that any usefulness I may have in this life is as a priest. As a layman I could not have helped anyone in that time of danger and fear. So I survived my storm. There will certainly be others but I believe I have come through the worst one. I read this again the other day in *The Imitation of Christ:* 'I have begun. I may not go back. It is not fitting to leave what I have undertaken.' He was a wise monk.

Yours in Christ,
Aloysius

247

He sealed and stamped the letter and wrote the address with affectionate memory. Then he went to find the mailbag. He passed Julia Hayward and said, "Good morning."

"Good morning, Father," she answered and there was a happiness in her voice that he had not heard before in their few conversations.

"Glad to be getting back?" he asked.

"Very glad."

"We've had quite an experience," he said and went on his way.

Julia wished she could have told him about the letter that had come this morning. She wanted to tell someone but not Alida just yet. Alida would say, "But you mustn't give up your lovely apartment!"

She was going to give it up and if she came back to New York she would live cheaply and simply. She did not have to think about that yet, but only be glad that she was needed. There was something she could do now.

She had been reluctant to open the letter addressed in Christine's sprawling handwriting. It would tell her that the divorce was final. It had told her that but Christine had also written,

I hope you won't think I'm just a marrying fool. But in Mexico while the legal things were being done I looked up some friends at the Embassy and met a man I used to know. He's in the Foreign Service. I always was a little in love with him and this time—maybe because I was at loose ends and so was he—anyway we are going to be married. Peter knows and I honestly think he's relieved to know I have someone else. The thing is, Julia, that Kent—his name is Kent Morrow—is due to go to South America in June for three months. He wants to be married at once and have me come with him and I don't know what to do about Tony. Peter is a little afraid of his child, and it was Peter who suggested that just possibly you might help us all out. If you could take charge of Tony for the months we'll be away it would solve everything. I don't know how he would fit into your elegant New York apartment and Tony does love the riding and swimming out here. Would you be angelic enough to consider coming out here and taking over—

In the foyer on the main deck Signe was reading the newspaper.

"You really are famous," she told Mark. "It tells all about the book that is going to be a motion picture and where your article is coming out—the one about the people on the ship."

"I've a smart agent. Milt Knott was right on the ball, taking advantage of our little squall to get some free publicity."

"*Bird of Passage* is a lovely name for a movie. I can hardly wait to see it."

"They probably won't use anything but the title by the time they get through with it," said Mark.

Hilary Chilton cut a path through the crowd of passengers toward him, with Cora in tow.

"We have to go upstairs and stand in line and then get off," she said. "My father is waiting for me. I came to say goodbye. I do not like goodbyes."

"There's no such thing. Goodbyes are illusions," said Mark.

"Illusions?"

"Things that seem to be happening but aren't. We won't fool ourselves with goodbyes. When I finish my job in California I shall come back to New York and take you to dinner and the theater."

"To a musical?"

"If there's one worth our while. I shall wear a black tie and you must wear your best dress."

"I've a black velvet dress for very best."

"It sounds perfect."

"You'll really come?"

"Of course," said Mark.

Cora said, "You must come, Hilary."

"I am coming," said Hilary with dignity.

"You're so good with the child," said Signe to Mark. "She adores you."

He shrugged and she said nothing more. She was rather shy with Mark this morning. Not that there had been anything to it really—he had been drinking quite a lot. But it was astonishing

249

even if he had not been quite himself.

They had been in the Seashell bar last night. For the last time. No bars would be open in the morning. And they had the place to themselves, for people were packing or being gay in the rooms where the orchestras played.

He had been silent in a brooding way. She had seen him like that before and always hopefully believed he was thinking about his work. Suddenly he said, "How would you like to marry me, dear? I know I'd be a hell of a husband for a good girl like you. But would you care to take me on?"

"Don't make fun of me tonight, Mark. We've had such good times in this room. This is where I first saw you. When you said that we were all refugees. You were so nice to me that night. Be nice tonight. Don't tease me."

"I am not teasing you. I'm proposing marriage. The holy state of matrimony. Which can be more unholy than anything else in the world."

"You've had a little too much to drink. But of course it is the last night. But, Mark, I hope you won't drink too much out there in Hollywood."

"Come along and stop me. I need your steadying hand. Repeat question. Will you marry me, Signe Goode?"

"I don't like jokes about things like marrying."

"I am not being humorous. I have been considering this very seriously for the last few days. And we haven't much time left to go."

"Even if you meant it for a minute—why should you want to marry me?"

"You want reasons? Well, I like to be with you. You have a curious way of stimulating me in reverse. You're learning to be handsome and you have a very pretty figure. And then—there's all your money."

"Oh," said Signe, "the money. But you don't need money now. You've sold things. You're going to have a movie."

"I'll be back on the rocks before long. That kind of money vanishes. You have a pocketful for a few months and then it's gone. Writers don't stay rich."

"I certainly wouldn't marry anyone who wanted my money."

"It's not the only motive. I gave you others. Don't you like the idea of marriage? Don't you like the idea of bed?"

She blushed under her sunburn.

"Why get red in the face about it? Everybody knows that's included. As a matter of fact I've wondered several times on this jaunt why I didn't take up the matter with you. There were good opportunities—"

"Stop," she said sharply.

"I'm sorry. That was off key. But getting married is decent. People do marry. Good-looking women like you. Bastards like me."

"The very thought of it," she said, "even if you meant it for a minute, I wouldn't dream of marrying you. I can't imagine ever— doing that with—anyone but Tom."

"I suppose he would be around all the time," said Mark gloomily. "Then you're turning down my offer?"

"Of course I am. And you didn't mean it seriously."

"Yes, I did. I anticipated possible rejection. But there's another thing. I don't like your going back to that apartment and being a lonely heart."

"Oh," said Signe, now on firmer ground, "the first thing I'm going to do when I get back is to get rid of the apartment. I hate it. People said that I should get an apartment and have a decorator and so I did but I wasn't happy in it. It never seemed real. I'm going to get rid of it, sublet it until the lease runs out. And I am going to buy a house. Not a big one but one with a real kitchen and an upstairs and downstairs and no elevator full of people I don't know."

"And hollyhocks over the back fence?"

"I never liked hollyhocks," said Signe, who was swinging a little now herself. "I like sweetpeas. I want to find a place near a lake where I could swim."

"Buy a lake," he suggested, "you've got the money."

"I'm going to spend money," said Signe. "I'm going to take more interest in things."

"What things?"

"Good causes. The night of the storm I kept thinking of all the things I could have done. Sins of omission, like the priest said."

"You're going to be a do-gooder? Take care. Tom wouldn't approve."

"I'll take care. And then every year I'm going to travel. Take a trip and learn something. Now that I know what clothes to take and about shore trips. I'll go somewhere every year."

"I feel better. Can I come to see you in the new house? And hear about the shore trips?"

"You'll be too famous. But it would be lovely if you did. And, Mark—I mean this. If you ever need any money—"

"I'll need you anyway, dear." He leaned over and kissed her in full sight of the barman.

The Commodore stood in his white uniform on the corner of his top deck and watched the ropes being thrown to the pier. He felt, with a quiet exaltation, the gentle shudder as the ship touched the moorings. They had made it. And Demarest had written that astonishing letter. If the company took his recommendations—and surely they wouldn't junk an investment like this—if they keep me on for even a couple of years I can increase its value. The commander of a ship can't have his wife as hostess of it. . . . But there would be ports. Ship or shore he knew he would not give Joan up.

From below Joan was watching him. He had shown her the report of Demarest and she had wept. Now she was looking at the Commodore with complete happiness and feeling the sapphire in her ring.

The passports were stamped. All the piles of luggage had been taken ashore, and the long line of passengers began to move down the gangplank. Reporters watched for familiar faces and cameras snapped pictures. The Nobel prize winner shook his head silently as someone asked him a question and hurried away. Alec Goodrich said, "Yes, it was a bad storm. My reason for taking the cruise? Well, I wanted to find out how the world is governed. Yes, I found out some very interesting things. Certainly I expect to stay in government service."

Mark Claypole, when he was asked about the price for the motion picture, said, "You'll have to ask my agent."

Ruby Canaday had been singled out by a reporter plus photographer. She swayed her figure in her habitual way and smiled enticingly.

"It was an awful storm," she said. "Some people were almost scared to death."

"Were you frightened?"

"No, I prayed," said Ruby.

"You were a friend of Mr. Demarest, weren't you?" asked the newsman, whose paper had told him to find out about the girl the financier was said to have had with him. "That was too bad about him."

"Yes, it was sad about Mr. Demarest. I met him on board ship. I was traveling by myself."

Jim Bates, who personally was taking a suitcase to the B section of customs for Mrs. Barnes because she had said it was full of fragile things, heard what Ruby said. The end of this voyage had been wonderful for Jim, for Alec Goodrich had seen no reason why Jim should not be informed of what he would get when the Demarest estate was settled. He turned and stared at Ruby Canaday with all the contempt he had withheld during the voyage, and anger at her denial of his benefactor, Demarest. His glance spoke, calling her a thief and a liar. Ruby's hand went to the string of pearls around her neck as the photographer snapped another picture.

71 72 73 10 9 8 7 6 5 4 3 2 1